Praise for *The Dreamca*

☾

"Imagination, adventure, and hope rests within these pages."
—**Great Grandmother Mary Lyons**,
Ojibwe Elder and author

"A timely and lushly drawn story about fearless young women
blazing new paths for themselves and Mother Earth."
—**Courtney Maum**, author of *The Year of the Horses*

"The essence of the divine feminine is captured within the
stories of *The Dreamcatcher Codes*. This creative force touches
the heart with visions of the natural world, and unity amongst
Earth's diverse plant, animal, and human nations. It is a call to
heal humanity's relationship with the planet."
—**Alexis Estes**, Lower Brule Sioux Tribe

"This book is a work of art. It is also timely and necessary for
it calls the inheritors of today's world home to the sacred
connection with nature. This book is a homecoming, it is
medicine for the soul, and it is frankly glorious."
—**Clare Dubois**, founder, TreeSisters.org

"*The Dreamcatcher Codes* is compassionate, wise, and
galvanizing, both a breathtaking adventure and an urgent
call-to-action. Not only will Barbara Newman's terrific debut
make you wish you had a magical flying horse, it will also
inspire you to do everything you can to save this gorgeous
planet we call home."
—**Lance Rubin**, author of *Crying Laughing*
and *Denton Little's Deathdate*

"Informed by ancient Earth wisdom, this magical story contains
potent medicine that's so needed in this time. Braiding
together a riveting journey for girls of all ages, *The Dreamcatcher
Codes* has all the ingredients to enchant and embolden
tomorrow's leaders. Filled with strong role models and mythic
trials, this beautiful book will help bring hope, vision, and
healing to all who read it."
—**Nina Simons**, co-founder of Bioneers, and author of
Nature, Culture & The Sacred: A Woman Listens for Leadership

"An empowering read, beautifully written, and a page-turner to boot."

—**Holly George Warren,** author of *Janis: Her Life and Music* and *The Cowgirl Way*

"Barbara Newman is a visionary. Using her pen like an artist uses a brush, she creates landscapes that take us out of ourselves and into worlds of wonder. I flew with the cowgirls through lush pink skies and over the stunning beauty of the open desert. And I didn't want to stop."

—**Jana Laiz,** award-winning author of *The Twelfth Stone*

"Barbara Newman's luscious words invite us, implore us, to look upon our beloved Mama Earth—as astronaut Alan Shepard did from his first steps on the Moon—with awe and majesty. *The Dreamcatcher Codes* is sure to imprint readers young and old with renewed wonder and respect for our sacred, natural world. Like a tuning fork, Newman's fantasy novel will resonate and activate your own inner guardian of Gaia. What a gift of inspiration to give our younger generations as they prepare to step forth into the world."

—**Deb Chamberlin,** singer-songwriter, and creator of *The Awakened Artist*

"Now, more than ever, teenage girls need to step into the possibilities of who they are and have the potential to become. *The Dreamcatcher Codes* invites them to cultivate their imaginative power and explore how Mother Nature, along with the deep and nurturing bonds of sisterhood, can guide them to know themselves, and connect to their own strengths. At an age when girls are seeking to belong, this mythic and empowering story helps them discover how nature is a part of all of us. Barbara Newman ingeniously interweaves messages of wisdom and insights from a culturally diverse array of ancient traditions that honor our common humanity as caretakers of our planet, and of each other."

—**Ellen Feig Gray, M.A.,** parent coach, developmental psychologist, author, and TEDx speaker

"Weaving magic and womanhood with love of our beautiful planet, the writer has brought a story to life I wish I'd been able to read as a young girl. *The Dreamcatcher Codes* will inspire you to speak up for what is right, to have hope and above all . . . be brave . . . just like a cowgirl."

—**Adrian Brannan,** singer/songwriter,
author *Dear Cowgirl*

"A rich, inspiring tale that reveals the power inherent in young women when they listen to their wild souls. A hopeful vision of cooperation, determination, and what we can become."

—**Kat Livengood,** renowned wild horse photographer

"Imagine Madeleine L'Engle and Starhawk merged with Joy Harjo. This story of the magic of nature and the nature of magic transports readers to some of the most beautiful and sacred places on Earth. And along the journey, the four girl characters learn lessons in diversity and biodiversity, humanity and humility, and the healing power of what is still here, still wild, still free."

—**Cassie Premo Steele Ph.D.,**
award-winning poet, novelist

"In this fantastical story, girls from all walks of life come together for the common good. By embracing diversity, equality, and inclusion, they become a stronger whole. It is my hope that every girl reads this book, and steps into her power to become a changemaker."

—**Ross Ellis,** founder and CEO, *STOMP Out Bullying*

"Barbara Newman has woven a tapestry of mythology and magic from cover to cover. Across time and space, the reader is carried on a journey of love for the natural world, while hoping that the four mighty heroines, who risk everything, will succeed in saving the planet. At this critical time in our endangered reality, this book is an urgent call for us to do the same." —**Hope Fitzgerald**

THE
DREAMCATCHER
CODES

☾

Alexis Estes

THE
DREAM
CATCHER
CODES

☾

A NOVEL

Barbara Newman

GREEN WRITERS PRESS *Brattleboro, Vermont*

Green Writers Press is a Vermont-based publisher whose mission is to
spread a message of hope and renewal through the words and images we
publish. Throughout we will adhere to our commitment to preserving and
protecting the natural resources of the earth. To that end, a percentage
of our proceeds will be donated to environmental activist groups and
social justice organizations. Green Writers Press gratefully acknowledges
support from individual donors, friends, and readers to help support the
environment and our publishing initiative.

GReen
wriTers
press

Giving Voice to Writers & Artists Who Will Make the World a Better Place
Green Writers Press | Brattleboro, Vermont
www.greenwriterspress.com

ISBN: 978-1-7336534-7-3

COVER DESIGN BY ASHA HOSSAIN, LLC

FRONTISPIECE ART:
ALEXIS ESTES, WOKSAPE OKE WINYAN
(SEEKS KNOWLEDGE WOMAN), LOWER BRULE SIOUX

A love letter to Mother Earth and all of her daughters

THE
DREAMCATCHER
CODES

☾

LASCAUX

WE JOIN THIS STORY in the moment that the world's first painting of a horse meets its destiny. Which is to say that we join an ancient story—a story that travels, like a talisman, through time into the hands of a woman named Sophia Rose.

That painting, on the walls of a cave in what is marked on our maps as France, shows a wild mane, a strong neck, a lean body outlined in black, legs in motion, hooves off the ground.

We view it from a distance of seventeen thousand years, in the moment that a crack in the stone lets a sliver of light seep in.

This light illuminates the crystalline deposits on the walls, layers that have built up for millennia.

This light, sizzling through the crack, lands on the horse's hoof with a power so intense that sparks ignite like firecrackers, activating a crystal buried underneath.

It leaves the smell of apricots.

What happens next might stun even those who believe in magic. The crystal, green as an emerald, dislodges from the rock, ricochets across the cave, and falls to the floor. It twists itself, stretches like hot blown glass into the shape of a U—a horseshoe that will change the world.

We are not told how it makes its journey around the circle of the earth, touching all the hemispheres, from east to south, west to north, gathering the wisdom of nature, the Codes that live in rivers and rocks, trees and wind, and the fire of the sun.

No human force carries this crystal, until it makes its way into the hands of chosen Guardians, women who understand the plant and animal kingdoms, secrets and symbols from gods and goddesses, myths and lore that evolve over time.

We meet up with it again in North America in the 21st century. This talisman, called the Crystal Horseshoe, named by Gaia, goddess of the earth, is under the protection of Sophia Rose.

The Thief

*T*HE AIR WAS THICK AND STILL, except for a whispering wind and the powerful pull of the full moon. Standing at the apex of Mount Shasta, Sophia held her hands high, offering the crystal to the sky. It was light and smooth to the touch, like glass. Strong and never broken, it was formed out of the natural world's most resilient substances. It would have to be to do its alchemy for Mother Earth.

Month after month, Sophia stood on this sacred mountain and performed this sacred ritual. The energy of the full moon recharged the crystal, renewing Sophia's feminine power as Guardian of Mother Earth. Together, they were a force, transforming greed and destruction into renewal and life.

The U-curved crystal was hollow, with small round openings at each end. Sometimes a green light, the color of new grass, shimmered through. Only a chosen few were taught how to see into its window of ancient worlds, which appeared as letters and symbols on a moving scroll.

These were the Codes, the Laws of Nature—messages from above and below—from the stars and the sun, the waters and the winds, and all living things on Earth. The Codes wove the tapestry of nature's DNA—threads dating back to the origins of time.

Eyes to the sky, Sophia stood straight-backed and purposeful, regal.

Two white feathers—a simple, well-earned crown—dangled from her long, braided, raven-colored hair, a black so deep that it shone blue in the moonlight.

A small medicine wheel was tied near the nape of her neck, and a soft cape, made from the skin of an antelope, rested on her square shoulders.

The old leather of her weathered cowboy boots was soft and scuffed, bald spots showing on the heels. These boots had walked many miles, on many paths.

Sophia's beloved horse, Apollo, stood close by, as always. He was strong and muscular, pure white, with a thick mane not of hair, but feathers of the golden eagle. Protector and friend, Apollo flew Sophia across the skies, transporting her to all corners of the earth.

The silence of this night was interrupted when Apollo began to pace. He sensed things before they happened, and loudly neighed. He tapped his front hoof—one, two, three times—against the rock.

Disturbed, Sophia shifted her attention away from Moon. Squinting, eyes straining, she saw a shadow coming at her from the west, a cloud rolling hard and fast with the force and fury of a giant wave.

The dark cloud eclipsed the moon, hiding its light, leaving the smell of burning iron in the air. As the cloud spread out, it boomed, a pounding sound so piercing that it shivered through Sophia like shards of ice.

The noise shook her, rattling her bones. Pressure exploded inside her ears. She was dizzy as the world spun around her and she lost her footing. Apollo saw her struggling and stood with his back to hers so that Sophia could brace herself against his body.

Sophia regained her balance. The sound of a hard wind crackled like lightning, and a relentless rain, cold as steel, stung like a thousand needles on her skin. Sophia had never seen weather like this. Usually fearless, she was unsteady and unsure. It felt as if the planet was being thrown off its axis, spinning into the Universe.

It felt like the world was coming to an end.

Sophia shuddered. She had to fight back. She could not let this onslaught scare her into backing down. She would not let herself or the Crystal Horseshoe be destroyed.

Determined, she grounded herself into the rock, imagining roots growing from her feet into the center of the earth. As gusts of wind lashed out, rocking her from side to side, Apollo moved in front of his charge. Feathers and tail moving like a pendulum, even his weight of two thousand pounds could not shield her from the squalls, not this time. He lost his balance and fell onto his hindquarters. As he struggled to get back up, Sophia bore deeper into the Mother, intertwining roots to weave a stronger web. It steadied her; she held her own.

As she watched the cloud morph into a Fire Dragon, her heart almost stopped. This was the kind of cloud that controlled the weather, the waters and the winds, the kind that manipulated oceans and floods, tornados and storms. It moved its head back and roared with a growl so deep that the Star People heard it across the galaxies. The echo shook Sophia with such force, it brought her to her knees.

She was a lone warrior—enduring the battle of her life.

Hands wrapped around the Crystal Horseshoe, Sophia called upon her own life force and her will to survive. She dragged her leg forward and, with invisible grace, got back onto her feet. In seconds, the storm pushed her to the ground again. Despite the wind's fury, she refused to lie helpless, but pushed against the brutal squalls, pulled herself up, and raised the crystal vessel, pointing the hollow ends of the horseshoe toward the Fire Dragon. The Codes inside had the power to neutralize all that was not good for Mother Earth. But Sophia's strength was slowly weakening. She was thrown, again. Apollo came and stood behind her.

All that was left was faith. Sophia held the Crystal Horseshoe to her heart, closed her eyes, called on all the knowledge within its scrolls.

"Show me how to fight this. Show me what I need to know," she prayed.

As the winds whipped her cape around her neck, she held the talisman tighter against her chest. Afraid that it would be swept away, she gripped harder, nails digging into her palms. She wouldn't let go—all of life depended on it, including her own.

When an angrier gust pushed against her, Sophia squeezed the crystal with a power she didn't even know she had, as if something outside of herself was forcing her hand.

The crystal cracked into six pieces.

The moment it broke, the storm stopped. It became quiet— so quiet that Sophia heard one of the pieces drop from her hands. In panic, Sophia scrambled, reaching quickly, but the broken crystal was out of her grasp. As she lurched forward, it slid down the slick, wet rock and began tumbling in slow motion. It bounced off the face of the mountain, catching the moon's light.

Sophia followed the crystal with her eyes until the strong green glow had faded. *It's gone*, she thought. As she stashed the other pieces into her pouch, a shadow crept over them. Horrified, she put the edge of her hand on her forehead, shielding her eyes against attack. The Shadow grew and turned into a black, green-eyed raven, the size of an elk. As he circled over her and dove, Sophia watched as Raven curled his talons, grabbed the crystal that had fallen, and flew to the North.

Apollo reared. Sophia jumped on his ready back and they took off after Raven. The bird, now invisible, left a slight scent. Apollo followed the trail, but the smell was too faint to be a compass. The horse moved through the air swiftly, against the racetrack of time. Sophia leaned forward, her hands clutching the feathered mane. The sky was cold against her skin, the only warmth coming from the moon. Sophia saw Raven fly across its face, like a witch on a broomstick. But in a blink he was gone, an illusion, like a mirage in the desert.

Sophia wondered how long his talons could stay curled. How many miles he could fly with the crystal in his grasp? What if he dropped it? Did he have a nest? Had the clouds put him up to it?

Of course, it all could have been happenstance: ravens were attracted to shiny and colorful objects, and the crystal was both.

No, he was sent by the clouds. Sophia was sure. She felt her weight sink heavier onto Apollo's back. They were both tired.

Horse and rider searched through the night, flying north along the coast. The search felt aimless, without direction— Sophia's feelings of helplessness could have come from shock, or the loss, or the panic, or the magnitude of looking for a tiny shard of crystal, or a trickster bird in a geography so vast and wild and dark.

After soaring over mountain ranges and rivers, rural towns and crowded cities, their energy was fading, like the glow inside the stones. Without that piece, Sophia knew the power of the horseshoe wasn't whole. The Codes could not be fully read. The messages that would preserve the world were as broken as the earth herself.

Sophia was broken, too.

THE GUIDES WENT SILENT

*S*OPHIA LAY ON THE FLOOR in front of her fireplace. It was not winter, but her bones were cold, and she felt limp, like an old rag doll handed down from child to child. Her body ached from the battle, and her tears pooled below the surface.

Those who knew her would not have recognized her in this moment of defeat. This was not who she was. Sophia had braved so much since she had been handed the role of Guardian of Mother Earth at fourteen.

Time and age had made it harder, and now she faced the greatest challenge she had ever known. Recovering the stolen crystal would test all of her skills. She had always been strong, resilient, agile, even powerful in her grace. Today, she felt faded.

As she lay on the floor, she recalled other clouds she had fought.

They had held all of the elements: dust, winds, lightning, rain. They were dangerous and getting worse. Some rained chemicals, others were laden with heavy metals, not easy for the Crystal Horseshoe to neutralize. But more and more, they were laced with a fifth element; greed—the desire for wealth, no matter the cost to human and planet.

Just four days before, Sophia had been in the Iowa cornfields. She had come face to face with Santomond, the viper cloud. He had changed into the serpent, but not the snake of lore who renewed the fertility of nature—no, this was a destroyer, voraciously disrupting ecosystems in and above the soil.

Sophia was tending the food supply. Santomond would have none of it, and Sophia would have none of him. She was being chased by a formidable enemy, one who wanted the horseshoe rendered powerless as badly as she wanted the earth to be whole. These clouds would destroy the Codes of Nature if they could; they did not care about the natural world at all.

Sophia ran through the maze of maize, endless corridors with stalks taller than she. She heard a hissing, then a slithering sound brushing against the earth. She felt hot snake breath on her back. But the land underneath her feet was solid, a springboard, and that gave her the physical power to keep moving while her mind honed its will and mental strength.

It was time to meet head-on.

She turned, straightening her arm, Crystal Horseshoe in hand. As her fierce eyes met the serpent cloud, she and the crystal became one single force.

She positioned the horseshoe, and as it sucked in the destroyer, the Codes inside transformed the cloud into a harmless mist of green.

❨

"Fearless," Sophia muttered, as she looked into the flames. She rolled over onto her aching back and looked at the ceiling. "I was fearless. But not on Mount Shasta. The cloud had a rage like I've never seen. How did I let him steal my strength?"

Five broken pieces of crystal lay scattered next to her on the wooden floor. She reached for them with sore arms, gathering them in her hands, inspecting each one, gleaning what power was left, if any.

A green light glowed around each cracked edge. It was pale, not nearly as vibrant as it had been, but it was still there. A bit more hopeful, Sophia turned onto her belly and began putting the pieces together, like a puzzle. The breaks were clean, they fit, and she could make out a few symbols through the widows of wisdom. But it wasn't whole.

She exhaled and put her head back down. She played the scene over in her mind, shivering as she relived the last night on Mount Shasta, when the Harvest Moon had bathed the northern hemisphere in an orange glow, when the dragon cloud had put a shadow on her life, and when a raven had stolen her peace.

Sophia rose from the heap in front of the dying fire and faced the future. She was tired. Was it time to pass the torch to those who were younger, stronger, and just as courageous as she? The answer would come. But now, she and Apollo must continue their search.

They combed Mount Shasta at high noon when the sun was at its peak. "Apollo, maybe Raven dropped it, maybe it will shimmer in the rays of Father Sun," she said. As the heat pounded down, they climbed the summit. Nothing. Not even the eagle perspective helped. Thirsty, they drank water from the falls. Sophia ate apricots.

Days passed.

In the mornings, Sophia lit beeswax candles, burned white sage, and called in the four directions. She sat at her altar, her personal temple, asking for contact from her spirit guides; these were the ancestors, animals, and higher beings that helped her make sense of things, of life. They were her North Star.

Staying true to her Lakota roots, she asked for White Buffalo Calf Woman, the vision who gave her tribe a way of peace. But this time, the vision didn't come.

She asked for Athena, the Goddess of Wisdom, and Demeter, Goddess of the Harvest, the mother of all growing things. She asked for Persephone, the Queen of the Underworld, who gave us the cycle of seasons. They were silent, too.

In the evenings, Sophia poured through ancient records that charted events from the beginning of time. She sought answers through stories of the knights of the round table, and even in musical scales. Sounds triggered memories. A high note could direct her to look to the North, where Raven had flown; a deeper tone took her to the South. She listened to Vivaldi's *Four Seasons* again and again, listening for patterns and clues. These were her favorite concertos, each season a color—like the gemstones found in the crust of the earth. Could the crystal be hidden in the depths?

She hovered over historical North American maps with a magnifying glass, hoping the names of lands and waters would become a trail of breadcrumbs. Exhausted, she closed the books, sipped rose tea with honey, and thought about where to look next.

Where were the messages? Sophia had asked for direction from the plant and animal worlds. If Fox came to her, it was a sign to be observant, quick, and adaptable. If Deer came, she knew to be gentle on herself, and everything around her. Normally generous with their wisdom, for weeks after the night on the mountain they didn't speak at all. Now they began to show up once again.

As she stood at the river, Beaver peeked out of his dam with a message. He was telling Sophia to be persistent. "Don't give up until the job is done," he said, speaking without words.

One night, White Lion came in a vision. Sophia was walking by his side through the desert in Egypt. They stopped in front of the Great Pyramid. Sophia counted seventy-two steps up to the stars. She knew just what the numbers meant: they told her to trust her own light, her own infinite wisdom.

Sometimes her great-great-grandmother came, usually when Sophia was at the hives. She placed her soft, elder hands on her sweet child's shoulders. When Sophia turned, her kind and knowing face put Sophia at ease.

Still, she was weary. She grieved and blamed herself. If the stolen crystal wasn't found soon, the Codes of Nature, which held the secrets to healing the *Anima Mundi*—the soul of the world—would be lost.

The color was seeping from her world, leaving only gray. Her spirit was leaving, too; she had not a bit of hope. She could feel Gaia's pain as if it were her own. The earth was crying, and so was Sophia. Mother Earth had chosen her to be a Guardian long before she was born, and now she was losing her will to live.

Tea and Trust

SOPHIA CONTACTED HER OLDEST CHILDHOOD FRIEND, the only one who held the secret of Sophia's calling. For the first time in a long time, Sophia asked for help.

"Anything," responded Keya, as Sophia knew she would.

"You might need a cup of tea," Sophia warned. "This could take some time."

Keya was wise, like her ancestors who came before. Sophia trusted the way Keya, with her Lakota traditions, looked at the world. The Lakota were taught to see through their senses, and believed the earth went far beyond the land; it traveled all the way up to the cosmos, offering great lessons in how to live life.

Sophia replenished her own cup and took a deep breath, unsure of how to tell this story. "I was on Shasta," she said. "The Crystal Horseshoe broke into six pieces. One of them was stolen."

"Stolen?" asked Keya.

There was a moment of silence.

"Stolen. By a giant black raven," said Sophia.

"Start over. Tell me everything."

"We were moon cleansing and a cloud came from the west, a Fire Dragon, the most vicious I've ever seen. The winds blew sideways like an angry god, too strong for me to neutralize. I was afraid the Horseshoe would be taken by the squalls. I tried to protect it, not realizing my own force, and it cracked into six pieces. Right in my hands."

"Oh, Sophia," said Keya.

Sophia knew Keya understood even the unspoken emotion of the story.

"One of the pieces fell. I went to reach for it, but it was too late. A giant Black Raven grabbed it and flew to the North."

"When did this happen?" asked Keya.

"I've been searching for weeks."

"Weeks?" said Keya.

"It might be time for me to pass the reins," said Sophia, her voice trembling. "I don't know how much longer it can wait." Over the years, Sophia had seen the climate change. Now ice was melting. Fires burned. Waters and woodlands were struggling. Species were dying. "The Earth is in distress. But humanity will suffer more. Without the Codes . . ." Sophia's voice trailed off. "Keya, I have to find it."

"Sophia, you don't have to take this on alone. Maybe you need a circle?"

"A circle?" said Sophia. The Guardians had always worked alone.

"Women were stronger when they held hands as one. It was how communities survived," said Keya. Keya's words brought Sophia up through the ashes of hopelessness, like a phoenix, emerging with a glimmer of hope.

Sophia was the Mother. She would not desert her children—all things alive—including the earth, herself.

A sisterhood. Maybe a young sisterhood, thought Sophia.

She continued the search. She looked in the spaces between rocks and trees, under sands, above the seas. If the crystal was of the earth, it must be hidden somewhere on it.

"You cannot do this alone." Keya's words played over in Sophia's mind.

But she was still alone. Except in her dreams.

Sophia tossed fitfully, wrestling with giant ravens in her sleep. One night she came face to face with the thief who had snatched the stone. She met his dead, green-black eyes with her own willful nature, and tried to convince him that he was being used, put up to thievery by the dark forces of greed that were breaking the planet.

"Don't you see?" she asked Raven. "Greed plays tricks. It makes you think you desire something. So much that you'd do anything to get it. Did it promise you power, or happiness?"

He didn't flinch.

Sophia had watched small corporations grow into giants, hungry to have it all. They polluted and poisoned—their huge appetites devoured the environment. They cared more about profits than people, or any kind of life.

"Raven, greed is a taker. It steals souls. It sucks you in." Sophia held her gaze steady. "Were you told you'd be granted a never-ending life? Or that your feathers would turn to gold?"

Raven stared her down, his curved beak almost touching her face. This was not the Raven she knew—the bearer of magic and light, bringer of cosmic messages and keeper of secrets. This was not the bird of creation. This was a bird of destruction.

Sophia changed her strategy, softened her tone. "Your real power is in being a healing force for nature. You must remember who you are."

Raven blinked.

Keya's words flashed through her mind: *Women holding hands as one.*

Sophia tried again. She could play tricks, too. She pleaded with the giant bird, begging Raven to be a messenger.

"Tell Dragon Cloud that I promise to sacrifice myself in exchange for the crystal." Sophia knew she would never end the lineage of the Guardians; it was a bargain as fake as the corn growing in Iowa. When the crystal was returned, she would have secretly prepared new Guardians, a new generation of Earth protectors.

Raven would not be fooled. He cackled—loud and wicked—startling Sophia out of her sleep.

She had this dream every fourth night.

Then one night, Sophia dreamt a more hopeful message.

She woke at 4:44, in a daze, and reached for her writing tablet.

I was on a mountain. The sky was like black velvet, with very few stars. There was a tiny green glow, far far away. I thought it was Ceres, the dwarf planet, named for the Earth Mother goddess. Then it moved. It didn't look like a comet, or a shooting star.

When it came closer, it appeared as a small constellation of orbs, transparent globes of light, like bubbles. They stopped in midair, as if to announce themselves. There were five of them. They were the pieces, the broken pieces of the Crystal Horseshoe. Inside each one was a little arrow, a copper compass that pointed to a direction. They formed a circle—and took their places in the North, South, East, and West. The fifth piece moved into the center. Dreamcatchers. I must call Keya in the morning.

Sophia placed her quill pen onto her nightstand, closed her eyes, and waited for the dusty pink of dawn.

In the morning, the women spoke for a long time, and Keya agreed that this was the guidance Sophia had been waiting for. Dreamcatchers would be important allies in the mission to find the stolen crystal.

They began to make a plan.

"So, a circle," said Sophia. "Guidance is telling me four girls."

"It makes perfect sense," said Keya. "The circle is the hoop."

There was a moment of silence on the other end of the phone. Sophia was deep in thought. "What if the girls came from the four directions," she said.

"That's perfect," said Keya. "But how will we find them?"

Sophia hesitated for a moment, "I think I know where to start."

Keya also knew but didn't want to say.

❨

Keya, who had made dreamcatchers all of her life, prepared to make five hoops. One for Sophia and one for a circle of strong young women. Four girls who would come from the four directions.

Keya would weave an intricate web. She would secure a single broken piece into the center of each dreamcatcher. The codes, even broken, would bring potent dreams and messages to the girls during their quest. It would be the perfect tool to bring home the missing piece, making the Crystal Horseshoe whole once more.

Turtle Creek

*M*AIA LIVED IN THE BLACK HILLS of South Dakota, where the earth and sky were so vast that they stretched to the edges of the world. Her Native ancestors roamed this land; it was a place of ceremony, both sacred and mysterious.

Sometimes Maia saw visions. Once, for forty-nine dawns, the White Buffalo thundered past her bedroom window, leaving streaks of golden dust in its wake.

The White Buffalo was a sacred being in Oglala Lakota lore. He was part of a story that had been passed down for two thousand years. Maia often wondered if her sightings were real or imagined. They felt real—she heard them and saw them with her own eyes.

Tonight, she was outside, wrapped in a soft blanket looking up. She loved being with Moon, she had become her friend.

Maia's mother liked to remind her that things take time, and that Mother Moon was the best teacher. Maia recorded her waxing and waning in her journal, with line drawings of crescents and half circles and cycles.

In winter, Maia noted the soft colors and patterns the moon cast on the snow, especially the long shadows. Sometimes they moved with the wind. Maia learned much from the North. Moon was teaching her to be more perceptive, how to watch change.

An only child, Maia felt the land was her sister. It was her place of comfort, a place where she had conversations with the natural world. She and her horse, Lune, disappeared for hours on end, exploring the hills and forests, taking in the shapes they made against the sky. Although she read time by the position of the sun, she and Lune often lost track of it.

Her horse was gray with white dapples and deep brown eyes. The first time Maia looked into them she saw a crescent moon looking back, and so his name. They were the best of friends.

Lune was more than fifteen hands from ground to withers. He was agile and fast and loved to run on open land. Today they were on the far side of Turtle Creek, where the mud was thick and squishy and fragrant along the river, smelling of earth and bugs and worms and all the things that live in those invisible places. She didn't want to head home, not just yet, but the sun was going down and she had to help with dinner.

Maia burst through the door. Her cheeks were smudged with dirt, and there were burrs in her hair. "Look," she insisted, both hands holding out medicine bags of arrowheads, stones, and other objects. "Look what I found," she said, out of breath, as she gently emptied them on the kitchen table.

Keya, her mother, smiled and exclaimed over the pile as she always did. Half of the day's collection would end up in a shoebox, and a few pieces would go on Maia's altar, reserved for special things, mostly treasures found on the land as she explored.

Maia's objects rested on a long rawhide that was painted by the loving hands of her grandmother. A fallen nest held a tiny blue egg, the shell strong yet fragile, once a protector for a life that wasn't birthed. Four hawk feathers spread out like a fan, their tips brushing against white birch bark, curled like parchment. A carved stone called the Twin Sisters kept watch over a small piece of red jasper, Mother Earth's nurturing stone.

After washing her hands, Maia chose a few of the things she had gathered and took them to her room. As she rearranged her cherished space, she spoke aloud to each piece.

Keya heard her from the kitchen. She wondered if her daughter would be a part of Sophia's tribe. It had been years since Sophia had held her goddaughter on her lap, telling her stories about secret codes, crystal grids, and the ways of the Universe. At the time, Maia was too young to understand. Maybe it was a language she would soon come to know.

STANDS IN THE CENTER WOMAN

WHEN MAIA'S MOTHER CAME OF AGE, she was given the name Stands in the Center Woman. She was fourteen. She was known by her tribe as the one who created quilled medicine wheels and hoops with intricate webs that caught dreams.

Keya was taught by her grandmother, who learned from her grandmother, of the Ojibwe, in the Canadian woodlands. Her band had migrated south, into the Dakotas, where she settled and passed the tradition down through the women, always the women, the protectors of children.

When Maia was little, she loved hearing her mom's soft voice as she told her the legend of the Dreamcatcher, how dreams held great power, how they swirled in the night before coming to sleeping children. Good dreams floated down the trail of beads, down the feather, and into the resting minds of those below. Bad dreams were caught in the web, never to be remembered.

Maia was just a baby when her mom opened a small trading post filled with objects crafted by Native artisans. Keya greeted the steady stream of customers while holding a chubby baby girl on her hip. There was no need to sway or rock—Maia was calm and peaceful. She followed people with her big round eyes, taking it all in, quietly listening to her mother's familiar voice, the voice that she had known from the womb.

Her mom, a storyteller like her grandmother, had something to say about each dreamcatcher. Maia didn't understand the words but later learned that her mother went into great detail—sharing how each dreamcatcher was made, why she chose the stones, the feathers, the color of the beads. No two were the same. The only thing they had in common was her Stands in the Center Woman mark, a small black hoop with a red SC in the middle.

As Maia grew older, she watched over her Keya's shoulder as she made the dreamcatchers. Her mother, hunched over the wooden table, showed her how to bend the pliable red willow and shape it into the hoops that captured stories of the night. Her little fingers followed along as she wrapped and twisted the softened branches. They listened to flute music as they worked—it had been a precious time.

Keya also made medicine wheels. These small circles represented the harmony in nature. Sitting cross-legged on the floor, Maia's mother taught her how to sort porcupine quills. They dyed them red, yellow, white, and black—the four colors of humankind, the colors of the four directions. Then they wrapped them around the small hoop and tied on an eagle plume.

Her mother explained that the circle was crossed by two roads—one for the spirits, the other for humanity. Where they met was called the *hochoka,* the center of all living things.

Young Maia had many questions about the ceremonies they were used for. Her mom told her that wheels were tied on a pipe stem or to the hair of the person when they were given their name. She learned that when her mom went on her vision quest—the *hambleycia*—she wore four medicine wheels.

The years blended, one into the next. Keya wove hundreds of dreamcatchers. She worked day and night, just to keep up. Maia rarely saw her mama smile—it seemed like her soul was gone. Her mother told her how commercialized dreamcatchers had become. They were being made by those who had no place making them, many from factories overseas.

That's when her mother came to the crossroads of choice, the center of the roads. Would she honor the Indian name she had been given all those years ago? Stands in the Center Woman chose her name. She and Maia would have to do with less as she moved away from crafting the sacred objects for sale. Keya was smart about saving, but they were very careful about what they purchased and lived with few luxuries.

Now, years later, Maia, stood behind her mother's chair, braiding her dark, waist length hair. When she finished tying a leather cord at the end of the braid, her mom turned to her.

"Maia, I need you to gather red willow."

"For dreamcatchers?" *I haven't gathered red willow in so long,* she thought.

Her mother didn't answer. Maia knew her mother's silence meant she shouldn't ask again.

Lately, her usually talkative mom had been quiet, almost secretive. Absent were the conversations about tadpoles or shooting stars, or why pipelines were being laid at Standing Rock. No more discussions about when they would next stand with the Water Keepers, protecting sacred lands from the oil companies that cut through the earth with no regard for human life—or the life of the Great Mother.

Her mom was removed. Maia was certain Sophia had a hand in it. The two had been speaking by phone every night. They hadn't been in touch like this for years.

Maia went outside, rolled up a worn woolen blanket and tied it with twine. She attached it to Lune's saddle, along with her trimming shears, then set out to gather red willow. It was plentiful near the banks of the creek, where the land felt most fertile. It was where her morning buffalo ran, the place where Maia heard messages from the winds, faint voices that said, "Be ready, a new world is on its way."

Maia found clusters of scarlet stems. The branches were naked as it wasn't the season for leaves. Maia buried herself in the woodsy fragrance, which intensified each time she cut a stem.

She and Lune lingered. A red-tailed hawk kept them company as did the field crickets in chorus. It was a welcome distraction from the questions in Maia's mind. *What is my mother hiding?* she thought.

Before heading back, she opened the blanket and placed the willow onto the wool, rolling it carefully so the branches wouldn't break. She knew her mother. Each branch had to be perfect.

When she got home, she put them on her mother's worktable. She looked at the pile and imagined strands of sinew threads tied in a web, in a pattern borrowed from snowshoes, the ones in the Canadian Woodlands, the ones that left impressions in the white carpet of winter.

KEEPING SECRETS

AIA HEARD THE PHONE RING before dawn. Her mother answered quickly. When she walked into the kitchen, her mother hung up.

"Was that Sophia?" she asked. Keya avoided looking at her, leaned her small frame against the counter, and wrung her hands. She needed a minute to come to herself.

"Yes, it was Sophia," she said. "I'm going to meet with her."

"When?"

"Tomorrow."

"Can I go?" said Maia. *Please, please, please,* she thought to herself.

Keya cocked her head. Her mother always did this when she knew she'd be disappointing her.

"I'm sorry, not this time."

Maia's lips got tight, and she turned away from her mother.

"But I'll only be gone for the day," Keya said, her voice trailing off.

Maia's throat burned from holding back tears. The dam opened and she wiped the tears with her shirtsleeve before her mother could see.

"Why can't I go? We always take road trips together. And I miss Sophia."

"It's not the right time."

"When is the 'right time?'" She looked at her mother in a way that demanded an answer.

Her mother said nothing.

"So you're driving all that way to see each other, and turning around and coming back?" said Maia, her voice rising.

"There are things I can't tell you, at least not right now," Keya said, softly.

"Mom, I am not a child."

"No, you're not."

"Something's changed. You're different. You're hiding something. And you don't trust me."

"Of course, I trust you," said Keya.

"If you trusted me, you'd tell me," said Maia, as she stormed out of the kitchen.

The screen door slammed behind her as she ran to Lune through a storm of tears. He always consoled her. He was sensitive, all horses were, and could read emotions before they even surfaced.

Maia didn't bother with a saddle, climbing onto his bare back. She needed to run, needed to feel the wind on her face and through her hair, she needed the sense of freedom she got when nothing held her back. This was her medicine.

She was gone for most of the morning.

They rode to the opposite side of the land, as far away from the creek as they could. She didn't want to be anywhere near the place where red willow grew.

They rode through sloping hills. Sprigs of prairie chickweed popped up through the grasses as they came to Maia's rock. They stopped so she could climb up and sit on the warm stone.

How could my mother do this? she thought. A doe and her fawn playfully pranced across the field. A mother and her child. Tears sprang like a faucet and Maia sobbed into her hands. She needed to get out every last drop of hurt, every last bit of disappointment.

Lune looked up at her with warm eyes.

"You understand me," she sighed.

Being alone, in this beautiful place, with her horse, the sun, and the quiet began to shift her mood.

She smelled a hint of pine in the air and looked over toward the evergreen forest. Usually a deep, rich green, the clusters of needles looked gray. Not all of the needles, but some. She walked over to the trees. *They look sick*, she thought as she touched the bark. There was a fungus growing. The winter hadn't been as cold as usual; she wondered if that was the cause.

❲

When Maia got home, the hollow feeling returned. She threw herself onto her bed. It was always her and her mother. The two of them. Like the doe and her fawn.

Keya came into the room and sat at the edge of the bed. She put her hand on Maia's shoulder. Maia didn't respond.

"Please," she said. "Don't be like this. You are my heart. We'll go to Sophia's for a long visit. I promise."

"When?" said Maia, thinking her mother would say next summer.

"Soon. She wants to see you as much as you want to see her."

"You're just saying that."

Maia turned to her mother and softened when she saw a tear collecting in her mother's eyes. Her mother. Her beautiful mother. Maia had hurt her, too. Her mother had always kept her promises.

Still, something was brewing.

The Golden Box

*A*THICK, WOOLEN BLANKET was folded around the Golden Box, the secret hiding place for the five broken pieces. Sophia had tucked it away years ago, this golden leather box disguised as a book. An artist had carved the cover with intricate designs of circles and hexagons, then lined it with a cushion of plush blue velvet. When she found it in an antiques shop, buried under a stack of medieval drawings, she didn't know that one day it would become the hiding place for one of the most sacred formulas in the world.

Sophia and Keya met at a lookout point on the highway. They had little time for talking. The box Sophia handed her wasn't heavy, but Keya felt the weight of it. She carefully tucked the package underneath the passenger seat.

Keya arrived home after midnight. Maia's bedroom was dark, but she thought Maia might be awake.

"I'm home safe," she whispered. "You can rest now."

When she was sure that her suspicious daughter was asleep, she went into her bedroom, closed the door, and carefully unfolded the blanket.

Sitting under a pool of lamplight, she examined the Golden Box. A green patina washed over the leather. She wondered how old it was, where it came from, whose hands had once held it. It felt warm and smelled of apricots. She took the key, placed it into the lock, and opened the box.

Nestled in a cushion of blue velvet was an old medicine bag. On the front was a thunderbird, sewn with tiny Venetian glass beads. She had given Sophia this pouch when they were young girls. She had forgotten about it, until now.

She looked over at the red willow sitting on her work table. Butterfly wings fluttered in her belly; her forehead glistened with sweat. She took a chest-expanding breath, held it for three long seconds, and let it go.

And then she felt them, her ancestors. They stood behind her—her mother, her grandmother, her aunts—the elders who wove the thread of her lineage.

Hands shaking, she opened the soft leather pouch and reached inside. She felt a jagged edge, uneven but not sharp enough to cut. She lifted out the first crystal. She tried to place it on her desk, but a strong magnetic force kept it in her fingers.

She tried to release it again. The stone didn't move.

Keya opened her palm and watched in awe as the clear stone began to change. A soft light, the color of tourmaline, glowed around the edges. It grew warmer and began to vibrate in her hand.

Keya had held many stones in her life and was sensitive to the power of crystals, but this—this was different.

Waves of warmth radiated out of the crystal, a starburst of light that made a green circle around her. It was a ring of protection, a shield, and it pulsed to the rhythm of her heart. Although the object was outside of her body, it was part of her, and she was part of it.

Convergence. The moment when all things come together, and nothing is separate. Not plants or rock, water or sky, or even humankind. It was a strange concept—the sky and water being one thing, humans and plants sharing DNA. Was this even possible? The answers *were* in the Crystal Horseshoe.

If this single piece has so much energy, imagine the power when the pieces become whole.

❨

Keya understood why she had only seen Sophia a few times in the past several years. After she was chosen to be Guardian of Mother Earth, the work required that she remove herself from the three-dimensional world, the everyday world that *appears* real. Solitude was the only way Sophia could stay clear, open to receiving instruction from nature, the ancestors of the earth, and the evolutionary guides. She sacrificed the material, the traditional life. She gave up becoming a mother. She lived, instead, with secrets.

But the time for secrets—all kinds of secrets, including those between Keya and her daughter—was coming to an end.

The sun lit the morning mist as it rolled along the hills. Keya went to Maia's bedside, got on her knees, and whispered to her half-sleeping daughter.

"We're going to Sophia's."

"When?" asked Maia, sitting up, awake and smiling.

"On the next full moon."

STORIES

MAIA PUT THE BURR OAK WALKING STICK into the loaded car. It had taken a month to carve. Her knuckles were scabbed from where the knife had slipped, though her mother's yarrow-root salve had eased the healing along.

Maia had spent hours watching the pile of shavings grow as her long, steady strokes made the gift for Sophia smooth. The final roughness was gone with the pass of a stone, and then she brushed the length with oil. Maia wrapped a thin, beaded leather thong around the grip. It was too tall to be a staff or a wand, but this gift was worthy of a queen.

"Are you ready?" asked Keya.

Maia noted the hint of hesitation in her mother's voice, as if she were asking the question of herself.

They had carefully planned the road trip to Big Timber, mapping out the safest routes, knowing that driving through some mountain passes could be rough in the wind.

Maia loved road trips with her mother. They had similar rhythms and read each other well. They knew when the other needed quiet, when it was time to talk, when it was okay to turn up the music.

Maia was in a reflective mood, thinking about how the trees talked, how the flowers got their colors, how the fish breathe underwater.

"Where is your imagination taking you now?" asked Keya. She loved her daughter's curious mind.

"Mom?"

Keya smiled.

"How come Sophia never married?"

"She devoted herself to other responsibilities."

"Like what?" asked Maia. Her mother changed lanes on the highway. "Didn't she want children?"

"Every living thing is her child—the flowers, the grasses, the waters, the winged creatures, and four-legged ones, too."

"Was she always like that?"

"Yes. Always."

Maia saw a wistful smile creep onto her mother's face, as she recalled the days of childhood.

"When we were young girls," said Keya, "we couldn't wait for morning to come. We grabbed handfuls of fruit and nuts, put them into our pouches, and spent the day exploring everything around us until the sun went down."

"Sounds like me," said Maia.

"We dug up worms, studied bugs—the soil smells so different after a rain."

"What else?"

"Animal tracks. Guessing who walked. Oh, there were so many—bear, racoon, mountain lion, and fox. Sophia loved the birds of prey—she watched them, learned how they moved, how they thought. She knew when an eagle or a hawk was about to swoop down and grab its meal, or just coast on the wind."

"Did you listen to the winds?"

"Yes. The ancestors live in them. They call out to us."

Maia heard the voices, too.

"Sophia and I hunted knowledge. Grandmother called us Twin Students of the Earth Girls. We were like sisters."

Maia felt bad about last month's moment of jealousy, when her mother had gone to meet Sophia.

"What happened to her family?" Maia asked.

"Her mother died when she was eleven," said Keya.

Maia watched her mom glance into the rearview mirror.

"That's so sad," said Maia. Her mother's eyes shifted back to the mirror.

Maia saw an expression of worry on her mother's face. She seemed preoccupied.

After a few moments, her mother continued.

"It was very sad. Just a year later her dad died of a broken heart. It was a hard time. Sophia's mom was the only one who knew just how strong her daughter was." Keya shifted her body, recentering herself in the seat.

"Mom, what's wrong?"

"Nothing. I'm driving."

Maia knew that when her mom said nothing, it meant something. She turned toward the back window. A grey cloud billowed in the clearest of skies. Just one.

"Didn't Sophia have brothers?" Maia asked, halfway remembering.

"They were older. They disappeared after their parents died."

"They just left her. Alone?"

"They did, and you know what? Sophia was relieved. When they were young, there wasn't a day when those boys hadn't made fun of her twig houses. They tore the grass garlands she wore, made fun of her beehives, and always commented on her feet—dirty from playing outside barefoot all day."

"If I had a brother, he'd never do that." But Maia didn't have a brother. Or a sister. And her dad had died in an accident before she could walk.

"Those boys didn't understand her rock collections or the herbs she collected and dried. And they laughed at her potions. They called her a witch. She used to tell them that if they weren't nice to her, she'd turn them into stone."

Maia took out the almost-empty bag of chocolate Twizzlers, her favorite. They were braided, like her hair, and she could take little bites at a time to make them last.

"Where did Sophia go after everyone was gone?" she asked.

"Grandmother was fond of her, and she came to live with us, until she was called to do her work."

"Her work?"

Her mother looked at the rearview mirror again.

"Mom?"

"Let's find a rest stop."

They hit the parking lot, stretched their legs, and made a beeline for the ladies' room. Maia closed the door to the stall and pulled down her white panties. No blood. Not one drop. All of her friends had gotten their periods. She prayed to the moon that hers would soon come.

Maia wandered through the aisles of the mini mart looking for something halfway healthy. For some reason, the donuts were tempting. She looked at the stacks of chips. She grabbed nuts and dried fruit, raspberry club soda, and gave in to another bag of licorice. She was at the counter when the Turkey Jerky caught her eye. She took one and handed it to the cashier.

Keya looked at her funny. "You rarely eat junk."

"I know," said Maia. "I liked the sound of it."

Back on the road, Joy Harjo's clear voice filled the car with songs that Maia remembered her mom singing when she was young. She hummed along to "Morning Song."

Maia appreciated the poetry that was grown out of a hard life. When her mom told her that Joy Harjo had been named the first Native American poet laureate, they danced in the kitchen. "She even plays the saxophone," Keya had said.

Time moved quickly, like the car on the road. The sun dropped before they pulled into a motel and crashed hard on a bed that was too soft.

❮

They woke to the sun streaming through thin beige curtains. Five hours of driving and two breaks later, they saw the sign for Big Timber, a tiny Montana town at the edge of the Crazy Mountains. They made a left turn after the Lazy B Bar Ranch, onto a narrow and nameless dirt road.

"Soon," Keya said, smiling at her daughter. "We're almost there."

The tires met the dry road, kicking up clouds of dust. Maia could tell that her mom was in her own cloud, somewhere else. "What are you thinking about?" she asked.

"When Sophia and I were young, silly girls, giggling about what it would be like to kiss," she laughed. "We scrunched up our noses at the thought, but secretly imagined canoeing on the river or sitting under a tree with the person of our dreams."

"Sometimes I think about that, too," said Maia.

"Boys?"

"No, just having a friend like that. Someone you can trust with anything."

"We had fun," said Keya, thinking of those carefree years. "I remember when winds whipped the plains and Sophia and I made indoor tipis out of our bedsheets, wrapping ourselves in thick woolen blankets. We drew on the fabric walls with charcoal, outlines of buffalo and elk and horses, Sophia's favorite.

"We played my grandfather's drum and the wood flute that belonged to your grandmother. We sang songs of the Sioux, passed down through the generations."

"What else?"

"We were explorers. We had collections, like you—plant bark, shed skins from snakes, sherds of Native pottery, stones. I taught Sophia how to braid lanyards out of long strands of sweetgrass, the hair of Mother Earth, as all of the grasses are."

"Did you make dreamcatchers out of red willow?" Maia didn't mean to ask about them, but the question slipped out.

Keya shifted in her seat. "We did."

Maia focused on the dark ribbon of road.

"See that up ahead? That's it," said Keya.

She made a sharp left turn into the long driveway and stopped. Maia jumped out of the car and trotted to open the black, hand-forged iron gate, welded at least a century earlier, then closed it behind.

Sprigs of blue bear grass grew at the edges of the dirt road; they swayed in the arms of a light wind, which also carried the crisp scent of ponderosa pine through the open windows.

The Crazy Mountains were no longer part of a distant landscape—they were right there, standing watch at seven thousand feet, sentinels on the horizon, white-crested peaks brushing the sky.

A dramatic transition from prairie to range.

Maia knew there would be trails that led to waterfalls, gushing creeks, and calmer swimming holes where tadpoles came to life.

As they drove toward the house, Maia pointed to the high-tech blades of steel.

"Wind gatherers," said Keya.

Maia remembered seeing them in *National Geographic* magazine.

"They have been around for a long time, my love, first made of wood, now made of steel."

Not far from the windmills, a small grouping of solar panels was lined up like dominoes in a field.

They passed a garden of beehives.

Bee technology, thought Maia. "The cabin!" she said, with the excitement of a child.

Built by hand with logs from the land, it was flanked by two stone chimneys and embraced by a wraparound porch. Chimes played like harps in the breeze. Just up the hill from the house, five horses grazed in the pasture, next to a weathered red barn with a large silo. A golden weathervane stood on the roof, a wheel that pointed to the four directions.

Keya pulled up in front of the house. Maia got out of the car. She stretched and walked to the porch. Then she rang the old cowbell three times.

WHISPERS

THE DOOR SWUNG OPEN to reveal an ageless beauty, otherworldly, with skin like coffee-dipped gold. Maia was awestruck as Sophia stepped onto the porch, barefoot, wearing a flowing dress the color of moss. As she turned, she surrounded them in her ethereal cloud, wisps of hair showing streaks of blue underneath.

"Sister," Keya whispered, as she and Sophia came together in an embrace that left Maia feeling awkward and on the outside.

When they stepped back, their eyes held a gaze for a long time.

Sophia turned to Maia and smiled, and without saying a word, acknowledged how grown up she had become. She opened her arms, and Maia fell into her softness. After their bodies parted, Sophia took Maia's hand and led them into the house.

The room was a mirror of Sophia. Flute music wove together the tapestry of drying herbs, books—so many books—and medicine bags. Old ledger art and narrative drawings by the Plains Indians hung on the walls. One shelf was lined with glass jars full of herbs with handwritten labels: dandelion, milk thistle, yarrow, echinacea, rose.

"I told you, Sophia likes collecting, too." There was a smile in her mother's voice.

Maia turned to Sophia. Just being in the room made her feel like a hummingbird, curious little wings flitting from here to there and back again.

"Will you show me everything?" she asked Sophia.

"I will, but there's a soup on the stove that needs stirring, and a bread to bake!"

"I'll give you a hand," said Keya.

The women went into the kitchen, leaving Maia to explore.

She walked over to the wall of books. They ranged from the practical to the magical. Among the collection were *Harry Potter*, *Narnia*, and *Lord of the Rings*, stories that took the reader into worlds of light and dark, quests and journeys, magic and fate.

There were stacks of books full of Native American plant medicine, sacred stories of the Lakota and the Ojibwe, and texts on Navajo astronomy. Maia saw an oversized atlas, dog-eared and worn, with page corners folded over into the tiniest triangles. A book about the canyons of the West was marked with dried floral stems, as was a book on the pre-colonial Mayan culture. There were books on the Egyptian goddesses, Jewish mysticism, and Greek mythology.

Maia hesitated as she pulled a small book about crystal grids from the shelf. She had wanted to learn about the power of laying out the stones, arranging them in just the right way to make their energies the most potent. She flipped through some pages before putting it back. She would ask Sophia if she could borrow it that night when the world was asleep.

She went to the car, got their luggage, and brought in Sophia's gift. The smell of warm bread made her hungry. Low voices came from the kitchen, but they sounded private, so she didn't go in.

Wanting to be useful, she found cloth napkins in a clay

bowl and placed them around the wooden table. Then she lit a beeswax candle.

Maia was glad that her mother had a sister-friend like Sophia.

As they came out of the kitchen, she wished she had one, too. It got lonely in South Dakota. She thought about her friend Ava. They had bonded over horses and their love of sunsets. They met at a wild horse sanctuary near Santa Barbara, where both girls had received a scholarship. That summer, they learned about conservation, rescue herds, and gentle ways of training horses to be adopted later on. When they got home, Maia and Ava began writing letters. It wasn't the same as seeing each other, but they became good friends through the written word.

After a dinner of soup and greens from the garden, Sophia showed Maia her collection of gems—giant amethyst, amber, and celestite, stones of turquoise, lapis, and quartz.

"Do you have a favorite?"

"This one," said Sophia, as she picked up the icy blue celestite. "It is the guardian angel's stone. It means purity to the heart."

She handed it to Maia. It was heavy, rough on the bottom. Inside, it looked like a mountain range of glaciers, clusters of clear blue ice.

Maia felt the presence of someone standing by her shoulder. Her grandmother. "Trust," whispered her grandmother.

She didn't want to put the crystal down. Ever. She wanted her grandmother with her all of the time. She had missed her stories, and her touch.

Sophia gave her time, as if she knew, then moved to another stone. "This is my power amethyst," said Sophia, putting her hand on the top of the giant geode.

Maia leaned over the wands of purple that lived inside the rock.

"To the ancients, this was the Gem of Fire."

"Why fire?" asked Maia

"It sparks creativity. It's the Artist's Stone."

Maia moved even closer, looking for the flame. "Would it work for a poet or a composer?"

"Yes," said Sophia, "it amplifies the life force. If a plant isn't doing so well, place an amethyst by its roots—it will grow."

"How?" asked Maia.

"I'm not exactly sure, but there is a spirit in all things, even stone."

Maia had questions. So many questions.

Five silver buckles next to the amethyst caught her eye. They looked like the winning buckles of a rodeo champion, big ovals with intricate designs, engraved by the finest Western silversmiths. But these were not rodeo trophies.

Each buckle had four crystals placed around the circle, with a larger stone in the center.

"Sophia, this stone could be on a crown." She paused. "Where did the buckles come from?"

"I made them."

Maia saw a sparkle in Sophia's eye, gratified by the response to her handiwork.

"They took me twenty-eight days."

As if she knew that was my next question, thought Maia. "May I hold one?"

Sophia hesitated, then nodded.

Maia picked up a buckle and cradled it in her hands. Etching surrounded each crystal, symbols that were familiar to Maia—the infinity sign, morning stars, three-dimensional triangles. Then she saw her two spirit animals, Buffalo and Turtle.

Maia's hands began to shake. She looked up at Sophia, whose eyes were closed as if she was in a trance.

Maia was afraid. What was happening? The buckle began to vibrate. It felt hot in her hands. Confused and scared, she put it down, pulling away.

Sophia opened her eyes.

Maia was stunned. "What *was* that?" she asked, her voice shaking.

"The crystals in those buckles have powerful properties, Maia. They send and receive messages."

"Messages?" asked Maia. "I saw grids and compasses and maps," she said.

She looked at her mom, then back at Sophia. She was confused.

"Tomorrow I will begin to explain it to you," said Sophia.

Maia didn't want to wait. She wanted to know now. She was about to ask a question when she noticed a beam of light moving around the room. The source appeared to be a dreamcatcher at the top of a small, hexagonal window. Four golden eagle feathers hung from the bottom.

The dreamcatcher hoop was made from the branches of red willow.

I recognize those branches, thought Maia. Inside, strands of sinew were woven into the Flower of Life, a geometrical shape of overlapping circles that formed a petal-like pattern.

Maia had read once that this perfect symmetrical form was six thousand years old, and was known to the great philosophers, architects, and artists of the world. She loved the idea that a secret symbol was embedded within the flower, holding sacred patterns of the Universe and life itself—from minuscule molecules to gigantic galaxies.

Maia stared more closely. She had never seen a dreamcatcher like this. The crystal in the center of the flower was clear, almost blinding. It glimmered like a thousand diamonds in the sun. Its edges had a hint of green.

Maia stood transfixed, looking into the crystal—not at it. She felt like she was pulled into a tunnel, a portal into other worlds. The room turned in a spiral; she felt dizzy, as if she were falling into the center of the earth. She sat down on the floor to ground herself and used her arms to hold steady.

Her mother called out to her, but Maia was in her own world and only heard an echo of her mother's voice.

Maia tried to avert her gaze from the crystal. She gathered her mental strength and tried again. She slowly managed to turn away from the dreamcatcher. She regained her balance.

Maia looked up at her mother's pale face, then at Sophia, then back to the dreamcatcher. This time she was prepared for its power.

"You made that for Sophia, didn't you, Mom?"

Her mother nodded yes.

Maia began piecing things together. Memories of hushed conversations, the quick meet-up, nights when her mother was up until the wee hours, the lamplight shining from beneath her bedroom door.

"You used the red willow I gathered. Why didn't you tell me?"

Keya started to answer, but Maia was too quick. "Where did that center stone come from? I didn't find that near the creek."

"It's ancient," said Sophia, calmly. "I can see you feel its power."

"Yes," said Maia, in a whisper. "I do feel it." She looked up at the dreamcatcher. "It has a heartbeat."

Sophia and Keya looked at each other and didn't speak. The silence was long, and awkward.

They know something. They're keeping it from me, thought Maia.

"Maia, I have a lot to reveal to you. I need you to be patient."

Her mother came to her, smoothing her cheek with her shaking hand. "Come, Maia, you need rest. Tomorrow is time enough for all of this."

Maia was too exhausted to ask more questions. Her mother walked with her to the guest room and lay down next to her on the bed. Maia felt heavy and limp and sank into the mattress.

Her mother stayed until she thought she was asleep, kissed her on the forehead, and quietly left the room.

But Maia was not asleep. She rewound the day—the moment her grandmother's spirit came, her hand so real on her shoulder, gifting her with the message to trust. She felt so safe. And then so frightened when she held the belt buckle, so hot to the touch, vibrating, like the rattle of a snake.

She thought about the collection of crystals, in particular the amethyst, the "Artist's Stone." She hadn't heard of it referred to in that way. And the dreamcatcher, the dizzying power of it, and the beauty, too. She had never seen or felt anything like it—or the web her mother wove. Not the typical pattern, it was the sacred symbol for life itself.

Her mother.

Maia was tired of secrets. Tired of feeling left out. She opened the book on crystal grids and tried to read, but couldn't focus. She slid out of bed and put her ear to the door, hating to eavesdrop, but wanting to hear the words under the whispered tones in the next room. It sounded so serious. When she gave up she crawled back into her bed and opened her journal.

There are secrets here. And they're about me. Sophia said that I need to be patient. But when will I know? My mother already knows. She's kept it from me, too. She says that I am her best friend. It's not true. Sophia is her best friend. Where does that leave me?

EARTH TEACHER

MAIA WOKE EARLY to a quiet house except for the greeting of birdsong through the open windows. She wandered out to the pasture. The dew sparkled in the pale light of dawn, tiny droplets clinging to grass like a mother holding her child.

The air smelled of pine and open sky, and she breathed it in as she walked toward the grazing horses. They heard her approach, and almost in unison, lifted their heads, welcoming her into their space. Maia nuzzled with each one, giving them a soft scratch behind the ears. It lightened her spirit like she knew it would. After giving them proper attention, she turned and walked back toward the house.

When Maia was small, she had sensed that Sophia was different. She was too young to understand why she felt that way. She later learned that you didn't need to find the logic—sometimes the knowing was enough.

Maia thought Sophia was the most beautiful woman who ever lived. Her name meant wise one. Her wisdom came from the ancients, yet she never seemed to age.

Sophia, dressed in a white cotton sleeping gown, stood at the counter in the kitchen, steeping tea. She smiled and motioned Maia to sit down.

"It's rose," she said, handing her a steaming ceramic mug. "It helps heal the heart."

Maia's heart was already softening with morning and the smell of horses. How could she not trust her mother and the woman who was like an aunt, the person who had midwifed her into the world.

I hope I learn the truth today, thought Maia.

"Do not be angry with your mother, dear one. This has not been easy for her," said Sophia.

"I don't understand," said Maia. "Yet," she added.

When Keya came in for her own tea, Maia saw the dark circles under her eyes. She stood behind her mother's chair and rubbed her shoulders. Tears gathered in her mother's eyes—gratitude for this gesture of forgiveness.

"Maia, would you like to take a walk with me later? I know you like creeks. I'd like to show you mine," said Sophia.

Keya looked up at Maia. "Go, my child, take time with Sophia. I will be here."

☾

Maia and Sophia sat beside the water, cold and timeless as it moved swiftly on its own way. Time was on Sophia's mind. She took Maia's hands in hers.

"Maia, it's time for you to hear this story."

Maia sensed that what she was about to hear would change her destiny.

Sophia told her story, as well as the story of those who came before her, and what their purpose was on Earth.

"It happened almost twenty thousand years ago, during the time of the Magdalenian," said Sophia.

"The Magdalenian?" asked Maia, rolling the word around.

"The cave people who lived in the southwest of France," explained Sophia.

"It was a cold era. When the climate warmed, the Magdalenian culture disappeared. What we know of them remains in a secluded cave called Lascaux. It was a sanctuary for initiations, with paintings of reindeer, bison, and wild horses."

Maia's eyes were wide and curious. "What happened after the people were gone?" she asked.

"Mother Earth saw the future. The climate warming told the story of what would come," said Sophia.

Maia nodded. She understood.

"She asked the wise women to be protectors. She called them her Guardians," said Sophia.

"Are you a Guardian of the Earth?"

"Yes."

Maia learned more about the cave in France, the primitive horse drawing and how, when lightning struck, it activated the crystal that shaped-shifted into a horseshoe.

"It's called the Crystal Horseshoe," said Sophia.

"What does it . . . do?" asked Maia.

"It is a container, a vessel. It holds the Codes of Nature: the ancient wisdom found in all of nature—in sound, in light, in the winds and stars, in all living things. The Codes are read as sacred symbols, languages, messages from the ancestors. Their teachings show us how to live without greed, with reverence for the earth and for each other," said Sophia.

Everything my ancestors passed down, Maia thought.

Sophia explained that her horse, Apollo, came to life that day too, and that he was eternal.

"Eternal," said Maia. "You mean he will never die?"

"He will never die," said Sophia.

Maia sat quietly. She didn't know if she was in shock or awe—maybe it was both. But she was without a doubt fascinated. She knew all kinds of creation stories, legends, and myths, from her own and other indigenous cultures. But this was not a myth, it was real. Sophia said so.

"How long have you been a Guardian?" she asked.

"For as long as I can remember."

It was an open-ended answer, thought Maia. *If Apollo lived forever, maybe Sophia was thousands of years old, too. Maybe she's been protecting the earth for many lifetimes.*

"Where is it? Where's the Horseshoe?"

Sophia took a deep breath.

"Three moons ago, there was a storm on Mount Shasta." Sophia retold the story of the evil cloud of greed, the six broken pieces, and the giant Black Raven.

"Apollo and I have searched for the stolen piece. But we haven't found it. The earth needs it in order to survive. Night visions brought me a message that dreamcatchers would be allies for this mission, which is why I called your mom, Stands in the Center Woman."

"So she made you the dreamcatcher . . ."

"Yes. And she made four more."

"Why five?" asked Maia. As soon as she asked the question, she knew the answer. *Five broken pieces,* thought Maia. *The center stone in each dreamcatcher holds a piece of the Crystal Horseshoe. That's what gave it power.*

Sophia saw the understanding on Maia's face.

"Maia, I need your help," said Sophia. "It is time to pass the reins, though I know you will question it the way I did when I was chosen."

"Chosen?" asked Maia.

"I have wondered, since you were born, if you might be the one. So has your mother. But I knew I would have to wait, these things reveal themselves. My suspicion was confirmed when you and the dreamcatcher recognized each other. You felt its power. And it felt yours."

Breathe, thought Maia. *Breathe.*

"I promise to prepare you," said Sophia. "I am your Earth teacher."

GOING HOME

*T*HE CAR HUMMED ON THE HIGHWAY, mixing Maia's thoughts with Sophia's words. *You have been chosen.*

Maia gazed out the passenger window. She spotted a herd of antelope running across the prairie—swift, graceful, confident as they moved, so clear about their direction. Was she? She hoped that on the long trip home, she could make sense of her time in Montana.

She closed her eyes, picturing the crystals, the dream-catcher, the books, the maps, the buckles. She went over the stories and the secrets the women had to keep. Sophia had shared every detail of the tragedy on Mount Shasta, including her painful truth. When the piece was lost, she'd lost a part of herself as well.

She had to fulfill her ancestral calling. If she didn't, it would be unbearable for her, for Mother Earth, for all things alive.

I've been called to risk myself for the greater good, thought Maia. *And I'm terrified.*

"Trust, my child." The words of her grandmother.

When she'd held the celestite at Sophia's, she'd felt her strong presence with that simple, one word message. *Trust.*

"Do you want to talk?" asked Keya. Maia had been quiet for most of the ride.

"Not really."

Keya placed her hand on her daughter's arm. Maia closed her eyes and retreated again into the last few days, spending time by the river that snaked over the land. She'd gotten lost in the hypnotic movement of tiny white caps churning around rock—so strong they'd changed the shape of stone. The water was cold and offered itself generously, a gift from the summit and the sun.

Sophia and Maia drank from cupped hands, welcoming the cold going down.

They swam in the beauty of the little things.

On horseback, they rode across that same river to the edge of the range, where waterfalls fell with great gushes, their deafening roars invitations to all who needed to drink.

At night they stargazed. Maia imagined she was on a swing attached to the crescent moon, exploring the heavens.

She saw Mother Earth from above, green and blue under silver light.

She told Sophia that she saw the earth breathing.

"Of course she is breathing," Sophia had agreed. "She is so alive."

Maia had lost track of the days and hadn't wanted the time to end. Now, on the way home, she thanked Moon for giving her an understanding of time. All things end. She faced forward with a mission, a mission to find and gather a tribe.

She closed her eyes again and thought of the place of bees and honey. Maia had thrown off her boots and danced barefoot in the tall, fragrant grass. Hands opened, she'd let the soft blades glide through her fingers, silken threads against her skin.

"You remind me of myself," said Sophia, "when I was young and free, and everything in the world felt new."

Sophia had held the walking stick that Maia gave her, saying it was the most beautiful gift she had ever received. They had sat together beside the buzzing hives. The colony was busy.

Maia peeked inside at their work. "Is it possible to see sound?"

"For some, yes," said Sophia.

"Well, I think I see it," said Maia.

"What does it look like?"

"It shimmers, the way sunlight moves through honey." Maia turned toward Sophia. "Does that make sense?"

Sophia laughed. "Perfect sense. It's Bee Wisdom."

"Bee Wisdom? I know they're smart little creatures—they would have to be. They have such an elevated stature as the pollinators of the world." Maia was pleased with her answer. It sounded grown up.

"You are also wise, my dear," said Sophia as she put her arm around Maia's shoulder. "Bees have an intelligence that is as intuitive as the flowers knowing when to bloom, as structured as the six-sided cell of the hexagon that holds the hive. The bee is the symbol of life, of immortality."

"You mean living forever?"

"In some ways, yes. In many places and in many languages, the bee is life itself."

"What places?"

"In Greece, the word *bios* is the verb 'to be.'"

"Do you know Greek?" asked Maia.

"I know all languages. But mostly the language of nature—The Codes that live in all of us. You will learn them too."

"How?"

"Some will come in dreams, some will come through observation, through study. You are learning them now."

Maia had turned to the hive.

"Look at them. So miraculous," said Sophia.

"And now they're dying of pesticides," said Maia, "It makes me so sad."

"That can change," said Sophia. "That's part of our work."

Maia had looked up with hopeful eyes.

"Like the bees, we need each other to do the work. Most of the healing will fall on the female. It always has. It's a guiding principle of life."

"Then why is the world ruled by kings and chiefs and presidents who are men? And corporations that make chemicals that kill things?" said Maia. *It's greed*, she thought.

"Women lost power," said Sophia. "And now it's our time to take it back."

In that moment, Maia had felt determination and hope, and she carried it with her as she headed toward home.

"Woman must rise as the fierce and divine healer that she is. Do you understand, Maia?" Sophia had asked gently. "I have watched you. Since you were a little girl. I have always thought you could be a Guardian."

Maia looked into Sophia's eyes. She *had* been chosen. She tried to stand tall. Maybe if she appeared brave, she would feel it, and convince herself.

"You cannot do this alone," said Sophia. "And you don't have to," she added.

"Well, we'll be together," said Maia.

Sophia took her time in answering.

"You'll be with me, right?" Maia sounded troubled.

"I will guide you from afar," said Sophia. "Four girls will come together from the four directions. They'll be powered by the elements—earth, air, fire, and water. I believe you can lead this strong young sisterhood to find the stolen piece. Dreamcatchers will be your guides."

"Who are these girls?" asked Maia.

"We will find the right ones," said Sophia. "Your mother will help, too."

Trust, trust, trust. Just trust, thought Maia. On their last night in Montana, they lay on their backs on the mossy edge of the creek, looking up at the northern sky. Ursa Major, the greater she-bear, was in full force, arrow pointing, seven brilliant stars shimmering. Maia wanted to climb an imaginary ladder, take one in her hand, and feel it as it turned to dust.

Sophia interrupted her gazing and gave strong and clear directions about what was needed for this new young tribe of Guardians. "These girls, Maia, they need to have courage. They'll be confronted with danger. Physical strength is not enough. They must be strong-willed, attuned to nature, deeply passionate about the earth. And horses—they must have a connection to horses. They will be your transport."

"Horses," said Maia.

"Yes. They were created by the gods."

"Anything else?" asked Maia.

"They must own the spirit of a warrior. They must be resilient and resourceful, and look fear in the eye, no matter how afraid."

"Like a cowgirl," said Maia.

Sophia mused for a moment.

"Yes, cowgirls have those qualities. And they do understand the horse, and the land, too," she said. "You'll have to believe in magic and mystery, and most of all, believe in yourselves."

Maia's heart beat faster, a mix of excitement and anxiety. She was learning that the two often felt the same.

"This mission will not be easy. You will meet ominous clouds, shape-shifters in the sky. These dark beings will do anything to keep you from the crystal," said Sophia. "But you will rise like the phoenix."

"What do you mean, 'rise like a phoenix?'" Maia knew that a phoenix was a mythical bird from Egyptian times, symbolizing life after death, a god of the sun. Would she and the tribe become giant sunbirds? Would their tears heal everything they touched?

"It means you will feel close to death, fight it, rise up, and return even more alive."

❨

The hum of the car went silent as it came to a stop. It jolted Maia back to where she was—on the road with her mother, going home. She asked herself, maybe for the hundredth time, if she was strong enough to take this on. Did she have the courage? Could she rise? She must. She would not let Sophia, her own mother, or Gaia down.

Maia looked out the window and saw the tumbleweed skipping like a carefree child. She thought about her grandmother, Soft Wind Woman, a storyteller and sage, a kind elder who guided her people to choose a wiser path. This was Maia's path. She hoped that her grandmother would guide her from the heavens, and that her wise ways would help Maia weave the threads of survival.

"Want to get something to eat?" asked Keya. "You must be starving."

"I guess maybe I am," said Maia.

She hadn't eaten for hours. Not even Twizzlers.

Keya saw the flashing neon sign. *Best BBQ in South Dakota. HERE.*

Maia hadn't realized they'd crossed the state line. She bit her lower lip, a habit she wanted to break. Keya looked at her daughter and took her hands in her own.

"Maia, Sophia trusts this is the right time."

"I know, Mom, but I'm . . ." She paused. "I just don't know."

"You know, Maia. . ." said her mother, with a sweetness for her only child. "Sometimes the things we are most afraid of are the things we have to do."

Letters

April 10, 2020

Dear Sophia Rose,
I have been home for less than a day and my mind is swirl-
ing. I loved our time together. Our walks were amazing. And
our talks. You know so much, I would say, about everything.

On the way back to South Dakota I couldn't stop think-
ing about the buckles, the dreamcatcher, and what it is that
you and the Great Mother are asking of me. But mostly, the
question: why me? There is so much I don't know and yet you
think I can lead the way?

Mom keeps telling me to "trust." I think she is a little
nervous, but trying not to let on.

How did you do it, when it was asked of you?

Love,
Maia

April 14, 2020

Dearest Maia,

I loved being with you and seeing the brave young woman you've become.

I asked these same questions all those years ago. Like you, I didn't understand why I was chosen. But I learned it was my destiny, the reason I was born. You will come to feel the same way.

It's natural to be afraid about what lies ahead. Even when I felt strong, there were days when I was uncertain.

But fear will get in the way of all the good you can do. Your mom's advice about trust is good. Listen to her. And to your ancestor. Know that, ultimately, you will be protected by higher powers. If you believe this, it shall be so. That is part of faith, a faith that has carried me, even in times of great darkness.

Maia, you must remember that this, too, is your destiny. You were chosen, which makes you more ready than you know.

With the purest of love,
Sophia Rose

P.S. Your handwriting is strong—there is a roundness to each letter showing that you are bold.

April 20, 2020

Dear Sophia Rose,
Thank you for saying that my handwriting shows strength.
I've never looked at it that way, but now I will :)

Your letter eased my nerves. Just knowing that I am not
alone, and that the Great Spirit is always with me, helps me
feel safe. My mom and I have talked a lot. She said when I
am in my truth, I can stand in my purpose. When she first
said those words, I didn't really understand, but now I do.
I am a protector. A guardian. When I accept this, I will
become it.

I think that makes sense. Ask me if I'll feel this way
tomorrow—maybe I'm just writing this on a good day.

Love,
Maia

P.S. Last night I dreamed I was standing on Mount Shasta. It
was cold and windy, and the high noon sun was strong. There was
a circle around it, rings of colors. I'd never seen anything like it.
I tried not to look, because I didn't want to hurt my eyes, but I
couldn't help myself. The rings started to move counterclockwise,
and when it went full circle and reached the top of the fireball in
the sky, they formed into a line headed toward the stars. I wondered if my eyes were playing tricks on me. The colors made a
sound. When I woke up, I looked outside my window and there
was a circle rainbow sitting like a crown above my favorite tree.

April 25, 2020

Dearest Maia,

Your dream! Such a beautiful dream. Our dream life is so important.. Keep listening to your dreams. And keep looking for rainbow light.

This is a short note, I must go to the hives today and check on the bees. The bears have been wreaking havoc. I will write soon.

With the purest of love,
Sophia Rose

Choosing

MAIA OPENED A NEW JOURNAL. She loved starting fresh, dating the page, then filling the unlined paper with ideas and little drawings. The pen she used was important. It had to feel good between her fingers; the ink had to flow with her thoughts.

"Journal," she wrote. *Jour* meant day in French. She wrote each day, in the morning, when her mind was just coming out of REM sleep, when she was still dreamy.

She scribbled: *Choosing the Circle*

They have to be:

Protective
Watchful
Brave
Strong
Curious
Fearless
Bold
Courageous (same as brave?)
Persevering
Spirited

Authentic
Passionate
Intuitive
Resourceful
Loyal
Humble
***Trustworthy
Trusting
Introspective
Inventive
Not whiny
Open
Won't give up (I guess that's persevering)
***Can keep a secret
***Trailblazer

They have to love:

Mother Earth
Magic
Science
History
Horses
Apricots (Sophia's suggestion)
Adventure
Dreaming
Stories
Stones
Plant Medicine (from Mom)
Animal Medicine
Protecting the environment
Each other

They have to be ok with:

Sweat
Going in the woods
No showers
Intense weather
Powering through period cramps—not that I would know :(
Can convince their parents to let them come (minor detail)

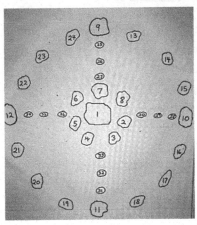

*Too complicated. ^^^^*

Creator: center of life/wheel itself
Mother Earth: gives us home
Father Sun: warms life, source of energy and light
Moon: guides dreams, visions

North: Earth, Wisdom, Elder, Dreaming, Regeneration,
Buffalo

East: Air, Innocence, New Beginnings, Planting Seeds,
Vision, Eagle

South: Fire, Energy, Growth, Trust, Transformation, Coyote,
Wolf

West: Water, Ancestors, Going Within, Heart, Introspection,
Thunderbird, Bear

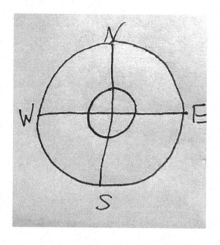

*Ava (S) (I trust her, wild horses) ————> *leads to YUE*
(W) Dad/horses
Brianna
Tory
Raina (smart but maybe too bossy)
Jamie (probably can't come)
*Sara/Falcon (E) (Mom found her poem about the horses)
Julia
Louisa
*Me (N)

North: Me, South Dakota

East: Sara/Falcon, New York City

South: Ava, New Mexico

West: Yue, California

(thinking. thinking. thinking)
I will ride today and listen.

April 28, 2020

Dear Sophia,

As soon as I got home from Montana, I started a new jour-nal. It has all of my thoughts about the tribe. I think of it as a sisterhood. I never had a sister, so . . .

I like making lists and drawing little sketches. Seeing it on paper helps. This is all I think about. My mom has been helping me, too. I will share it with you.

Love,
Maia

April 28, 2020

Sophia, my dear soul friend,
This morning I woke up in a pool of sweat. I had dreams only you can imagine, compounded by the darkness of night. I talk to Maia about trust. And yet, sometimes, when I utter those words, they sound empty. I am frightened for my only daughter, the one who still sees the world through the eyes of a child, though she is a young woman.

Yes, she is wise, and there are days when I know she is ready. But still, as a mother, the thought of her in danger frightens me. I wish I could go in her place, but it is her destiny, not mine.

So, I ask you, dear Sophia, what happens if she goes too soon, before she is ready? I tell myself to trust, the same words I say to her. I know that you would not have called her unless you thought she was ready. Leading this mission is her purpose. The Codes come first, as hard as it might be. I trust you, Sophia. Please watch over her. Watch over them.

Nothing separates us, not even time.
Your Keya

We must become*May 1, 2020*

My Dear Keya,
When I read your letter, my throat tightened. I understand
your fear. I know it's not easy. There is danger in this mission.
I cannot promise safety, I can only promise to be a guide, the
way others were for me.

We must become Grandmother Trees for Maia. Rooted in
grace and wisdom, with strong upright trunks for her to lean
on. She will climb the many branches—each one represents
a different direction. She will find her way. I know this in
my bones. The ancestors told me.

We will keep talking and writing, my darling Keya.

Nothing separates us, not even time.
Your Sophia

Together we walk
as sisters of the Earth

SARA

They come from the brightest star in the sky,
the one that sparks a constant ring of fire.
It makes a circle of hope . . .
each ray a shimmering sunbeam . . .
a golden promise of possibility.
Beyond oceans of light
the thunder roars
four white horses
soar,
eagle feathered manes
carried by the winds of time.
They have come to transport the Crystal Warriors,
four girls powered by the elements
and unwavering cowgirl spirit.
These brave young beacons of light
were chosen to heal humanity
restore Mother Earth,
and enlighten this age to be new again.

—Sara aka Falcon

RAYS OF DAWN kissed the dreamcatcher that hung in Sara's window. Made by the hands of a Native woman from South Dakota, it caught the fiery colors in its center stone, spreading a prism of light that fluttered like wings. The colors left patterns on the ceiling that looked like a firebird.

She was mesmerized by the movement. Long feathers danced like flames. Sometimes they turned into symbols. Yesterday she saw a pyramid. This morning, a horseshoe.

Today, the wind was like a rushing river, rattling against the panes, booming through the canyons of New York. Sara felt it originated from far away, from a place she didn't know.

Sara lived on the top floor of a glass-and-steel building, sometimes touching the clouds. She was usually fearful of big winds, but an energy she couldn't explain enticed her out of bed. Pressed against the glass, she squinted, second-guessing her own eyes. In the distance were the four white horses she dreamed about almost every night, horses with eagle-feather manes. This time, the vision was more than a dream. These horses were real, coming toward her in slow motion, galloping like thunder through the morning sky. Today they were face to face, soul to soul. The reflection in their eyes showed a compass which changed into the face of a clock, which turned into the earth, rotating.

"What do you want to tell me?" she whispered.

Maybe they had come to show her the way to a new world. But what kind of new world? Would it be a world with cleaner oceans and air and enough food for all of humankind? A healthier planet? Would the bee population rise again, pollinating fruits and flowers, the way they had in the past? Would the ice stay frozen? Would there be enough rain? Would the corn be real?

The horses turned and headed back towards the sun, leaving a trail of light behind them.

Dazed, Sara sat down on her bed. Gazing out the window, she watched the light expand like watercolors on wet paper, brushstrokes of yellows, pinks, and golds, gentle hues that painted each new day with possibility. The colors of the eastern sky soothed her; they told nature's story, how layered it was, how one thing blended into the next and couldn't exist without the other.

And then, horses.

I don't want to go to school today.

Sara looked around her room. Tiny porcelain ballet slippers hung by a pink silk chord on a hook, along with other remnants of her childhood—beaded necklaces, a feather boa from a dress-up kit, a birthday crown studded with plastic gems and rhinestones.

Time to give this stuff away, she thought.

Her tiny desk, out of a catalog, was piled high with a messy stack of books: *Weeping Under This Same Moon, Brown Girl Dreaming,* and *Youth to Power—Your Voice and How to Use It.* A portable reading light sat on top. Mixed in were a few used books she'd picked up at a street market, one about the life of trees, another about rooftop gardening.

Luna Magazine, the issue containing one of her poems, was on her dresser. An old *Teen Vogue* lay on the floor.

Why are these walls still pink? she thought. She had covered them with posters and photos, sticky-glued images of owls, hummingbirds, and deer, a tribe of Maasai women, Malala, and Greta Thunberg. Sara loved Greta's fierceness; she was like the Fearless Girl statue on Wall Street, only real. Next to Greta was a quote from Pooh: *As soon as I saw you, I knew an adventure was going to happen.*

Her Museum of Natural History button was pinned to the lampshade by her bed. She knew every nook of that cavernous place, and the security guards knew her name. She spent hours at the Planetarium. Her dad was a cosmologist, an expert who gave talks at special exhibits. Sara wished she were seeing the universe for real, perched on a mountaintop at night instead of in an enclosed dome. The telescope she'd gotten for her birthday was a good start.

She looked at herself in the mirror. She saw a girl with hazel eyes flecked with gold looking back at her. She touched her latte-colored skin and grabbed a scrunchie. Kinky curls, she thought, as she twisted it around her honey-brown hair, then piled it on top of her head. She was a mixture of both parents. People say I'm beautiful, but I don't get it, she thought, then turned away.

Her private school uniform, which she detested, hung on her closet door. It was in a plastic bag from the dry cleaners that made her loathe it even more. Her school's mission statement was about inclusivity and being citizens of the world.

"So why are there only six Black students?" she asked her dad who taught Intro to Astronomy and was on the school's advisory board. It was a topic she brought up at dinner at least once a week.

She looked out the window, wondering if the horses would return.

Last summer, on a forest walk at farm camp, Sara had seen what appeared to be a white horse coming out of the morning mist. When she called out to Diana, her counselor, all traces of the horse disappeared, except for a golden eagle feather left on the ground.

The forest had secrets—at least, this one did.

She had begged her parents to let her go to camp. They'd wanted her to go on a young person's tour of Europe to learn about art history.

"I don't need to get on a plane for that," she told her mom, who worked at the Metropolitan Museum of Art in the Egyptian wing.

After reading the book on gardening, Sara had longed to walk barefoot on the earth and trade blue nail polish for dirt underneath her fingernails. She wanted to learn how to grow food, and grow herself, too. She reminded her parents about their trip to Costa Rica, how it had changed her view of the world. Central Park, the largest green space in all of New York City, was hardly a rainforest. Central America was a universe.

And the birds. She was drawn to them; the feathers and distinctive calls were far more interesting to her than the pigeons on the streets of New York. Sara was most fascinated by hummingbirds—the buzz of their tiny wings, how they zoomed through space, changing direction in a split second. How could something so small be so fierce? She thought about the cloud forests, hanging like misty blankets, cool and wet on her skin. And the soil. It had a heavy, musky scent, damp and earthy, old and fresh all at once. Everything had felt more real in the rainforest. Even the mangos. They were sweet and ripe, sold from baskets on the side of the road. Nothing wrapped in plastic and shipped thousands of miles to a grocery store. And no pesticides.

Sara's passion convinced her parents. She went to farm camp, worlds away, just two hours north of Manhattan.

She had been the first to arrive at her cabin. Sara quickly scoped it out and threw her overstuffed backpack onto a top bunk. She liked being up high, closer to the stars. She had sewn half a dozen patches on the canvas bag, badges that proudly told the world who she was, a mirror of her bedroom at home.

The cabin smelled of pine and time. The knotty wood walls were covered with scribbles from summers past, campers leaving their mark.

Coco loves Doug. I AM HERE. Beyoncé Rocks.

As she was settling in, the screen door, patched in four places, creaked open.

"Hi, I'm Diana, your counselor." A tall, lithe girl stood framed by the doorway.

"I'm Sara. Wait, do I know you?"

"It does feel like we've met, doesn't it? But that's impossible. I just arrived from Australia." She was older, maybe eighteen. A dark brown pixie cut framed her heart-shaped face, showing off blue, doe-shaped eyes. She wore an olive-green tank and a necklace with a silver stag.

"You have tiger eyes," said Diana.

Sara blushed.

❨

All through that summer, Diana had shared the secrets of mud and mushrooms, trees and roots, and the underground road-maps that generated life. She pointed out orb-weaver spiders building circular webs, and how the best time to find them was morning, when droplets of dew still glistened on the silk threads in the sunlight.

Diana belonged there. Sometimes Sara thought she must have been born in the forest.

Diana taught her how to see, and they inspected every-thing—crevices in oak bark, frogs clinging to trees, ant mounds, pine needles, moss that grew under rocks. Sara looked at it from every angle and began to understand that the real architect of the world was nature herself.

Mornings and late afternoons, when the sun was low, Sara and her bunkmates worked in the fields, crouched over rows of neatly aligned crops.

Sara marveled at how fast things grew from one day to the next, seed to fruit, driven by adaptive natural intelligence. "You're closer to the earth when you pluck it off the stem and the plant is still in the ground," she said proudly as she handed Diana an heirloom tomato—red, plump, and ready. The girls both took a bite, juice squirting and dripping down their chins. Sara wiped it with her forearm, laughed, and took another bite. Uncomplicated perfection.

Diana taught Sara to become an observer of life, of time, of how things emerged. She watched in awe as the natural world watered and fed itself through the rains, the sun, and the winds.

Diana pointed out nests, the different barks, and the holes of the woodpecker. She had laser focus when she was in the forest. She watched over it like a mother protecting her young.

At the edge of that forest lived a red-tailed hawk. Each day she circled the camp, watching over her domain. Sara got lost in how the wind carried her, how she floated on air, a weightless dance that could shift in one quick movement—hawk swooping down toward her prey, and as sad as it was to see the mouse's end, she recognized that the hawk must eat.

Diana told her that trees whispered to each other through entangled roots. When one tree was failing, the others sent nutrients through their underground arms.

And the mushrooms. Sara had never liked them, but now she had a new appreciation for the power of their ways. The hidden fungi had the most important job. They balanced the soil, flushed out toxins, and were a safeguard during a drought.

Sara promised Diana she would give them another chance and try them in her next omelet.

When the end of August came, quiet tears fell onto Sara's pillow, tears she didn't want anyone to see. Diana gave her a parting gift, a book by Rachel Carson called *Silent Spring*. The book was about the future of the planet and all life on Earth, and how, as humans, we must be stewards of the land.

"What's a steward?" Sara asked.

"Someone who looks after Mother Earth," answered Diana. "And all living things."

Diana also gave Sara a necklace with a falcon charm.

"I see you as a falcon," said Diana. "It would be a good name for you."

From then on, Sara asked people to call her Falcon, the strongest and fastest bird in the world. She ignored her parents when they rolled their eyes.

She treasured Diana's gifts, trusting they were important, maybe even life changing, just like those two months on the farm. When she returned home, her priorities changed. Now getting a new cell phone or shopping for clothes or the latest sneaker were not at the top of her must-have list. Instead, she thought about the animals, the birds, the waters, and the Earth—and what she could do to care for all of it. That fall, she pounded the streets at the Climate Strike March.

❮

Now, the strong wind outside the apartment window shook her back to the present. She looked through the glass to see if the horses were somewhere in the distance. She knew they would be back.

The promise of a new adventure stirred inside her. This summer she would be going to a ranch in Montana. Keya, the woman who'd made her dreamcatcher, had read her poem about white horses in *Luna Magazine*. She'd shared it with her daughter, Maia, who'd sent Falcon a handwritten letter.

Dear Falcon,

First, I love your name. I've never done this before, written to a total stranger, but my mom showed me your poem in Luna. *As you know, she spoke to the editor, who got in touch with your parents.*

I'm glad you said it was okay for me to write. (I don't have a cell phone, by choice, or social media accounts—I know, you probably think I'm crazy, but . . .)

I loved your poem, and it hangs on my bedroom wall, and I want to build a new world, too.

Wopila (Thank you in Lakota!)

Maia

Falcon wrote back to Maia about her newfound love of nature and the responsibility she felt to care for it. Maia wrote about her Lakota roots and her connection to the earth. She told Falcon that sadness lived in the hearts of her people, and all Natives. She wrote of the Trail of Tears—when 60,000 Native Americans were forced to relocate from their ancestral homelands in the Southeast. They were moved west of the Mississippi River, by the American government, to a place called Indian Territory. Children were sent to boarding schools—their culture and identity denied and buried. Traditional clothing was replaced by uniforms. All things associated with Native life—their songs, their languages, their hair, their way of being in the world—was stripped away.

Falcon realized that she had only learned half of that story in school.

She wrote to Maia about the Holocaust, how family members on her mother's side were killed in the camps. The lucky ones escaped and immigrated to the United States from Russia and Poland. Arriving on Ellis Island, in New York Harbor, they were given new names, sometimes based on the names of the villages where they were born.

Maia had read about the recent rise in anti-Semitism but had never known someone of the Jewish faith. She and Falcon felt a shared suffering. Both of their tribes faced annihilation. It wove a common thread of connection and loss between them.

Sometimes Falcon stood on the outside for other reasons.

I'm a mix of Black and White, she wrote. *In New York, I blend in. But in other places, not so much.*

Sometimes people were rude and asked, "What are you?"

I am both. I am neither, I am everything. And nothing,

When Maia and Falcon spoke about their pain, some of it melted away.

In the night, they even had similar dreams—Maia of White Buffalo, Falcon of White Horses.

We are destined to meet, thought Falcon.

Maia invited Falcon to join her and two other girls to stay for the summer with her godmother, Sophia, at her Montana ranch. After some pleading, and many conversations between her parents and Maia's mother, Falcon got her wish.

It was hard for her to tell Diana that she wasn't returning to farm camp. They spoke almost every day. But the Pooh Bear quote reminded her that adventure called. She finished getting ready for school and grabbed her favorite necklace, the one with the silver-tipped wings. She hadn't worn her Star of David in months. She grabbed that, too. Then she was out the door.

AVA

The southwest sky sparkled
with a thousand stars,
each one its own world
of luminous light.
These worlds spoke to one another,
for they were messengers
of the sounds and secrets
that breathe through the Universe.
A sun path lives in these stars,
an Angel of Fire as ancient as time.
Her arrow points and shoots.
One star becomes two,
and then three,
and then a thousand more.
They light the sky with sparks of fire
that tumble down,
to become the morning stars of dawn.

—Ava

*T*HE COYOTES SANG, nipping Ava awake from a deep sleep. She looked up at her dreamcatcher, a red willow hoop connecting a web of sinew strings crafted by Maia's mother in South Dakota. There were no coyotes caught in the center. They had come for a real visit. Ava loved their trickster spirit—smart, clever, sometimes disruptive. They were playful and hard to pin down, a cover-up for the seriousness that lay beneath the surface.

She stared into her dreamcatcher, which hung from the apex of the tent. The center stone was clear, with rough, uneven edges. It had an aliveness to it, a hypnotic power she didn't understand. If she looked at it long enough, she fell into a dream state where nothing else mattered and time did not exist.

At the midpoint of the stone, intersecting lines formed a tiny morning star. It beamed green lines of light onto the white canvas. Each time it shimmered, she wondered if it were a lost star that had dropped out of the Milky Way.

Ava drifted back to sleep in her place of solitude. When she and her mom had set up the canvas tent for her fourteenth birthday, neither had any idea how often Ava would retreat to her private space, the place where the silence gave her room to hear her own thoughts.

But the night had a voice. While the world slept, Ava lay awake, listening for the desert animals, the ones that came out of hiding after dark. She tuned into the scurry of lizards against rock, barely audible, and the louder white horned owl, and the mating calls of the foxes, and the snorts of wild javelina—aggressive beasts that ran in packs, known for chasing even the toughest cowboy up a tree.

More than anything, she longed to hear the call of the gray wolf—rare, and at one point almost extinct. She would wait for as long as it took.

The night was when she could feel her life-spark most, the little flicker that burned inside, the flame that nothing could put out, not even fear. No dragons, rattlesnakes, or obstacles could dim it. Fire gave Ava her fierceness. It burned stronger when she was hiking in red rock country. She never tired of how the southwest sun lit each ridge into a blaze of orange layers, each with a history, a paleogeology, a timeline that reconstructed the evolution of the earth.

After the coyotes retreated at dawn, cooing doves sang her awake from her second doze. Ava wiggled out of her snug bedroll of canvas and wool. She untangled the long black strands of hair that clung to the salty sweat on the back of her neck. She arched her back, stretching like a cat, then opened the tent and peeked out. Two ravens perched on the chipped mosaic table in the courtyard of the house that had been in Ava's family for generations.

Ravens, she thought, *messengers of magic from the great void where all knowledge waits for us.* She remembered those words from her grandmother, a great storyteller.

She looked at the sun. Time to get ready for school.

But something was odd about this morning. The air smelled of iron. Dark clouds were gliding in from the west. It didn't make sense. It was early for the monsoons that blessed the desert in summer, that turned the slot canyons into rushing, dangerous rivers. Ava had been warned to stay away from them, which made her want to go even more, just to see the floods. But she respected the power of nature. Now she glanced at the sky, wondering about the iron. *I've never smelled that before.*

She brushed off the mysterious odor as nothing, and made her way into the small adobe house, carrying her pillow, blanket, and journal. As she walked through the stone archway, it reminded her of the burnt-rust settlements—Pueblo communities—that were built thousands of years ago from earth mixed with water and straw.

Ava lived in the Land of Enchantment—in Nambe, a little town north of Santa Fe, at the foothills of the Sangre de Cristo Mountains. She didn't need a GPS to navigate the rocks and crevices of the high desert. She had climbed and hiked in them since she could remember.

She walked over to the kiva fireplace, also made of clay, that was built into the corner of the room. Her precious guitar sat on a woolen blanket, leaning against the wall. An old and sacred instrument, it had been handed down to Ava by her Great Aunt Rosa, who inherited it from *her* aunt, a wanderer who traveled from town to town, making her way to the United States with the rest of her family.

Ava often thought about the courage it must have taken to flee Mexico in the early 1900s, escaping the country's civil war, leaving everything behind for a strange new place with nothing but hope.

"But hope can take you far," her mother reminded her.

Her mother explained that many people, all over the world, left their places of origin, making hard journeys toward better lives. Ava knew her mother was grateful to be here, in this small sun-filled home, with her only daughter. She tried hard to hold onto the customs of her ancestors, but as time went on, they had begun to fall away.

Ava loved the stories about her grandmother's sister, Rosa—how she played music in the streets, mesmerizing crowds, transporting them into a trance that kept them dancing well into the night. She imagined the bright, floral colors on ruffled skirts and the sound of shoes tapping on cobblestone. She could smell the spices—cumin, chili, oregano.

How free she must have been, Ava thought, wistfully.

She wished she had known her.

Ava picked up the guitar and ran her dark, slender fingers over the rosewood. It had lost some of its shine, but not its sparkle. It had seven strings, not six. She plucked the F with her thumb. She heard the note, clear and strong. It was energy in motion, a field that started small and compact, expanding into silence, like ripples on the surface of the water. She plucked the A string, and then another, creating a cocoon of sound that vibrated through her body in waves, touching everything—a sound bath that washed over every cell of who she was.

The more she strummed the catgut strings, the more familiar she became with their powers. The notes were carriers of ancient knowledge—messengers sending and receiving information from the stars that came in dreams and images and sounds. Ava listened intently. She had promised herself that she would become fluent in this new language, and for her, it sounded like the language of survival. Survival was on her mind. Summers were hotter, drier, stretching longer. Storms were harsher and more frequent. Recovery from loss was more difficult.

Raging wildfires ravaged lands—savage beasts destroying everything in their path. The year before, the entire West Coast had been in flames.

Ava set the guitar down gently. The morning in the desert was chilly, so she moved closer to the fireplace to warm her hands. In the flickering flames, she saw the shape of a bird, wings moving. It sparked a thought about the music of animals—the chorus of sounds that make up nature's symphony. Rocks and winds and water—they had voices, too. They were the songs of the earth.

Ava looked at her most treasured silver ring, the one she called the Angel of Fire. Sparks of light were carved as lines coming out of the angel's wand. Five tiny morning stars were engraved on the side, going from top to bottom, symbols for Heaven and Earth. It was handmade by a woman in her little town, who ran a trading post along the High Road to Taos. The designer had grown up in South Dakota near her friend

Maia and knew the Lakota way. She'd thought the Angel of Fire would be the perfect mirror for Ava—a reminder of who she was.

As Ava spun the ring on her middle finger, she heard her mother in the kitchen. Typically, her mother would be chopping vegetables on the old wooden table for *chile verde*, or standing at the sink, washing dishes.

Today her mother, Isabella, was at the sink, water running over lined hands that told the story of a woman who had not lived a pampered life.

Ava knew that her mom had given up much for her family. One day, her own mother had turned to her, a girl who loved to learn, with a veil of sadness on her face.

"You need to leave school for a while," she said. Isabella hadn't even finished the eighth grade, but she was needed at home to help care for her younger siblings and her aging Abuela. The good daughter had put away her pencils and left her childhood behind.

The night became her constant and soothing friend as Isabella traded some hours of sleep for time to read.

She had studied books on ancient textiles, nature, poetry, the history of the world. Later, Ava had been introduced to faraway places, places that her mother had seen through her travels on the page. They had long conversations sitting outside by the fire. Isabella shared secrets with her daughter, secrets like her decades long crush on Pablo Neruda. She knew his love sonnets by heart and memory, as if he had written them just to her, his darling Isabella.

It had been Ava's idea to dig a hole and make a firepit. Now she often sat looking into the flames, daydreaming.

Ava loved three things . . . playing guitar, listening to her mother recite poetry, and working with Lucas at his small ranch down the road. For a long time, she had simply been a visitor, leaning on the fence, watching the old man work his magic on the horses he rescued, big animals that were fascinating, intimidating, and strong. They were the wild horses from the mustang bands that roamed the West. Herds that foraged the land, pulling grasses up from their roots until there was nothing left. Many of the horses were starving and close to dying. People like Lucas saved them from slaughter, a different kind of death.

Ava longed to spend more time with these horses. Little by little she began helping out around the ranch, and now she had a real paying job.

She fell in love with a colt named Tolusa, young and stubborn. Ava saw in him a fire that matched her own. Time and work and trust brought the two of them together, and changed them both. Ava sang to him, noticing how the music calmed all of the horses in their unfamiliar captivity. She understood. She didn't like being fenced in, either. At night when Ava played Aunt Rosa's guitar, she would leave her window open, gently strumming a lullaby for the horses who were once part of a herd and were now adapting to a new family.

Ava's mom turned off the faucet, dried her hands on her apron, and took a letter out of her pocket.

"This came for you in yesterday's mail." Isabella smiled as she held it out to her daughter. "I meant to give it to you last night."

Ava recognized Maia's handwriting and tore open the envelope, almost ripping it in half. Maia's letters were like songs, and Ava savored each note. They had been writing since meeting at the horse sanctuary in Santa Barbara.

Over time, Maia learned how Ava's inner fire was lit by nature, by sound, and by the stories of the Mexican traditions that had been passed down through the generations. Maia understood how crossing the border all those years ago had left part of Ava's heritage behind. So much had been sacrificed to live here in America. And now, America was sacrificing itself. Money ruled, corporations took the land, poisoning it with greed.

Ava's hands shook when she read Maia's letter. Maia told Ava about her godmother, Sophia, and her ranch in Montana. Maia had confided that she had been asked to carefully choose three girls. They had to be adventurous and strong, and have a connection to horses, the land, and one of the four directions. Ava was South. She was fire. Ava understood magic. And Maia trusted her.

Inside the envelope, wrapped in a small square of tissue paper, was a necklace. A tiny wolf charm hung between the beads.

Ava held it in her hand, feeling the importance of this gift. The wolf was intuitive. A pack leader, a wayfinder. Wolf was about loyalty. Ava was honored that Maia saw these qualities in her.

That night, Ava asked her mother about the proposed trip to Montana. She told Isabella everything that Maia had written to her. Her mom said that she would talk to Keya but thought this was part of Ava's path. It was her mother's way of saying yes.

Ava was already packing.

YUE

A fish of shimmering gold swam across the western sky,
pulling a lotus flower made of glass.
Thousands of stars nestled amongst petals.
When the flower of purity crossed the full moon,
the stars fell,
sprinkling onto the snow-capped mountaintops.
As the sun rose from the east,
the warmth melted the ice
and the stars became sparkling falls,
which became a river,
which flowed into the ocean of all things.
In the depths of the waters
streaks of sunlight lit the fish of a million colors,
a kaleidoscope dancing in the waves,
moving to the currents of change.

—Yue

*Y*UE WOKE IN THE DARK, grabbed a pencil, switched on her night light, and began writing in her journal.

I am a river, she wrote. *Flowing and bubbling—I gracefully twist and turn and move from here to there. Nothing gets in my way. Water is curious about what's ahead and uses its intuition to follow itself. It is strong. It softens and smooths the hard edges of rock. Water makes its own music. When I am still, I hear the dolphins singing their songs.*

The fish with the glass lotus made Yue think of the oceans. Water was her peace; fighting to keep it pure was her personal war.

She touched the orange starfish that hung from a frayed cord around her neck and went back to her journal.

I wish I could regrow parts of myself that are torn. Yue wrote the wish as she held the star, five points resting on her chest, moving slightly with her breath. If only it were still alive. Once, she had watched a tiny sea star—without a brain—regrow a leg that had been eaten by a hungry crab.

It always amazed her. How did any creature know how to do that, or anything at all, if it didn't have a brain? Yue was sure that this ability was the most gorgeous and remarkable miracle in the ocean, second only to the life cycle of the coral reefs. Underneath the hard, calcified skeletons were clusters of soft, complex sea creatures. These living organisms, colonies of them, made up whole systems of underwater landscapes that spanned hundreds of miles. Maybe thousands.

They were in danger. Climate change, acidification from CO_2 in the atmosphere, along with microscopic bits of plastic, were slowly taking the coral's colors, first turning them gray and then white.

That's what death looks like under the sea.

Bleached.

Yue went back to her journal and the ocean's lullaby. A night star sparkled through the dreamcatcher on her window, the light coating her bedroom walls. She put her pencil down and got out of bed, pulled to the window by the full moon and the hoop of red willow that was a gift from her friend Maia.

She caught its eye, the crystal in its center. Some would say that a dreamcatcher can't see things, but Yue would disagree. This one could. Whenever the moonlight hit it a certain way, the reflection shimmered on the walls like sparkling water. Sometimes she saw letters on the walls—ancient Chinese calligraphy, or symbols from cultures she didn't understand. Sometimes she saw the color green in a line that moved like an eel.

Yue lived high up in the hills above the Pacific Ocean, close enough to the beach that, when the waves were wild, she could hear their voices. Tonight, she followed the song of the tides, their rhythms both constant and changing. She breathed in sync with the waves, to calm her inner storms.

It was spring. Yue had trouble sleeping this time of year when things sprang forth and came to life. There was so much to see that had been hidden underground. Yue deeply cared about the planet. She often asked herself what she could do to help fix the damage that humankind had done. Huge, billion-dollar corporations cared about one thing: profits. Over-consumption of plastic, deforestation, emissions, fracking, drilling for oil and gas—didn't businesses see that all of these things had an impact on the future of every living thing? It had to stop. Yue burned inside.

As a small child Yue had been shy, but now she found herself speaking out. At the beginning of the school year, she gathered her nerve and made her plea to the principal to start an offshoot of the Environment Club to boycott single-serve water bottles.

"I won't take no for an answer," she said. "Everyone should all feel as outraged as I do." She got permission and went to work.

"I'll get these posters made if it takes me all night," she said to her dad, who was proud of his feisty daughter. The next morning, she woke at dawn and got to school before the bell. She put up signs everywhere. Two days later, she stood on stage at morning assembly and looked out at a sea of eight hundred students and pleaded her case. Nobody noticed her shaking.

She read Amanda Gorman's poem, *Ode to Oceans*, and then said, "We can do this. We must do this."

Within hours, she had a battalion behind her. Within weeks the school banned plastic water bottles. Eventually, so did the town. She found her voice, and eventually convinced the grocery stores to stop using plastic bags. She was tireless in her efforts to see change.

Yue watched all of nature the same way she watched the oceans. She saw firsthand how a three-year drought had devastated the cattle ranches, vineyards, and farms that dotted the California coast. She saw how the drought hurt the grasses, which hurt the animals, which hurt the balance of nature. She saw the wildfires and floods and erosion. She knew that the ice caps in the Arctic were melting and the polar bears struggled for food.

Yue was most concerned about her beloved oceans—home to the fish of a thousand colors, the coral reefs, and the plant life that lived and breathed in the depths. It was its own world, its own beautiful planet. She knew when she saw a whale, dead from ingesting plastic bags, that protecting water was her calling.

Her adoptive mother, the only mother she had known, had been a marine biologist. They had spent a lot of time on the beach, looking at crabs, watching turtles, identifying different kinds of seaweed. She'd loved Sundays with her mother. It was their day—just the two of them. She missed her. She had died less than a year ago, and Yue still saw her ashes drifting on the wind and the waves.

Yue's dad was a quiet man, a horse whisperer, someone with a tender touch who used the gentlest methods of training. Like Lucas, he worked with wild mustangs and ran an organization that saved them from euthanasia and prepared them for adoption. There were so many horses—too many—and as beautiful and free as they were, the land could not sustain them all.

It made Yue sad that any horse might have to die, but she understood that if there was no grass to graze, they would starve. So would the coyote, the gopher, the snakes—the entire ecosystem would be thrown off balance and many species would perish. Yue believed that everything was equal. No one creature more important than another. No matter how big or small.

She thought about the coral. Minuscule life forms that grew stronger when clustered together. They formed a community. Like bees. She had formed a community, too, a community around fighting for change.

Her guidance counselor was concerned that her fierce passion was a guise for hidden anger. Well, yes, she was angry. She'd lost her mother. And now, she would do what she could to save the oceans that had been her mother's love.

Besides her dad and the kids at school who gathered around her fiery passion, there were only two other people who understood, two people who knew the deepest parts of her heart. Her new friend, Maia, who never judged, and her friend Jake, who stood by her side at every school rally and every Friday Strike for Climate. He helped make signs and phone calls and write letters to Congress. They took long walks together on the beach, dreaming about one day sailing in New Zealand or

Hawaii. They would be forever friends, or maybe more. They hinted at it from time to time.

Yue went back to her journal and scribbled a heart and wrote Jake's name inside. Then she drew a blue infinity sign.

"I will have to be a river," she declared. "A strong and mighty river." She would navigate the rocks and deftly move around anything that got in her way. There was no point in trying to go back to sleep. She would check on the horses. She shimmied into her jeans, put on Jake's old moth-eaten sweater and her bear pendant, her most cherished gift. She looked at the porcelain statue of Kuan Yin sitting on her dresser next to a small jade jewelry box. She kissed her own fingers and placed them on the lips of the Goddess of Compassion, the one who hears the cries of all beings. As Yue left her room, she hoped that Kuan Yin would hear the cry of the fish in the oceans of the world.

She slowly walked down the narrow hallway, stepping around the spots where the wood creaked. Holding her breath as she tip-toed downstairs, she opened the back door, an inch at a time, hoping it wouldn't squeak. She didn't want to wake her father. He wasn't strict, but he was cautious, more protective now that it was just the two of them. He would rather Yue not go to the horse barn alone at night. *Well, it isn't quite night*, Yue said to herself. The moon was setting over the hills, and soon it would be hidden—the day was rising, and the year was getting warmer. Summer was coming, and soon Yue would be gathering around a campfire in Montana with three other girls. One of them was Ava.

Yue's dad had placed one of his horses with his friend Lucas in New Mexico. The horse's name was Tolusa. Ava heard about the girl who fought to get an entire town to ban plastic bottles. She was a water protector, and she was West.

She and Yue wrote letters, forming a strong bond.

After spending time at the barn, Yue walked back down to the house. She was grateful for the horses, and for her Dad.

She wouldn't have met Ava, or Maia, had it not been for them. She climbed back into bed and opened her journal.

Dad finally said I could go to Montana. It was because of Lucas. I didn't tell him about the mission. He would have said no. He comes from the world of science, not magic.

I am the fourth girl, making the circle complete.

Maia didn't promise it would be safe, but I'm willing to take the chance. Do I have a choice? The world needs us. Time is ticking.

The dreamcatcher that her mom sent after I said yes is already bringing me messages. Thank you, Kuan Yin, for answering my prayers.

Maybe the coral reefs will get another chance.

MAIA

I am not the woman from the sky.
I am but a girl
who walks by her side.
I can tell her story,
which is our story,
the one about trees and roots, mountains and rock,
and how the Earth came to be.

—Maia

Counting the Days

MAIA SAT UP SLOWLY, arched her back, and rubbed the sleep out of her eyes. She swung her legs over the side of the bed, stepping onto the cool floor, the wood smooth against the soles of her feet. She gave quiet thanks to the hardy pine that was once a tree, a mighty tree with roots that went deep into the earth.

The morning chill made her reach for the woolen blanket at the bottom of her bed. She wrapped herself in its rich earthen colors—reds and oranges and browns—and stood tall.

Maia glanced at the calendar that hung on the wall above her nightstand. The days were getting longer—only a few more weeks until the summer solstice. She took a brown marker and put an "X" into the little square of the day before. She was counting the days until all four girls would meet at Sophia's.

Maia let the blanket fall to the floor. As she put on a flannel shirt, she looked up at her dreamcatcher. She, her mother, and Sophia had had long conversations about its power. Maybe the words on the winds were right. Maybe she was ready.

Today she would look for stones. Maia grabbed her silver necklace, the one with the turtle charm. She flew into this new day. Nothing to fence her in.

Lune ran through creeks and around the rocks toward the faint beat of a drum. The sound led horse and rider to what they thought was the source. When they got there, they were met with silence. Maia thought she heard a drum as she rode

Lune through the water under the towering cliffs of stone. The sound lead them on but they never quite found the source.

"My imagination playing tricks," Maia said. "It does that, you know."

Lune snorted—he understood her words. It didn't matter if the drum was real or not. The essence of it was. It spoke to Maia as if it were her own beating heart—the pulse of the earth, the perfect place to find stones.

They came to the river. Maia picked up a rock and rubbed the smoothness between her fingers. It was an old stone, maybe even ancient. Years of water had washed over the rough and ragged rock, turning it to silk. The stone was in the shape of a circle—a small crystal embedded in its center. When she raised the circular stone toward the sun, the rays shone through like an arrow, beams of light that felt clean and clear and important. She stepped into the cool water. It bubbled with magic, and she reached down to pick up another stone. It also had a crystal in its center, but this one was the color of gold. Maia collected four stones and placed them gently in her medicine bag—the one that her grandmother had given her.

Four girls. Four directions. One purpose.

Maia was imagining a naming ceremony to solidify the bond of their first meeting.

These would be perfect.

CIRCLE OF FOUR

SOPHIA'S HAIR BRUSHED against her cheeks as she gathered sweetgrass, pulling the long silvery strands from the dry earth. She filled her old basket, woven by a neighbor on the other side of the canyon. When it was heavy and could hold no more, she walked down to the river. There, at the edge where earth and water met, the river's rush was musical. She bowed her head, thankful that it was clean and running strong—but questioned how long it would last. She said a prayer as she placed the fragrant grass into the water. Sophia didn't rush. She waited until every last strand was soaked through before hanging them in the sun. When they were damp, they were ready for braiding.

When Sophia was a child, her mother had explained that sweetgrass was a part of their medicine. The sweet smell of sweetgrass smoke called the spirits to their sides. Her mother showed her how to weave wreaths. Sophia loved making garlands and wore them like crowns. In summer, she slipped tiny blossoms into the crevices between the strands. She never cut the stems of flowers until they began to fade, for they were needed by the hummingbirds, bees, and other pollinators. Sophia didn't pay attention to time, at least not by the clock, but rather, let the cycles of nature dictate how she lived. When the firefly lit up, she knew it was July. When cicadas shed their skins, she knew it was August. Late spring was the time to plant the seeds.

A quick, biting wind interrupted her peaceful moments beside the river. The mistral lasted for just a few seconds, and then all was quiet again. The leaves on the trees hadn't moved in the strange wind, nor had the tall grasses swayed. The wind had only touched Sophia, chilling her, and not because of its temperature, but in warning.

Sophia walked swiftly to the barn and felt a quickening in her belly, a tightness, a knot, an urgency. Time felt more compressed—and it was closing in on her and the earth she was called to protect. Dark, powerful forces of greed were swirling in the atmosphere. She knew their brutality and their capacity to destroy. The clouds were on their way again, and the girls would be coming just in time.

☾

Maia's mom had brought her to Montana a few days earlier so she might prepare herself to be a leader. She hardly slept. In three days, the others would arrive at the ranch. They were brave to be coming so far, or even at all. They knew that the search would be a mix of danger and adventure, but their higher purpose was stronger than either one. Still, they had no idea what was in store. Only Sophia knew.

Maia had told them about Mount Shasta, the clouds, the Horseshoe, and how Sophia needed help.

Yue had been tentative at first. *I don't know*, she thought, but the images of the dying coral haunted her. Her love for them was stronger than any fear of the unknown. Ava never hesitated when she received Maia's invitation. And Falcon had been ready to spread her wings. They were all sworn to secrecy. "Not a soul," said Maia. And she trusted them.

Now Maia lay in bed. The window framed a crescent moon, with Venus to the left. Usually, she would be staring at the display, falling into space, and then sleep. But not tonight. Tonight, she looked at the ceiling, a white screen where she projected the movies of her mind.

She rewound to her first time at Sophia's . . . the iron gate that led to the driveway, the windmill and solar panels, the bee garden, the falls, the river, the sweetgrass, the streak of blue in Sophia's hair. When Maia had gotten home, she'd added a streak of green to her own hair, and now she wrapped it around her finger.

She thought of the books, the crystals, and her grandmother standing at her back, whispering. She saw herself picking up that belt buckle for the first time. Now she wondered how the others would feel when they held one. Would their hands buzz, too? Would they be afraid? They understood the power of their dreamcatchers, how the light danced on their bedroom walls—but what about the buckles?

She grabbed a piece of licorice and bit into the chewy chocolate. The bag was almost empty. *I shouldn't be eating this, anyway.*

Maia had ruminated on everything—the sisterhood, their purpose, whether everyone would get along. They had already established an important rule: No gossip. No talking behind each other's back. If there was a disagreement, they would hash it out, no matter how long it took. They would pass the talking stick and hear all sides, and if needed, agree to disagree. They made a pact.

Their secret group chat, "CIRCLE OF FOUR," had serious threads of conversation. They were already weaving their story cloth. Some days, they talked way past midnight, their keyboards clicking, until every parent threatened to take their computers away.

Their chats covered everything: family, school, being only children, books they loved and hated, favorite things and pet peeves, music, rooftop gardens, coral reefs, the climate, bees, dreamcatchers, trees, the zoo in Central Park, the homeless, the hungry, immigration, adoption, fracking, the food supply, floods, and wildfires. Falcon told them about Diana, and Yue confided her crush on Jake. They discussed how to tell a boy, or a girl, to back off, school strikes, and Greta, their collective hero. Maia admitted that she hadn't gotten her period. She had kept it a secret from everyone at home, but here, with these girls, she was real. They declared sister love.

Technology was new to Maia. She used her mom's computer. She was the only one without her own. Until now, she hadn't wanted one. She preferred to be where her feet were, not somewhere in the cloud. No phone lived in her hand or back pocket or under her pillow, either. She used a walkie talkie to communicate with Keya when out exploring. Now her mother insisted on the phone. She played with its functions and posted on their group text.

Three days, 72 hours. xoxo

Maia loved this circle of girls, but the movie reel replayed inside of her head, and she asked again: *What if it's different in person?*

Maia knew what was at stake. Then she remembered her mother's words.

"You will be guided, Maia."

They would be there in three days, just enough time for Sophia to finish instructing Maia in leadership. Just in time to finish up the work Keya started in the silo, the perfect place for their circle of four.

Airport and Nori

THE FOUR GIRLS wrapped in a team huddle, jumping, squealing, and carrying on in an airport terminal as if they had just found a long-lost family were hard to miss. Sophia watched from a few feet away. The girls spoke so fast that she couldn't make out a thing, but they understood each other perfectly.

"Falcon, you're even more beautiful than your Insta photos," said Ava.

Falcon laughed, embarrassed by the compliment. She took a group selfie. She was the tallest, her long arms reaching up to fit them all into the frame. She wore a white T-shirt with the "coexist" design. Symbols of faith and unity emblazoned in blue. From conversations with Falcon, Maia understood that Falcon was street-smart. That she had to be to live in the city. Her antennae were always at full attention. She took everything in, including the people at the airport—the parents and children, the businesspeople, the security guards with their guns. Maia saw how Falcon watched, her eyes darting from here to there. Falcon could sniff out trouble even before it happened, a valuable skill.

"Yue, you're tiny!" said Maia.

"And mighty." It was a comeback that Yue used often. Her petite form was more obvious when she stood next to Falcon. "Am I really here?" said Yue, looking at Maia.

Ava touched the dolphin and starfish charms on the frayed silk cord around Yue's neck. "You are, Water Girl, and I will write your song." Ava's dark hair was woven into a long thick braid. She wore a straw cowboy hat—its brown leather band studded with silver stars. Her jeans were worn thin from riding, as were her boots. She carried her guitar on her back in a soft black case, the colorful strap embroidered by her mother's hands.

"Will you play tonight?" asked Maia.

"I will," she said. "But now I'm *starving*. Plane food is terrible, and I couldn't have eaten anyway. The turbulence was crazy. Especially over North Dakota."

"It was bumpy on my flight, too," said Falcon. "I've flown a lot, but this was weird. The sky was clear, except for a little black cloud near my window, as if it were chasing the plane."

Maia glanced over at Sophia and saw that she had heard what Falcon said.

"Want some?" asked Maia, holding out a bag of licorice to Ava. "You said you were hungry."

"Twizzlers! I forgot you love them!"

"Did you expect me to eat tree bark?" said Maia.

Ava laughed as she put her arm around her friend's shoulder.

"Try this," said Yue, pulling some chips out of her bag.

"Nori? What's that?" Maia took one and felt the thin, crispy seaweed soften in her mouth.

"You like?" asked Yue, hoping she would.

"I'm not sure yet." Maia ate another. "Sea bark," she said. "Not too terrible."

They laughed the kind of easy laugh of people who have known each other for a long time.

Sophia walked toward the girls leaving the scent of rose petals in her wake. People stared. One woman gasped and dropped her water bottle. Another looked at her from different angles, as if Sophia were the Mona Lisa. Sophia paid no attention. But Maia did. She watched Sophia cast a spell without even trying. She called it The Sophia Effect.

"Ready to get your bags?" asked Sophia.

"I'll grab them," said Falcon, as she expertly moved through the crowd to take them off the carousel.

"Is that a New York thing?" asked Maia, laughing. She was happy to see Falcon taking charge. Maia heard that people from the city were always in a hurry to get things done. Things moved fast. She didn't see Falcon as pushy or bossy, but focused and capable. She was on a mission. Yes, that was it.

While they waited for the last of the bags, Ava shared photos of her horse, Tolusa. "She and music are my life," she said. She opened Spotify on her phone. "I made a playlist for us," she said. "Our songs."

Maia noticed all these little things . . . How Falcon took charge and helped. How Ava gathered music, *their* music. How Yue had brought enough Nori chips for everyone.

The private group chat was Falcon's idea, though Maia had resisted at first—she was a letter-writer—but her mother had encouraged her to try something new. To her surprise, she'd spent many late nights in bed with her mom's laptop, the screen lighting her face as the sound of the keys went *tap-tap-tap*. And now here they were, no screens or miles separating them, arms linked as they walked.

Sophia had warned Maia that there would be times when things would get intense, maybe even stormy, after the four strong personalities, like elements, gathered together. Forever a peacekeeper, Maia worried about this. She had written in her journal: *We are like colors on a wheel, different, yet complementary. I know we will have our moments. The colors will get muddy when we're not in sync. I hope it will be okay.* As Earth, she knew she had to stay rooted, bring in stability. But even the earth cracked.

The girls threw their luggage in the back of Sophia's Jeep and squeezed in.

Ava whispered to Yue, nodding toward their mentor, "She's beautiful, like a queen."

They arrived at the ranch and quickly pulled their bags out of the car. Maia led them toward the barn, a red structure with an earthy patina, humbled by years of sun, wind, and water against wood. The silo looked like it was painted onto the blue sky. Before she returned to South Dakota, Keya had helped set up the girls' sleeping quarters.

"Is that ours? Is that our barn?" asked Ava, with excitement in her voice.

Maia hoped the other girls would love it as much as she did.

As the girls rambled over to the barn, dragging their belongings, Sophia walked toward the house, giving them a chance to settle in. Maia looked back and saw that Sophia had turned, too, her expression wistful.

Maia wondered if being with them brought Sophia back to her own childhood, before she grew into her role, a time in her life when all she wanted was to feel as if she belonged. She'd told Maia that, even as a young girl, she knew she was different and there were things about her that others didn't understand. Keya had been the only one. Maia heard stories about them praying to the North Star. They were smitten by the Milky Way, just like she was. They learned all about the constellations, and imagined the stars speaking to one another. Three blinks on Archer's bow were an SOS to Pegasus. Archer would climb onto the horse's back and take off into the celestial sky. As he rode, he would release his arrows, making starbursts of falling light.

Tonight, when all is quiet, maybe Sophia will pray on the North Star, thought Maia. *Maybe she will ask for direction as she folds four girls into a circle.*

Maia wondered if tomorrow Sophia would introduce them to the horses who would become their chariots.

Maybe it was too soon.

FALCON

writes

I HAVE BEEN DREAMING. On the way to Sophia's, I closed my eyes and saw her standing in a field of grasses. They were tall, almost to her waist. She held a basket of wheat, long stalks cascading over the sides.

She was the Roman goddess, Ceres, protector of the grain. She wore a crown of baby's breath. Bluebirds and butterflies danced around her, like in *Snow White*, but Sophia isn't a fairy tale, or a goddess—she's real.

It would be no surprise if I saw her standing among the wildflowers, wearing a wreath, with fawns and squirrels and other wild things coming to be near her, as if she were their mother. I think Sophia is of the earth, not born to flesh and blood, although she seems otherworldly. But I know that can't be true.

I'm strange, I know. I dream about mythic horses. Diana is of the forest, and now I think Sophia is Snow White. What will be next?

In the Silo

I T WAS THEIR FIRST NIGHT as a sisterhood. They had counted the days leading up to this moment when the silo would become their haven, their safe cocoon—a respite before journeying into the unknown.

A round staircase curved up to the loft. The girls followed Maia, hauling multiple duffels and backpacks, bags bursting at the seams with things they would have to leave behind.

Falcon gasped when she saw the hexagonal skylight, the portal into the astrological world, the sky that was her heart.

Yue followed. She looked up at the unbroken lines of streaming light, an extension of the sun. She was looking forward to seeing the moonbeams that would flow in during the night.

"We're here," said Ava, softly, almost to herself. "I can hardly believe it." She heard the echo of her words bounce off the cylinder walls. "The acoustics in here are like the canyons. I love this place."

The circular room was set up like a medicine wheel. There were four twin-size beds, each draped with a different colored throw. Curved headboards were placed in each of the four quadrants, and the foot of each bed extended into the center of the room. A table of thick pink glass, shaped like a hexagon, was aligned perfectly beneath the skylight. Four small triangular windows were set into the walls above the beds—the perfect spots to hang the dreamcatchers they'd brought from home.

The girls didn't have to be told which beds were theirs and quickly claimed their spaces. Falcon gravitated toward the one with the yellow throw, the color of the East, where the sun came up. Ava went to the bed with the red blanket in the South. She gently put her guitar against the wall. Yue placed her journals underneath the pillow that sat on a black woolen throw in the West. Maia's bed, in the North, was covered in white.

"It's like being inside a dreamcatcher," said Yue.

"Let's put them up while it's still light," said Maia, eyes sparkling. *I wonder how much more powerful they will be when they're together in the same room*, she thought.

The girls had been given instructions on how to safely transport their dreamcatchers. Sophia had sent them thick silk and flat protective boxes. They were instructed to tuck them inside a small blanket in their carry-on bags.

The girls stood on their beds and hung the hoops on the tiny golden hooks above the windows. Sophia and Keya had thought of everything.

Falcon reached into her bag and brought out some gifts.

"Not yet!" said Maia. "First we open the medicine wheel."

"Oh, I'm sorry, Maia," said Falcon, blushing, thinking that she already messed up. *Why do I always have to rush things?*

"You don't have to be sorry. It's my fault. You didn't know."

Ava looked at Falcon. "It's nobody's fault."

Maia appreciated Ava for pointing out neither of them had fumbled, and so what if they had.

"Let's try this again," said Maia, and she began. "Great Spirit, thank you for today's sunrise, for the breath and life within me, and for all of your creations."

This was new for Falcon and Yue. They had never been part of a circle where the four directions were called in. The girls followed Maia as she turned to the West.

"Spirit keepers of the West, Brown Bear, Thunder, Wild Horses, be with us." Maia continued with the prayer, turning in all four directions. After she completed the circle, she bent to the ground where she laid both hands. "Mother Earth, thank you for your beauty, for all you have given. May we always give back more than we take."

"Did you learn that from your ancestors?" asked Yue.

"Yes, but not all tribes do it the same way. Many open with the East."

"So different from my custom. I say a prayer to Kuan Yin. She's the Chinese Goddess of the Seven Seas." Yue took out her phone and showed them an image. "She's also the Mother of Compassion."

"What's she holding?" asked Ava.

"Pearls of Illumination."

"Does she watch over the oceans the way Artemis protects the forests?" asked Falcon.

"I hope so, but I'm not really sure. I have no ancestors to ask. I was a baby when I was adopted from China. But I feel safe with Kuan Yin around. She feels like my mother." Yue showed a picture of her mom. They were standing on the beach, arm in arm. Her mother's windswept hair was the color of sand.

"I'm glad you have Kuan Yin," said Ava, grateful that her own mother was still alive. She handed the phone back to Yue.

"Who's ready for gifts?" asked Maia. She bounced onto her bed and they all laughed at the joy of finally being together. The girls started rummaging in their bags.

Maia looked at Falcon and nodded. "You want me to go first?" asked Falcon.

Maia saw that Falcon was hesitant and coaxed her. "Go on." She finally felt like a leader, putting people at ease.

Falcon stood up straight, moving to the center, and unfolded the pages of her poem *The Sun Horses*, the vision that had brought her to this room. She cleared her throat and paused before she began to read. She captivated them with a spell, almost before she could get out the words.

> *. . . beyond the oceans of light,*
> *thunder roars.*
> *four white horses*
> *soar.*
> *eagle feathered manes,*
> *carried by the winds of time.*
> *They are here to transport the Crystal Warriors,*
> *four girls powered by the elements,*
> *and an unwavering cowgirl spirit.*
> *These brave beacons of light were chosen*
> *to heal humanity*
> *retore Mother Earth,*
> *and enlighten this age to be new again.*

Falcon had made copies of the poem that had brought her here, writing the lines with her quill pen, dipped in gold ink, on marbled paper she made by hand. She'd carefully folded each page into the shape of a crane, adding a tiny sapphire crystal for the eye.

"Are we the Crystal Warriors?" asked Yue.

Maia knew that the question was for her. She wasn't sure how to answer. "Sophia will guide us."

None of them, not even Maia, fully understood how Falcon's vision would inform the world they were about to enter.

"I have something else," said Falcon. She handed her friends packets of sunflower seeds. "They come up every year, and will remind you of the sun, and the East."

Ava was next. She thanked Falcon. "I love them both." Then she brought out a small canvas. "This is a painting of a gray wolf standing high up on the mesa. Sometimes I think she follows me."

"Dolphins follow me, too," said Yue.

"Wolf represents the South. They have strong instincts and are good hunters. They are pathfinders and members of packs. That's what we are—a pack," said Ava. She reached into her jean pocket and took out silver wolf charms, one for each of them. She went around the circle, also handing each girl a red rock gathered on her walks in the high desert.

"These rocks don't look all that special, but they symbolize layers of time and strength. They formed over millions of years from sandstone and the rich red color comes from iron. Keep it with you to pull up your own power."

Ava turned and picked up her guitar. "This is the other gift."

She plucked a string as she sat cross-legged on her bed. The silo filled with sound. It traveled like a wave to the edges of the walls, expanding them. The room felt bigger as the reverberation moved through and around everything.

Falcon was stunned.

"That was crazy. I've never felt sound."

"I think we *are* sound," said Yue, crossing both hands over her chest to hold in the vibrations.

"This guitar has seven strings, not the usual six. And the weird thing is that I never have to re-string it." She plucked a few more notes. "I think this music is magic and that this guitar speaks many languages." The girls were silent as the notes faded. They would come to depend on this music in the evenings, for mystery, encouragement, and strength. Ava laid the guitar aside and looked over at Yue.

"What I have isn't much," Yue said. "Not like all of you."

"I'm sure that's not true," said Maia.

Yue reached into her sweater and pulled out a small bear. It was hand-carved out of black onyx by a woman who lived in the woodlands of the Northwest.

"I brought Bear because she's fiercely protective. Bear is a strong leader. She's introspective and takes her time."

She brought out four green silk pouches. Inside were light-blue dolphins, hand blown from sea glass.

"These are amazing creatures. They are communicators. Dolphins use sound to tell stories. Like whales. They're playful and energetic." She handed each of them a dolphin, and they held the glass up to the light.

"The dorsal fins shimmer." said Yue.

"Like the moon on water," said Maia.

"My name means moon in Chinese."

"I didn't know that! It makes total sense, Yue!" Maia said.

"I love my dolphin," said Ava. "Thank you."

"Me too," said Falcon, as she held it in her open hand.

"And I have one more thing," said Yue. She walked the circle with small seashells cupped in her hands. After each of them chose, Yue brought out her conch shell. "Listen," she said as she passed it around. "You can hear the ocean."

When it was her turn, Maia reached into the medicine bag made of buffalo hide that hung around her neck. She took out four round stones, each wrapped in its own beaded chamois cloth. "Falcon, you're from the East, so I give you this stone, the one with a golden center, the color of the rising sun. Yellow is also for the spirit of the eagle for sharp vision."

Falcon took the stone and felt the warmth of the Universe in her hand. "I will keep this with me. Thank you."

Maia turned to Ava and pulled out the stone with the red crystal. "This belongs to you."

Ava gasped as she took the stone. It reminded her of the Angel of Fire ring that never left her hand.

Maia brought out Yue's stone with the dark blue center, the color of deep rivers and oceans and the sky at dusk. Yue placed it over her throat, closed her eyes, and took a deep breath. She felt understood and heard by her sisters.

There was one stone left, for Maia. It was the very first stone that she had found. She called it Opal Moon. It had a clear center, but when tilted, it made the colors of the rainbow.

Ava looked at the skylight and then back at walls. "What's that?" she asked.

"It's like a thousand hovering hummingbirds," said Falcon.

Yue shivered. "I just felt goosebumps."

Maia pointed to the dreamcatchers.

Four beams of light erupted out of the center crystals, meeting in the center of the room. Where they touched, cascades of green formed into petals in a delicate circle.

"It's buzzing in here," said Ava.

"We're inside a flower," said Maia. "The Flower of Life."

"You can't make this up," said Yue.

"No you can't," said Ava, as she twirled the ring on her finger.

"I wonder what my Dad would think," whispered Falcon, the daughter of a man who studied light patterns in the cosmos.

That night, when the girls were finally tucked under their covers, Ava whispered into the dark. "Yue, are you still awake?"

"Shhh, I am."

"So am I," said Falcon.

"Me, too," echoed Maia.

Laughter bounced off the walls. The chatter of a new sisterhood went on deep into the night until one by one they fell silent.

The Ways of Gaia

SOPHIA OBSERVED THE GIRLS CLOSELY. In less than two days, she knew Maia had chosen well. For the first time in a long time, the Guardian began to have hope.

These girls were already fierce with a hunger to know what they didn't know. They were learning the ways of Gaia: her nature, her moods, her responses, the human qualities many never see.

This morning, on the hike to the falls, Sophia casually said, "The land feels things. Even the rocks are alive."

Falcon had the most trouble with this concept. Rocks were hard and impenetrable, cold and unfeeling. How were they alive? But the stones in the dreamcatchers told her differently, and so did the stone with the golden center, the one Maia had given her in the silo.

"The earth has a spirit, a soul," said Sophia. "Some say there is a fifth element. It's more subtle than the others. You can't feel it, but you can sense it."

They talked about the elements and their places within the wheel of life.

"These elements can work together or become enemies," said Sophia.

"Wind makes fire rage, and water puts it out. Is that what you mean?" asked Ava.

"But fire destroys forests," said Yue, thinking about California.

"Yes, but it also regenerates the soil and drives seeds deep below the surface. Often, new growth is even stronger," said Sophia.

"The earth has emotions, like we do," said Maia.

"She quakes, she cracks, she breathes, she hurts, she's volcanic. She's soft and nurturing and grows things. She makes oxygen, holds water with her rivers, and makes food for the world," said Sophia.

"And medicine from her plants," said Maia. Maia knew about the healing ways of flowers, herbs, and barks. Her grandmother had taught her mother, who passed it down to her, like recipes in a family cookbook. She crushed yarrow root, made tea from echinacea, used ragweed and sagebrush, and of course sweetgrass, whose smoke rose to the heavens with messages more powerful than words.

"Maia, choose some plants and tell us the ailments they help with. It will be useful on your journey," said Sophia.

"This is balsam poplar. See how the buds are covered in resin?"

Falcon leaned over and felt the stickiness, then inhaled. "It smells familiar, like Christmas."

"It's good for the lungs, when you have a cold," explained Maia.

Beside Yue, a butterfly landed on a dark-pink flower that looked like a daisy, except for the color.

"That's pink coneflower," said Maia. "It's a prized medicine—Nature's antibiotic."

Falcon and Yue had grown up going to doctors when they were sick and getting drugs from a pharmacy. They were fascinated by this other way, the way Maia had grown up with.

Falcon recalled a walk in the forest with Diana, who said that mushrooms had medicinal powers. Diana also told her that dandelion leaves were a superfood that helped heal the body.

"What else is balsam good for?" asked Yue.

"You can take the buds and make them into a salve to treat wounds. You can also use it for sprains and sore muscles. We'll take some with us. We will need others, too." The girls helped Maia gather plants as they walked.

In this place, doing this task, Falcon felt Diana's presence. She wasn't there, but she was.

"These trees, all trees, are the lungs of the earth," Sophia said.

"They have spoken to me," said Maia.

"Yes, if you listen, they will share what they know. The Grandmother Trees are wise," said Sophia.

"I've never heard trees speak," said Ava.

"Neither have I," said Yue.

"You have to be with them for a while. Sit against their trunks, feel the bark against your backs. See the designs in the leaves, the roots in the ground. Honor them. You have to want to hear what they have to say."

"How do you see roots if they're covered up?" asked Yue.

"You imagine them," said Sophia. "Follow me."

They went deeper into an old-growth forest near the river where the air smelled of earth and moss, wood and leaves.

"See these big trees? They are the Mothers," said Sophia, as she looked up at the canopy. "They take care of their saplings, and in the dense parts of the forest, baby trees get nourished by the fungi in the soil."

"Mycorrhizal networks," said Falcon.

Yue was surprised. Falcon grew up in concrete and steel. How did she know about mycorrhizal networks? Yue couldn't even pronounce the word.

"They're crazy vast underground systems of roots and fungi, all connected to each other. They send signals," said

Falcon. She couldn't help but blush. "My friend Diana told me all about it."

"What kind of signals?" asked Ava.

"They release chemicals. I don't know which ones. But they warn about drought, and disease, even attacks from insects."

"Then what?" asked Yue.

"When the trees receive these messages, they adapt," said Sophia. "They change their behavior. They live in communities. If one isn't getting enough nutrients, the others step in."

"They help each other," said Maia.

Falcon was glad she wasn't the only one who knew something about trees.

❰

When dusk came, and the sun began to drop, they gathered up kindling for the evening fire.

Ava was in charge of the flames. To call herself a firekeeper would not be right. It was an art and a ritual and a title that didn't belong to her. She was riveted when she saw her friend's uncle tend fire, keeping it burning and alive for four days during a Sun Dance ceremony. She'd been an invited guest, not part of the tribe. Now she did her best to move the ash within the circle, a constant motion that drew them all into the power of the flame, into community.

On some nights they drummed and danced with the fire and the moon. Falcon felt awkward at first. It wasn't that she *couldn't* dance, it was just that she felt inhibited. Maybe even silly. She watched how free the others were, which helped her unleash the wild in her own nature.

Soon she was twirling, too.

Yue felt the moon in her body, as she always had. The moon guided the water, pulling the oceans, and people, too. Some said dolphins were messengers of the moon.

Maia loved the different names for the moon, names that depended on the seasons: Wolf or Harvest, Strawberry or Hunter. In Lakota, all moons were Hanhepi-Wi, and married to Wi, the sun.

The girls studied the constellations and their shapes, and in the darkest of summer skies they could practically taste the Milky Way. It wasn't made of chocolate and caramel. It was a spiral band of stars, billions of them, a whole galaxy of lights and dust and colors. And mystery, too.

Falcon had only known the stars in the Hayden Planetarium. The lights in New York City made the real stars invisible to the naked eye. She had loved the lack of light pollution at farm camp, and it was the same here. Now she understood why her father made the cosmos his life's work.

Their days were so full of learning and new information that after they danced, they slept like babies.

☾

Summer was hotter than usual for Montana. As they swam in the rushing stream of high, quick waters, Falcon splashed, laughing and licking droplets as they flew from her hands.

Not Yue. She stood still, waiting for dragonflies to land on her outstretched arms. She looked closely at the iridescent, stained-glass wings as they caught the light. Yue thought they were magical beings, faerie-like. And they were blue.

"There's sweetgrass," said Maia, as she ran toward the silvery strands. She loved combing it in her hands, her fingers moving over and under. It smelled of vanilla, sweet, like its name. Braiding the grasses was second nature to her. Like her mother and her grandmother, Maia had twisted her hair each morning, since the age of four, into a single braid. Now it ran down her back, long like a horse's tail.

To many Native people, hair had feeling powers, like the whiskers on many animals, horses in particular. Braids were woven, one piece holding another, making it strong. The same thing was happening in this tribe.

That afternoon they collected honey from the hives and learned that the hexagon is a sacred form of geometry, not something taught in a standard math class.

"Numbers and formulas shape everything," said Sophia. "Do you know what a nautilus shell is? It's the Fibonacci code, the golden spiral, a mathematical pattern," explained Sophia.

This is better than school, thought Yue. She thought of all of the shells she had gathered from the shore.

"The golden spiral is everywhere, from the shape of our galaxy to the petals of a pinecone. Have any of you looked at the skin of a pineapple?"

"Triangles?" said Ava.

"Yes, those patterns are reflected all around us. All we have to do is learn to see."

Hunger for the natural world grew in the girls like blades of grass in spring. That night, they sat on Sophia's porch and talked about crystals and stones.

Sophia told ancient stories about the goddesses, the faerie realms, and symbols found in nature, in myths, and in tribal drawings on rock walls.

"When you are out there searching for the missing piece of the Crystal Horseshoe, you'll see petroglyphs that go back thousands of years, carvings that tell stories without words. Pay attention to the symbols—they will give you insights."

Ava thought of petroglyphs as the first graphic novels. As a young child, she and her family had taken trips to the Pueblo settlements. She would stand, staring at the walls, trying to figure out what the pictures meant. She used her vivid imagination and made up her own stories from the images of wind and rain, sun and stars, animals, hunters and the harvest.

"How did the Pueblo tribes survive?" asked Ava.

"Community," said Yue.

"Not everybody has one," said Falcon. "In New York City, there are many people who don't have homes and are living on the sidewalks. They're invisible. People walk by, pretending not to notice, moving on with their lives, doing nothing to help. They don't acknowledge the suffering. I think people say, 'As long as it's not me,' or, 'It's just hard luck.'"

"It's sad," said Yue. "I see the same thing in California."

Falcon told the others about the man she passed every day on her way to school. His name was Andrew. She had asked. He was somebody's son, maybe even a brother or a father who was desperate to see his kids. Maybe Andrew had helped discover a cure for some crazy disease. Maybe not. Maybe he once worked at the corner deli. To most, Andrew was "that man on the street"—dirty, hair wild and unkempt, with nowhere to go, and nobody to turn to for help.

"It's unfair," said Falcon. She hated that some people had what they needed while others didn't. It made her furious and determined to make a difference.

Every night, the conversations swirled beneath the stars and around the fire while Ava stoked the flames.

"Fire is beautiful when it's contained," she said, "but when the wind blows, it gets out of control fast."

One bolt of lightning on a dry desert floor could burst into sizzling flames, destroying miles of plant, animal, and human life. She understood why people said fire was alive. Ava had seen it happen in Arizona—slithering like a snake, rattling with the power of a dragon's roar. It had killed nineteen fire-fighters. And now Australia was burning.

Yue knew fire, too. She folded her arms against her chest, not because she was cold. She looked serious and stern. "My dad's friend lost his ranch in Ojai. The horses had to be moved and two died before anyone could get to them. It sounds terrible but trees can regrow, and hopefully people can build new houses, but the ocean reefs can't come back. So many are gone. It's the plastic. It's ingested by fish, and then by people."

There was silence.

Maia and Sophia encouraged the others to pray to the Great Spirit, always, asking for guidance.

The girls spent their nights with the flames, sitting on wooden thrones, their passions lit—heated conversations sparking their warrior sides. As future light workers, they talked about what love could look like in the world. Many of their sentences began with, "What if . . ."

On some evenings Ava played her guitar. Sometimes Maia joined her on Sophia's drum. The thump, thump, thump on the tightened skin, in synch with their heartbeats, opened the girls' memories.

Mostly Sophia stayed in the background, observing. She liked that they listened to each other and took turns speaking. They weren't trying to out-do one another. They were discovering the common threads that wove their special quilt.

One night, Sophia pulled Maia close and whispered in her ear.

"*Mitakuye Oyasin*," she said in Lakota. "We are all related. I think you are ready."

Maia's heart pounded.

"Are you sure?"

"Yes, my child. I am sure. Besides, we cannot wait any longer." Sophia turned to the girls. "It is time to get to know your horses."

They tried to contain their excitement, to appear mature, but it didn't work. They had a little four-person party with Maia in the center.

"Tomorrow morning," Sophia said. "First light."

Eagle Feather Manes

SUNBEAMS LIKE ARROWS through the windows coaxed the four girls awake. In the night, white horses had come to Falcon, and Maia had heard a buffalo run. Ava and Yue dreamed about wolves and dolphins, and songs of those who had passed.

Falcon and Yue opened their journals and began to write. It was a morning ritual they never missed. When they were done, they tucked their books under their pillows and slipped into their jeans. On their way out, the girls grabbed handfuls of fresh apricots from the ever-present and always full basket.

Sophia led them past the barn and into the pasture. Five white horses were silhouetted against the morning sky. Their bodies—lean, muscular, and strong, walked out of the mist.

Falcon stopped in her tracks and grabbed Maia's hand. "My dream," she whispered.

The fifth horse was taller than the others. He paced back and forth, restless. "His name is Apollo," said Sophia. "He has been with me for a long time.

"Is he . . . from the cave?" asked Falcon. "Is he the one who came alive seventeen thousand years ago?"

"Yes, he is," said Sophia.

A horse came toward Falcon. As their eyes met, Falcon's pulse quickened—she could barely catch her breath. "I've seen her before. She came to my window with the others. But where are her feathers? When I saw her last, she had feathers."

Sophia put her hand on Falcon 's shoulder. "Touch her."

Falcon reached over and began finger-brushing the horse's thick mane. It was coarse and wiry. She felt a strange heat in her hand. Falcon looked at her palm. "What's happening? My hand is hot, tingling."

Maia took Falcon's hand in her own. A soft electrical pulse moved between them, an energy they didn't understand. The air felt charged. The ozone was strong, and it smelled like a swimming pool with too much chlorine, not the crisp Montana air they had gotten used to.

The horses were no longer calm. They felt the wind barreling down the mountain before it began. Now it hit, strong and spiraling.

"It's okay, shouted Sophia, over the wind.

The girls squinted, placing their forearms over their eyes, and huddled together for protection. The horses reared and whinnied. It was pure commotion. Then the wind stopped, leaving complete silence.

The girls opened their eyes. The horses stood before them... changed. From ears to withers their manes were transformed into feathers, those of the golden eagle.

The girls were stunned. Maia was the first to step forward. She took a feather in her hand and examined it. The spine was white, slightly curved like the foot of a dancer, graceful, with a rounded point at the end. The markings were rich browns and golden tans, patterns of light and dark, opposites, a balance of both.

Falcon moved closer, recognizing that these were the feathers on their dreamcatchers, and the manes of the horses she wrote about, those she named Horses of the Sun.

There was magic here. Real magic, not the kind in movies.

Maia had told them to be ready, but nobody was prepared for this. Not even Maia.

Sophia watched the girls looking into the eyes of these beautiful creatures. Most relationships take time to form. Trust is built slowly. But in this instance, the bond between each girl and her horse was immediate.

Falcon had no experience with equines except for those that had come to her window far above the street. In the days ahead all the girls would come to understand the language of these strong, mythical animals that would become their protectors, chariots, and fearless allies.

FALCON

writes

I DIDN'T THINK I could see into the future. I'm not like the psychic on 72nd Street who tried to lure me into her storefront, promising me that her crystal ball held the answers to my life's questions. I didn't even know what my life's questions were. I was only eleven at the time.

Now I have so many.

How did I get here? How did I foresee the horses that stood before us this morning in the pasture?

They were white, like in my dream, but it wasn't a dream... and they had manes made out of feathers—hundreds, maybe even thousands of eagle feathers, gold and brown with gray. And the wind carried them.

I have always believed things happen that can't be explained. I think I have a power that I don't yet know about. I can see things. I remember when Diana was teaching me about hawks. She said that they see things far into the distance. Maybe I am a bird.

You will never see this, Diana. I have been sworn to secrecy and must honor that promise, but I will write these private journal entries as if they were letters to you. Maybe you will receive my words in another way, in a dream, or while you are walking in the forest—I don't know. But I will trust that you're on my shoulder, the way the owl rests on Athena's, and can hear my whispers in your ear. I need you with me.

I am learning that I have other guides, but you were, and will always be, my first, the one who showed me the forest and the hawk, the seed and the sprout. The one who showed me roots and leaves, and soil—all which made me fall in love with Mother Earth. I am here because of you and the horses that came both to my window and to me in the forest that day. Remember?

I am here because I wish, with every breath I take, that the earth be healed, the air purified, the oceans cleansed, the fires calmed.

There are four of us. We come from the four directions. I am East. My power is air. When you told me that the eagle is a sacred messenger and carries our prayers on its wings, something fluttered inside. When you gave me the necklace and named me Falcon, it was no accident.

I will use the vision of the raptors—the eagle, hawk, and falcon. You said that life looks different from up high where one can see the bigger picture. I asked if that meant patterns, too, and you said yes. It is true.

I need to make friends with the wind. This is not an easy thing. Because I have always lived in glass and steel on the thirty-sixth floor, it scares me. I remember when I was little, I spent many nights with my head underneath my pillow, singing to myself to muffle the rattling. I prayed the glass wouldn't shatter. When it shook, I wondered if it were me and not the glass.

I have trembled, like a train whizzing at high speed on electric tracks. In my imagination, I hear the thunder of jet planes flying into my building, like they did in 2001, when they crashed into the World Trade Center. My parents say the world as they knew it changed that day. I wasn't alive yet, but it feels so real that I wonder if I was looking down from the cosmos, watching.

I am afraid of wind, and yet air is my power. I must become the circling hawk, the soaring eagle, the falcon, the goose gliding home for winter.

I can look to the pollinators for comfort. The little winged creatures—hummingbirds, honey bees, the seeds of a dandelion being blown and wished upon. They need the wind. The good, benevolent wind. The kind that moves water, sparks fire, and has shaped the geology of the earth.

The wind I fear creates hurricanes, tornados, tsunamis, and heartbreak.

Maybe I am the calm in the storm.

We are leaving soon . . .

I love you—when I close my eyes to sleep, you are the light underneath the darkness.

Training Ground

*T*HE GIRLS WOKE BEFORE DAWN and climbed to the highest point of the hillside. The morning was cool, but the girls wore thin clothing, with nothing for added warmth. They needed to build resilience to the cold for their mission ahead. Rising during the darkest part of the day also helped to sharpen their vision so that they didn't need to rely on flashlights or headlamps. Falcon still felt unsafe in the dark after having lived in an ocean of man-made light all of her life.

"You've communed with the land, learned her ways, and now you know your horses," said Sophia. "But you haven't met your adversaries, those that come in the form of dark clouds full of evil. These clouds have created floods and fires, earthquakes and droughts," said Sophia. "They've awakened volcanoes, poisoned oceans, the air, our food supply. They represent the desecration of Mother Earth through greed. The crystal is the antidote. The horseshoe holds the truth."

Falcon took in a deep breath and exhaled slowly. She didn't know how much she would come to rely on her breathing.

"What do the clouds look like?" asked Ava.

"They change," answered Sophia. "Sometimes they're dark grey and turn to deep purple. Sometimes they're the color of rust. They always smell like iron."

Ava fiddled with the end of her long braid.

"When they stay clouds, they're damaging, but not as destructive as those that shape-shift into the Fire Dragon. Or Santamond."

"Santamond?" asked Ava.

"The Viper Cloud. A symbol of big business slithering in, telling us they are doing good, when in fact they are doing harm."

Yue shivered. She didn't like snakes. Not even eels.

"The clouds are getting stronger," Sophia continued. "They're being called out by groups that see the effect they have on the environment. They're fighting to remain in control. They wanted to break the Crystal Horseshoe because they knew it would weaken the Codes. When you are out there, searching, watch for them following you. They will trick you, try to knock you off course. They want to exhaust you, to discourage you from this mission."

Falcon swallowed hard.

"But you won't walk away. I know you won't. I believe in you," said Sophia. "I cannot call the clouds in, but I can show you ways to protect yourselves, and each other. We need to practice tapping into your elemental powers, your individual forces."

As if on cue, a cold wind circled down from Canada.

That came out of nowhere, thought Yue, shivering. They stood, looking up, riveted to invisible shears of ice, crystal plumes that had a life of their own. They moved swiftly from right to left, with no set path.

"Falcon, use your breath to make the winds change course," said Sophia.

Falcon inhaled and blew outward from the deepest part of her lungs. The winds retreated for a moment, then returned even stronger. Falcon wanted to quit right then.

"Up," said Sophia as if Falcon had crumpled to the ground. "No time for being a heap on the grass."

Sophia's sharp tone and the insinuation got under Falcon's skin. She'd only tried once . . .

"Inhale up, into your crown," said Sophia. "And ground your feet into the earth."

Falcon took a deep breath with a hint of fury. She expanded her lungs with as much air as she could gather and pushed it out with all of her strength.

The wind shifted and turned. The ice plumes retreated. The gale force weakened into a mere breeze. She took another breath, and then another, until she mastered her own power.

"Good," said Sophia, her eyes sparkling. "Do you feel the difference?"

"Yes," said Falcon, a look of accomplishment on her face. Secretly she thought getting a little mad helped.

"You are East, of the Sun," said Sophia. "When darkness arrives, in whatever form, see your air, your breath, as light. Envision light."

Breath as light, thought Falcon.

Sophia turned toward Ava. "Your power comes from fire. It can transform anything. It shows up as passion, as rage, as impulsivity, and you will need to know how to temper it. Like all of the elements, it is energy. Control what's inside of you and use it for good."

A red-orange creature scurried across Ava's bare foot. "A salamander!"

"A fire symbol," said Sophia. "Telling you to use your own."

"How?" asked Ava.

"Use your *will* to transform. Use the intention of your mind to change things. You can move things with the power of your thought. See that stone?" said Sophia, pointing to a small gray rock. "Make it move."

Ava's determination rose. The small stone shook beneath Ava's still and intense stare. The slight movement fueled Ava's fire. Her breath was steady and strong. She didn't blink. The stone moved three inches to the right.

The girls stood, open-mouthed, almost in disbelief. But not Ava. She was filled with a sudden knowing, a sudden understanding.

"Ava, do your fingers ever feel warm?" asked Sophia.

"When I play guitar, yes."

"You may see heat come out of them, like the glow of fire. It won't hurt, but it will help you be a warrior."

Ava looked at her hands. The thought of fire coming was both encouraging and scary.

"Keep practicing, dear one. And drink water."

Sophia faced Yue.

"It's hard to define how your powers will appear, because they will change, like a shifting river. But, oh, they are strong. As strong as the tides. As strong as the water that smooths stone, as strong as the pull of the moon," she said.

"How will I feel them?" asked Yue.

The ways of the water will tell you what is needed for each situation. You will know. You'll use intuition," said Sophia.

Yue nodded. She understood.

"There are times to be still, like a mirror to the sky, or ferocious, like an untamed wave, "said Sophia.

"How do I practice?" asked Yue.

"It is best to practice with the moon, We will work with her tonight, at the creek."

Yue was disappointed that she didn't get to still the wind or move a rock. But she trusted her mentor. She would wait for night.

Maia was ready for Sophia's wisdom.

"Earth," said Sophia. "You are her, all of her, the rivers and winds, waters and landforms, the fires that burn in her belly. As her Guardian, you carry her soul, the *anima mundi*, and you feel what she feels."

"The elements bring balance," said Maia.

"Exactly. You will come to know all of the mysteries, the symbols, the patterns, the connection between living creatures.

For you to do your work, you must ground into her, take root. You're already doing this and now you must teach the others."

Sophia looked at each of them. "I have used grounding to keep me steady when confronted with the clouds. It will be a valuable tool. And so will these . . ."

Sophia took her dreamcatcher out of her medicine bag. It was now the size of a quarter. "Always keep them with you."

"How do we make them small?" asked Falcon.

"The infinity wave," said Sophia, as she drew a figure eight in the air with her finger. "Imagine it as light. Now imagine it inside the hoop. You can expand and contract your dream-catchers. There may be a time when you'll need to make yourselves smaller, too." Sophia handed Yue the hoop. "Try it," she said.

It took Yue five tries before she got it right, but eventually the dreamcatcher grew and shrank before their eyes.

"The apricots you have been eating also have powers. Have you noticed how you feel after you've eaten one?" asked Sophia.

"Things are moving inside, buzzing," said Yue.

"I feel more focused," said Falcon.

Maia took a moment to reflect. "My senses are more intense. Everything is just . . . more."

"Ava? What about you?" asked Sophia.

"I'm physically stronger. And more clairaudient. I hear sounds before they happen."

"What's in the apricots?" asked Falcon.

"Even I don't know," said Sophia. "But the story told by the Guardians is that they hold some kind of light. There is energy in the seed, which seeps into the flesh of the fruit. I promise you will have everything you need waiting at your ARIA cave, the secret place I've prepared for you. It's a hidden cave deep in the red rocks of the Southwest. It will be your haven, your home. Everything you need is there. Everything else is inside of you."

AVEER. AZE. TERRA. MAZU.

*T*HE MORNING SUN KISSED the dew as the girls gathered in the pasture. They were silent as they walked the hill, the usual chatter among them stifled by anxiety and anticipation. This ceremony would be the last before they were on their own, facing the dark forces Sophia had been warning them about.

"You know why you've been called here," said Sophia.

They all nodded.

"You have a big mission. Maybe the most important of all time. The health of this planet is at stake. Humanity has lost its way, and your generation is not blind to this."

Sophia stood facing them, wearing an animal skin on her back, the one she'd worn standing on Mount Shasta the night the crystal was stolen.

"I have watched you all. Maia has chosen well. You have been warned about what you will encounter. Finding the crystal will not be easy. But you are strong. You will be protected by forces that you cannot see."

Yue touched the bear on her necklace.

"You can do this. I know you can. But time is also your enemy. There is one more thing," she continued, handing Maia the Golden Box. "Today, you will receive the buckles."

Maia knew how hard Sophia had worked on them, head bent over for forty nights, scalpel in hand. She had carved intricate lines into the silver ovals using steady, tiny movements with just the right pressure. Crafting communication systems like this took intense focus. Sometimes Sophia had been so focused that she forgot to breathe.

The girls stared at the Golden Box as Maia opened it with care.

"These buckles, worn on leather belts, store data—ancient, current, and futuristic. They use the physics of light, sound, and minerals from the earth to send and receive messages."

Maia took one out of the box. Four crystals surrounded the oval. The center piece, the power stone, glowed like amber.

"When you press this crystal," said Sophia, "a GPS system will be activated. Watch."

Chimes sounded and images moved inside the crystal screen. "The technology measures distances, tracks ley lines, earth grids, and constellations," said Sophia. The girls leaned in for a closer look.

"Information is downloaded in symbols and other languages, interpreted, then transmitted through the amber stone."

"Incredible," said Ava, under her breath.

"This higher intelligence will guide you, give you direction, and be a lifeline to me," said Sophia. "I've made one for each of you."

Maia wondered if the other girls would have as powerful reaction to the buckles as she did that first evening in Sophia's den.

"You are brave young Guardians, each with your own strengths. Use your gifts. Be vigilant. Look out for each other."

Falcon's gold-flecked eyes focused on Sophia, then shifted to a dark shape in an otherwise cloudless sky. It was small, hovering behind Sophia. It looked like a serpent. Falcon felt a chill. *This is not a normal cloud*, she thought, as she looked over to Maia.

Maia was watching, too. *Is that Santamond?* she wondered. But the wind carried it away, or it disappeared because they had seen it. Either way, Maia took a breath. She imagined a white light above her head, coming into her body. She focused on it traveling down, resting at her feet, then moving into the soil of the earth. She rooted herself and the others.

Apollo whinnied now as the horses gathered around the girls. They smelled sweet and pungent. Sophia handed a buckle wrapped in thick purple silk to Falcon.

"You bring seeds of possibility, and hope. You have great vision to see ahead. This will also guide you," said Sophia.

Falcon bowed her head slightly to Sophia, acknowledging the gift she had just been given.

"This is your horse. Her name is Aveer—the Hebrew word for 'air,'" said Sophia.

Falcon felt seen. And proud. Closer to who she really was.

Sophia turned to Ava. "You are fire, you ignite. Your passion can get in the way of your brilliance, but you are wise."

Ava understood Sophia's gentle warning. She knew the power of the flame.

"Use your music," continued Sophia. "Follow the gut of the string—it is also your intuition." She handed Ava her buckle and turned toward Ava's horse.

"This, my child, is Aze. In Old Norse, it means 'flame.'"

Yue was next.

"You are Moon, and the color of water. I see you as a river of energy, with great depth. You are a small but mighty force. You learned that last night, at the creek." Under the moon the night before, Yue had practiced the power of ebb and flow, pushing and pulling, releasing and holding back. She had practiced stillness and listening, the art of reflection.

"Water is life," said Sophia. "Your horse is named Mazu, after the great sea goddess in Chinese myth."

Sophia handed Yue her buckle and turned toward Maia.

"Maia, your name means Earth. Stay strong, like a tree, roots embedded deep into the womb of the Mother. May your name always remind you of who you are, and why you are here. Terra, your horse, will carry you," said Sophia. "Her name means planet."

Terra's gentle gaze reminded Maia of Spirit.

The buckles vibrated in the girls' hands and there was a few minutes of confusion and activity as they helped each other thread them onto their belts and buckle them on.

"These buckles are your navigators," said Sophia. "As valuable as the stars."

Maia had prepared one last thing for this ceremony. The night before, she had used short, hard strokes against a granite stone to sharpen a steel blade. Now she slid the knife out of its leather sleeve.

"This will bind us," she said. "Ava, you first. Stand still."

At first Ava thought Maia would prick her finger and they would become blood sisters. Then she heard the slice of the knife as it cut through strands of her long, dark hair.

"Here," Maia said, "hold this until I'm finished." She went through the same careful task, cutting eight-inch hanks of hair from each sister and Sophia. When she was done, she clipped her own. She and Ava worked together to divide and braid the hair into four braids, tied with red thread and silent ceremony.

"We are stronger together," said Maia, "Connected as one." The girls secured the braids to their horses' manes.

Sophia took four tiny medicine wheels out of her bag, a gift from Keya. "We cannot forget these," she said. One by one, Sophia attached them into the girls' hair. "The four directions will always be with you."

"We've been decorated. The Crystal Warriors!" said Falcon.

Sophia spoke ceremoniously. "You each have powers that were given to you. Use them. There are four of you, eight counting the horses. The power of eight is the infinity wave on its side. It corrects imbalance. This is what our world is suffering from. Nature is not in balance, because humanity has lost its way. I'm sorry that this is what your generation has to face. You are the voices. Use your dreamcatchers. I love you as my daughters."

❨

Sophia stood tall like the Earth Goddess she was, with Apollo by her side.

Before the girls mounted their horses, she hugged them each goodbye. She and Maia clung a bit longer than the others. When they finally separated, Sophia brushed her lips on Maia's forehead, "Trust, my child. You have been chosen."

As the girls and horses lifted into the sky, Sophia knelt, kissed the earth, and prayed.

"And one day she discovered that she was fierce,
and strong, and full of fire, and that not even she could
hold herself back because her passion burned
brighter than her fears."

—MARK ANTHONY

First Flight

THE HORSES LIFTED OFF like jets from the runway. Thousands of pounds of solid muscle became weightless. Half equine, half bird, they thundered through the air, golden feathers swinging like pendulums as they caught the currents of the wind.

Trails of screaming laughter echoed through the mountaintops. The girls were flying high in their saddles, holding tightly onto their silver reins.

Maia was in front. She had never seen the country from on high. It was as if she could see the edges of the world.

Falcon, accustomed to heights, saw ahead with new eyes, her vision as sharp. Familiar with horses only in her dreams, she held on for dear life and prayed she wouldn't fall.

Yue, more at home on the water than in the sky, imagined she was on an equine surfboard.

Ava, cowgirl that she was, screamed "Yay ha!" across the canyons. The faster the better.

Maia touched the center crystal on her belt buckle. The GPS system lit up and buzzed, homing in on Compass Point 5.05, flashing their estimated time of arrival at ARIA.

And the bundle of eight—four horses, four girls—were on their way.

ARIA

THE MONADNOCK, bathed in pink light, jutted up from the flat, high desert plains. It was an isolated peak in the rugged four corners of New Mexico called Shiprock.

A rock with wings.

A runway for the horses led up to the mountain. At night, it was lit with stones that glowed in the dark—a rainbow of colors. The lights appeared only when the horses needed them, keeping the remote location difficult to detect. The girls named it Crystal Ridge.

As the horses slowed, the wind picked up. It was turbulent, making the landing hard. Falcon fell off of Aveer. She held on tightly, but the bump threw her. She twisted her body, landing on her knee.

Damn, she said to herself, shaking her head.

"Are you hurt?" Maia shouted.

"No. I'm just mad at myself," Falcon shouted back.

As the girls and horses gathered together, Ava encouraged her. "You're new to the horse and you are doing great. But there's a rule: If you fall off, you have to get back on."

"Do I have a choice?" Falcon joked. She dusted off her jeans and took in the landscape. "This is right out of *Lord of the Rings*," she said.

"Let's settle in," said Maia. Her questions began to build. How would their first night be? Would they be all that Sophia was hoping for? Then she heard her mother's whisper: *You must trust.*

"Let's go," said Ava in a ready voice, as she unstrapped the guitar and lifted it off of Aze.

They walked single file up a narrow red-rock path that spiraled up the mountain to a broad, flat resting place. The view was endless, an ocean of desert.

"This is a great lookout point," said Falcon. "And a good place for the horses to stand watch."

Maia turned and pointed to a crevice in the rock that was just wide enough for them to enter. "I think this is it." She peeked inside. It wasn't cold or damp, like most dark places. The temperature was perfect, dry and not too warm. It smelled of apricots. The girls filed through the split in the rocks.

The cave was round, like the silo. Shafts of light streamed through a natural, open skylight directly above a large compass carved into the floor. A copper arrow sat in the center of the four directions.

"Did Sophia make this?" asked Yue, in awe as she turned in a circle.

"She must have," said Maia. Nothing about Sophia surprised her anymore.

Usually, Maia would have smudged a new space with white sage. That ritual wasn't necessary here. ARIA was warm and safe, a cocoon of protection. A soft light flickered on the walls. It came from seven stones vertically embedded in the rock. The colors descended, from violet at the top to red at the bottom, a rainbow glowing on burnt-orange walls.

"I know this sounds crazy, but have you ever wondered what it would feel like to be inside a diamond?" asked Falcon.

"You mean actually *in* the facets?" asked Yue.

"That's what this place feels like to me. Do you feel it?"

"It's like water," said Yue, "shimmering in the sun."

"I feel it, too," said Ava.

She looked at the copper arrow on the floor. It began to move. Ava wondered if the power of her mind had made it turn. Without words, she spoke to the arrow. *Move counterclockwise.*

The arrow turned left.

"Arrow," she said out loud, "go to the North."

The arrow swung to the north.

"Arrow, where is the East?"

Arrow showed her. This game was good practice.

Ava touched each stone embedded in the walls and held her hand firm against their vibrations. She immediately thought of the music of the stones and recreating it with the strings of her guitar.

The girls settled into their new world. Everything they needed had been laid out . . . shelves of books, empty journals waiting to be filled, a basket of medicine bags, each with herbs, elixirs, and botanical oils. They found mini telescopes, charging stations for their buckles, and special hooks on which to hang their dreamcatchers.

Baskets of apricots were scattered around the room. Called "Moon of the Faith" in Arabic, Sophia's small, velvety golden fruits were infused with all the nutrients they needed. Along the way, they might find seeds and nuts and berries. If they wanted meat they would have to kill and cook it themselves, but the golden fruit was the only thing necessary for their survival.

As night fell, ARIA's thick walls blocked out all nocturnal cries. For the first time, the girls were on their own, without Sophia nearby.

I feel closed in, thought Yue. *It's so dark. I don't know if I can handle this.*

"Yue, are you ok?" said Ava. "It's dark in here. I'm not afraid of the dark but this is different. Like there's no way out."

Falcon wasn't uncomfortable with confined spaces. New York could be claustrophobic. "Imagine that you're in the ocean, scuba diving or something," she said. "Isn't it dark underwater?"

"Good reframe!" exclaimed Ava.

Yue closed her eyes, and went deep down, with the dolphins that gave her comfort. She also sent a prayer to her mother. *Watch over me, Mom.*

Maia thought about her grandmother. *Trust.*

"We need to get some sleep," said Maia. "Tomorrow is almost here."

CATHEDRALS IN THE SKY

*M*ORNING WASHED THE WALLS with pink light, stirring Falcon from sleep. She always woke first. As she wrote in one of the unlined journals, the others woke around her and soon the silence was gone with the chatter of excitement.

Today they would train. Ava suggested the heart of red-rock country, where the vortexes were strong, and the climbing was rough. Nobody else had experience in this kind of terrain, but Ava knew it well and would be a good guide.

They gathered their packs, belts, boots, pouches, and the cowgirl hats that Sophia had placed on hooks in the cave, grabbed some apricots, and went out to the ledge. The horses stood and stretched, ready to transport them to one of the most powerful rocks in the Southwest.

Maia's home had many shapes. The Black Hills, in the middle of the Northern Plains, was a heart-shaped island mountain chain, known to the Lakota as the center of the universe, the heart of all that is. The land was marked with Devils Tower, also called the Bear Lodge, and Mato Paha, another name for Bear Butte. There, the plains sloped away from the mountains in all directions. They were flanked by wide river valleys and a sea of grasslands in gentle waves.

This new red-rock landscape, shaped by billions of years of wind and water, was totally foreign to her. These cathedrals were tall and jagged and rose to the clouds as if they were touching heaven.

Falcon's cathedrals were very different. They also stretched to the sky, but the New York City canyons were made of concrete and lined up along a grid. She had hiked before, in the woodlands of Upstate New York, in the rain forests of Costa Rica, and in the desert of Jerusalem, but never on land like this.

Yue's world was shaped by water and dunes and hills that met the shore. She loved seafoam on her feet, the grit of sand between her toes. She had climbed over the waves, but never over red rock. It was her first time navigating giant boulders, deep crevices, and veined stones—some hard, some so soft they crumbled in her hands.

They were at Bell Rock, Compass Point 9.28, one of the five vortexes in northern Arizona, a place of imposing strength that vibrated with unseen forces. Ava's grandmother had explained the power of vortexes to her—she had said they were swirling centers of energy coming out from the surface of the earth. They were natural healers and could recharge the body.

"Ready?" she asked. "If your heart starts beating faster, don't worry. It is because the air is thin at this altitude. Breathe deep and slow."

They all looked up at the giant castle in the sky.

Maia sensed that Yue was intimidated—she was unusually quiet.

Maia took her hand, "We have to do this, Yue."

"I know," Yue said. She stood behind Ava.

"One foot in front of the other, Yue," said Ava. "Look for natural steps as you climb. You can balance yourself with your hands, like this." Ava leaned into the mountain, in a way that made her seem a part of it, no separation between human and rock.

Yue followed her lead. She placed her foot in what seemed like a good spot, but the red sandstone crumbled with her weight and she slipped. Falcon, behind her, quickly put her hand on the small of Yue's back, steadying her.

"Grab that rock—use it to lift yourself up. You can do this!" Ava shouted.

Yue saw another way. Determined, she pursed her lips and focused on a small hole in the boulder. She stretched out her hand, placing it inside. Using her arm for leverage, she raised herself up, and then slipped, her fingers scraping the rock before she quickly grabbed it again. This time it held.

"Yue, what were you thinking? That could have been a mistake!" yelled Maia. At six thousand feet, any false move was dangerous. There were stories about Bell Rock—about the energy being so powerful that people fell to their death. Yue should have listened to those who knew better. But she was trying to prove to herself that she wasn't afraid.

Ava, who knew these rocks like her own hands, continued in the lead. The higher they climbed, the easier it became. Not because it was less steep, but because they were connected to the bones of the Mother. The earth held them the way Yue's hand had held her.

Maia saw an ant—tiny, shiny, and black. She watched as it climbed the rock, carrying fifty times its weight on its back, moving around whatever got in its way. Maia thanked it for reminding her what it looked like to persevere.

Falcon hoisted herself up, catching her shirt on a narrow limb that grew out of the rock. The thin white cotton ripped, but she didn't care. She thought about how this small, twisted tree had pushed itself through, and how hard that must have been, how much strength it took to emerge against such odds. Trees did that in concrete, too. It was a good reminder to push on.

Ava was slightly up ahead, scouting the terrain. The sun was strong, and the hot, dry, ninety-degree heat that reminded her of her own fire.

"Come on," she called, as she waved to the rest. They continued their training by moving onto the second leg of the climb, building endurance and strength while learning how to maneuver in these conditions.

After another two thousand feet, Yue was out of breath. Her hand hurt. She was secretly glad that the light was changing—a signal to start heading back. When the sun set, the temperature could easily drop fifty degrees.

As they began to descend, Maia looked up at the formations. There it was, clear as day. On the face of the mountain, sculpted into the rock, was the face of a turtle. There was no doubt in her mind—the Great Spirit was watching over her. What she didn't know was that the clouds had been watching, too.

MAIA

writes

MY SLEEP WAS RESTLESS. I dreamed I was in the forest, standing in front of an old oak tree—my feet firmly planted on the earth. I felt something move beneath the surface.

I thought it was a mole, or a chipmunk—some creature that burrows underground. Was I standing on a den?

The dirt rippled slowly, like pudding on a stove when it's hot and thick and just starting to bubble. The bubbles got bigger, faster, and a giant turtle pushed through in slow motion, three times the size of a sea tortoise.

A turtle, in the middle of the forest? I didn't think it strange to see Turtle shaped in stone, like the one I saw yesterday at Bell Rock. There are lots of faces in rock, but this was alive.

I was more intrigued than scared, and held up my new phone to take a photo. I heard a crunch and a sizzle, teeth against metal. The turtle ate my phone!

I had questions for Turtle, but she disappeared back into the underground. What did this mean? Was it about technology? But what kind?

A phone is a whole computer we can hold in our hands, but there are whole worlds of natural technology, like the communication of trees—without phones or wires—whole communities with a complicated network that sends signals that help them thrive.

Grids crossed my eyelids, and I saw technology everywhere, in the stars, the pyramids, the plants. I saw the mathematical codes in spirals, in shells, in waves—technical patterns that revealed themselves in nature, everything Sophia showed us in Montana.

When the images stopped flooding my brain, I had the answer.

Turtle was reminding me that I should not forget the ways of the Universe. She wanted me to see how the modern world was consuming itself. Hold onto the sacred. Isn't that what Sophia said?

I need to sleep a little more. We have to be strong today. We're going to the mesa. Last night the arrow on the compass pointed to 3.03.

SHAPE-SHIFTERS

"*A*VA, ARE YOU READY FOR THIS?" Maia asked.

"Do I have a choice? What about you—are you nervous?" asked Ava, her voice cracking.

"Yeah, but mostly no. I mean, a little, but we've been chosen because some power in the Universe sees the power in us. We lose sight of that."

Maia turned to Falcon and Yue. "Are you good?"

They nodded. The horses stood, ready.

"Let's do this," said Yue.

Maia stroked Terra's neck. "Here we go."

Falcon saw the Mesa first. It jutted up from the flat desert, like a lookout with no walls or moats or guards. It stood naked and vulnerable, unprotected.

The girls paused in the shadow of the mountain. The hair on Ava's arms was standing straight up, and she could smell the electricity building in the air.

Iron, she thought. She looked toward the West. "This is not good," she said.

"I know," said Maia. "I feel it too."

Moments before, the sky had been filled with clouds of white cotton. Now they looked injured, like a black-and-blue mark spreading on the surface of newly bruised skin. One of the dark forms picked up power and speed, changing as it moved, becoming a massive wave. It changed form again, shifting into layers of gray and purple, with markings of black and white. It wasn't shaped like anything from the animal kingdom, but it had a hungry maw, vicious, ready for the kill. The horses reared.

Bolts of lightning zig-zagged down to the ground, cracking like massive shards of glass. Smoke rose as the land sizzled. This cloud was not a force of nature, but a villain to be reckoned with.

Sophia had prepared them, but now they were facing it for real. With a shaking hand, Maia pressed the red crystal on her buckle and radioed for help. She hated to do it. This was their first encounter, but they were panicking.

Sophia's voice came across the distance. "Maia, what is it?"

"It's the cloud. It's here!" Maia shouted.

"Show it that you're not afraid," said Sophia. "Look it in the eye, use the power of your mind, and make it change direction."

Ava understood. If she could move a copper arrow or a pebble, maybe she could shift the cloud.

The girls linked arms, focusing on their goals, and as they would talk about later, they felt their horses' energies join their own.

The cloud didn't move.

Sophia, watching through the amber stone, spoke words of encouragement.

"Don't stop. Keep going. And Falcon, use your breath. Yue, push it back, like a wave."

The girls could barely hear her through the winds, but they held strong. It took much longer than shifting an arrow and more strength than they knew they had, but eventually, the cloud turned and disappeared into itself.

Sophia's voice finally became audible. "Now you've seen what you're up against!"

"The clouds will do anything to keep us from finding the crystal," shouted Maia, still intense, but now triumphant.

"Yes. You are the Crystal Warriors," said Sophia. "You were meant for this."

Then her voice was gone.

❆

They crawled through the opening of mica and gold into ARIA, and fell onto the floor, exhausted.

Earth, Air, Fire and Water had been tested. *Round One,* thought Maia. *It is too big.* The girls broke down, crying in each other's arms.

Ava

writes

YESTERDAY WAS INTENSE, and so was my fire. It showed up as fierce determination. I refused to let the cloud have its way, all of us did. It is together that we can do anything. Not as individuals.

My fire lives deep inside my belly. It rises, like passion. Not the kind of passion for a person, I don't think. I don't know what that is. I've only kissed a boy once, and it wasn't very good. He slobbered.

My Angel of Fire ring reminds me that fire is the spark of life. That—to me—is passion. I've been thinking a lot about fire, how it changes. The shapes move, colors flicker—white is the hottest. I wonder what the science is behind that.

The sound fire makes changes, too, depending on the wood and the size of the flames. I like not knowing when the crackle and pops will come. Not like a song, when you know what note is coming next.

But there's a shining and a shadow to everything. And I think Sophia wants us to discover that about ourselves, too.

Fire destroys. So does water when it's too forceful. And wind. An out-of-control fire ravages forests, displaces people, kills wildlife. The climate crisis lights wildfires that rip through the Amazon, Australia, California, the Southwest. It has a temper.

In Montana, we talked about its other side, how its wildness can be good. After a fire burns, forests regenerate, new growth rises from black ash. Like the phoenix. The ash is a fertilizer and the flames drive seeds deep.

In some ways, the land is indestructible.

My fire builds up like a musical crescendo, then drops down into a gentler place. When I play guitar, the vibrations soothe the world.

Yue

writes

I AM AFRAID OF SCORPIONS. They are transparent. Light glistens from inside the layers of its milky skin, gooey and pliable, like a worm, like the jellyfish I once almost stepped on. But that sea creature doesn't scare me the way the one in the desert does, its tail curling like a fiddlehead—venomous stinger waiting for a victim.

I am not anything like Scorpio, my astrological birth sign.

If I got stung, I imagine myself dying in the hot sun, writhing in pain, foaming at the mouth. I know I am exaggerating, but still.

Ava told me she sees them all the time. Before she goes into her house, she opens the door and looks up to see if they're hanging at the top, ready to drop.

Some people smash them. They won't hurt another creature, but they will smash a scorpion.

I remember in biology class waiting for my turn at the microscope. We were studying amoebas. The light goes through them, too. I didn't want to just look at them, I wanted to see *into* them.

Do they think? Do they feel? Are they afraid of anything? Fear isn't such a bad thing. It can protect us, save us from making mistakes. What if it's an ally, not an enemy? It keeps us awake, makes us brave.

Ava said if we had a black light and lit up the desert at night, we would see the scorpions glowing blue.

That might be beautiful.

I'm still nervous.

Maybe I'll be okay with the scorpions tomorrow.

Ava says that I'll be fine, that this is their home and they were here first.

FALCON

writes

THIS MORNING, Maia gave me a quill pen with no ink-well. Words drip from the tip—teardrops of ink that flow faster than my thoughts.

I hold the hard shaft with my thumb. The center spine is stiff and strong, smooth between my fingers, almost like a bone. But it is not bone. It's made of keratin, a protein helix that's found in hair, nails, horns, claws, and hooves.

Usually when I write, the pen moves as I direct it—from thought to hand to paper. But this feather writes by itself, and the scribble does not look like my handwriting. It looks like the Old English Latin alphabet from the 12th century. Gothic and beautiful.

I wonder if I am to be a scribe, like those in ancient Israel who studied and copied the sacred texts. I don't know what kind of pens they used—or which plants made the ink.

I am not afraid, but not overly confident to say that I am fearless. That would be irresponsible. Having no fear at all can get us into trouble. But this feather. This gift from Maia. I don't know what to make of it.

I can see you, Diana, holding it in your hand and righting the world. We are leaving tomorrow for a few days. The wheel pointed to the southwest, Compass Point 9.28. Again.

FEATHERS AND WIND

*T*HE WIND BLEW FOR TWO DAYS STRAIGHT, sucking every morsel of moisture out of the air. It wasn't like the winds on the prairie, where tumbleweeds lift out of the dry dirt, gather speed, and skip over the flat terrain like roadrunners. This was a hot wind. A brutal, relentless wind.

"I need water," said Yue. She struggled to get the words out. She didn't want to seem weak.

Maia licked the sweat that dripped from her own brow and saw that Yue was parched. Her lower lip was cracked in four places, and her tongue was covered with lines, like a map. Yue told her it was called geographic tongue and happened when she got stressed or ate pineapple. Yue stuck it out for Ava to see.

"It looks like a map of Australia. Does it hurt?" asked Ava.

"No, but I need water."

Ava handed her the extra hydration pack.

"Not the kind you drink," said Yue. "I need bodies of water."

They had been searching for the stolen piece of the horseshoe on foot, looking between rocks and in the dry creek beds.

Maia put salves on their blisters so that they could keep going. The compass in ARIA had pointed them in this direction, but so far, nothing. The girls picked up everything that glittered, but still, nothing.

Maia prayed for rain to fill the creeks and cool the day.

Ava was resting in a puddle of shade when she saw a flat dark cloud, three shades away from black, hovering over the range. *That is a good cloud*, she thought, *a monsoon cloud*. She loved the season when buckets of water fell from the sky in the afternoons, sheets of water so thick you couldn't see through them. But now, the monsoons she knew so well failed to come.

The sun beat down around them. Maia noticed Terra favoring her left front foot. She got down on her knees to see what was wrong. The titanium horseshoe was so hot, it was dripping, like melting wax.

"Falcon, come look at this."

"I know what to do," said Falcon. She got underneath Terra, bent her leg at the knee, and pulled her foot toward her. She took a deep breath. Wind power came from her lungs. It cooled and reshaped the soft metal until it firmed and fit the hoof. Maybe not the conventional method for shoeing a horse, but for now, it would have to work.

Ava looked at Falcon in disbelief. "What made you do that?"

"I'm not sure," said Falcon. "Instinct, I guess?" She had surprised herself, too.

As they moved on, Yue was third in line. This was challenging land, with twisted trails and thorns that tear. Yue was watchful for scorpions but so far hadn't seen one. They were smart little creatures and hid themselves under rocks in the daytime. Yue was glad—and also a little disappointed.

Ava spotted a prickly pear. The syrupy fruit had to be extracted carefully or tiny hair-like spines went into your skin like splinters of glass. Ava was good with her pocketknife but getting around the fine spines was nearly impossible. She wished she could do it for Yue and give her the sweet and sticky pulp.

Maia looked at the sky and saw a new cloud on the horizon, a smaller and darker cloud, a cloud that didn't move like the rest. She swallowed hard. *Do I hold back? Do I let them know now? Or wait until I'm sure?* she thought. She didn't want to alert the others until she had to. She kept a vigilant eye.

"I can smell water," said Yue.

"What do you mean?" asked Ava.

"What does water smell like?" asked Falcon.

"It's what's around it. The banks of a river sometimes smell like moss or mud, and wet sand can smell like fish or kelp.

"Kelp?" said Maia, with her eye still on the cloud.

"Seaweed," said Yue. "Sometimes it can be giant, like the coral reefs, or it can be so tiny, it's almost microscopic. Algae live in the water. It grows and blooms when the sun shines on it. Off the coast of Puerto Rico, plankton glow in the dark, like little green stars in the water."

Maia knew the trees and plants that grew in the soil, but she didn't know much about things that grew in the sea. Her attention was still on the cloud.

"I smell wet clay," said Yue.

As they walked toward where Yue pointed, Maia saw a feather drop from Terra's mane.

Falcon picked up the feather and looked at the gold and brown markings. She placed her finger on the stiff vane.

"Feathers are stronger than they appear," she said. The central shaft was hard and resilient, like the spine of a book, each page stitched and bound. She reached into her pack for the quill Maia had given her.

Maia loved watching Falcon write, her pen dripping with words. *Her poetry soars like a bird. Falcon says there are times when her quill pen writes by itself, warning her of things to come. Maybe that's why Terra lost a feather*, thought Maia. *Was it a message for Falcon to use her own?*

It is illegal for a non-Native to possess an eagle feather. One must be a tribal member. The eagle is sacred. Falcon had no indigenous blood, but Maia had heard a voice that echoed from her dreamcatcher. It told her that Falcon needed the feather of a golden eagle to help her with their mission.

Falcon held her quill and knelt down. The feather moved, writing a message in the sand.

Compass Point 6.50

Maia leaned over Falcon's shoulder. It took about two seconds for her to press the red crystal on her belt buckle.

"Star People?" asked Ava.

"Yes," said Maia. "They'll show us the exact positioning of 6.50 on the earth's grid." The Lakota Oglala saw the Star People as great messengers. High in the Milky Way, they looked down on Earth, seeing things humans could not. Some came down to Earth in human form. Others remained in the cosmos.

Yue was disappointed... she wanted to see the water here in this desert land, but she knew when a compass point appeared, the girls must go.

As they mounted their horses, Maia turned to look at the cloud. It wasn't far behind.

White Buffalo Calf Woman

*T*HE HORSES MOVED IN A HARD GALLOP—gaining the speed and power that would propel them into the sky. As they rose through the clouds, sixteen hooves thundered across the sky. The Northern Plains were a long way from the desert. The steep mountain passes through the Rockies were treacherous.

When the horses flew like this, Yue thought about the golden fish pulling a glass lotus that carried the moon and stars, leaving trails of dust that sparkled on mountaintops, which melted to become the rivers of the world.

They were headed toward the Star People, which made Yue's dream a kind of prophecy.

Maia saw Harney Peak in the distance. The Black Hills were the heart of the Plains, and according to myth, the center of the world. The girls sank deeper into their saddles, holding onto reins of braided silver, and prepared for landing.

Terra arched and twisted, rearing in the air, her sudden movement spooking the rest. After Maia regained her balance, she turned and saw two eyes staring back out of a thick black cloud. The Fire Dragon had caught up to them.

Yue turned in the commotion, too, and saw a tiny flicker of a flame nestled in the middle of the purplish-gray mass.

The horses split up and formed a circle, each girl in her direction. They would need the powers from all of the elements to slay this Fire Dragon, the one Falcon named the Dragon of Greed.

Ava usually fought fire with fire. Maia didn't think that was always the answer—sometimes that inflamed things even more. But right now, they needed strong medicine.

Sophia watched the unfolding drama from her home, through the crystal in her dreamcatcher. The crystal whispered to Sophia in a language she remembered from long ago. *They need to read the Codes. But they're broken*, she thought.

She heard another whisper. *It doesn't mean they don't have something to say.* Sophia translated the message and sent it to Maia, who reached for her medicine bundle. She pulled out her dreamcatcher, now the size of a large coin. Maia looked into the center of the crystal. She saw a mathematical equation—a Code. She wasn't sure what it meant, but it looked like a shell.

She yelled out to Yue. "Take out your dreamcatcher." Maia knew that she would understand the message. Yue recognized it as the nautilus spiral and quickly signaled with a circular hand gesture. They linked energies, and together, as one human medicine wheel, began to spin, like the design on the nautilus, into a downward spiral.

It was not a smooth ride. It felt like riding the whip in an amusement park, where just as one becomes accustomed to the circular motion, it shifts in the opposite direction.

Yue flowed with the motion, going with, not against, becoming the wave in the midst of the storm. In the swirl of chaos, Falcon used her wind breath to center herself, and Maia rooted herself in earth energy, grounding herself so that she wouldn't shift as they spun. The fire in Ava's center gave her the focus she needed to remain steady.

Their spiral became a funnel that spun downward, and as it did, a field of energy pulsed outward, surprising the Fire Dragon into retreat.

The Crystal Warriors landed at Compass Point 6.50 with the feeling that they had barely escaped something dark and evil. Drained of energy, they had nothing left. They lay down in a cushion of tall grasses on the plains and fell into a deep sleep that lasted until sunrise. And they dreamed.

*

Maia dreamed about a white buffalo. The one who ran by her window for forty-nine days. When her eyes opened, a real calf stood beside her. Dense white fur hung from its body. Its eyes changed color from black to blue. For Maia, it felt like the answer to her prayers.

Am I imagining this? she thought. She gently tapped on Yue's shoulder.

"Do you see that?" whispered Maia, as she pointed to the sacred animal.

Yue nodded silently. The other two girls stirred and, half-awake, stared in awe at this stunning creature, a creature whose appearance could change the course of humanity.

Sioux prophecy foretold that the birth of a white buffalo calf would be a sign that White Buffalo Calf Woman would return to purify the world. Wasn't that what the Codes were here to teach? Was White Buffalo Calf Woman returning now? Maia knew the legend of her arrival, the story passed down through the generations.

The girls couldn't take their eyes off the white calf. A white mist rose as the young buffalo turned into a beautiful woman. White Buffalo Calf Woman was the mystic who brought the seven sacred ceremonies to the Sioux, showing her people how to live with honor. She also came with the sacred *channupa*, the pipe to hold tobacco. As the tobacco burned, the smoke carried the prayers to the heavens, to the grandfathers, and to the Great Spirit. She was clothed in white leather embellished with abalone shell and horsehair. Her long, silken ebony braids danced on the currents of the wind. A white eagle plume adorned the crown of her head. She was not of flesh and bone.

White Buffalo Calf Woman spoke. "You are here as Guardians of this sacred land. You will save it by awakening the heart of humanity."

Yue was flooded with doubt. She wasn't so sure she could live up to this. Finding the crystal was one thing, but awakening the heart of humanity?

"The buffalo was put on earth by Wakan Tanka, the Great Spirit, at the making of the world," said White Buffalo Calf Woman. "It gave the people everything they needed to survive. Food. Shelter. Clothing. Warmth. Bones to make into tools. Nothing was wasted. People took what they needed, and no more. The buffalo is a symbol of self-sacrifice, giving until there is nothing left," she said.

"Is this what Mother Earth is doing?" asked Maia.

White Buffalo Calf Woman nodded. "Greed is destroying what is essential."

Falcon understood this well. She lived in a city where money and power ruled. Most of the kids at her prep school were privileged, but like her, they wanted change. They were inheriting a mess. They had conversations about truth being power and which climate groups to join. Her friends signed up for Zero Hour. Other warriors were rising up, fighting for change—like Greta Thunberg, the teenager on strike for the planet, and Tokata Iron Eyes, the voice for Standing Rock, and Jamie Margolin, the unstoppable activist for climate justice.

White Buffalo Calf Woman said, "Humanity has become separated from what is essential, has ceased to honor the earth."

The girls could barely breathe with this new presence.

"Maia, one of your ancestors saw four generations into the future. He saw adversities that he had no power to change awaiting your people. But you have the power. You have been chosen by Sophia Rose."

Maia was shocked that White Buffalo Calf Woman knew her name, and the story of Sophia.

"Look to your dreamcatchers for guidance. Keep looking for answers in nature. When you mend the horseshoe, and make it whole again, the Codes will reveal themselves. Then you will understand the teaching."

White Buffalo Calf Woman took out her bundle—a white leather bag that held the sacred pipe she had brought to the Sioux nineteen generations earlier. Each holy ritual began with smoke that billowed to the heavens, asking Great Spirit for guidance and answered prayers. She did not use the pipe today. Instead, she pulled out a red stone, which symbolized the earth. She placed it at Maia's feet, then bent down and drew a red circle around them for protection.

"The circle is the road," she said. "*Mitakuye Oyasin*. We are all related."

MAIA

writes

MAMA, SHE CAME TODAY, to me, to us. She came. Who am I but just a girl? A girl who loves Mother Earth. A girl who sees all things as kin, as family. Is that enough?

She was beautiful.

The girls thought they had seen the face of the goddess. I knew that it was spirit.

She said we have separated from the essential, that purity of heart would heal the world.

That is the message Turtle also gave me. When she cracked my phone she said to stay connected to the earth.

I have known this all of my life, but now it feels different. It feels different. It's an in-my-bones knowing, an ancient knowing passed down and down and down again.

Mama, am I making sense?

I wish you were here. I know you are with me. With us. Have you known all along what my purpose was?

Help me to breathe, to neutralize the things that I fear.

I am still just a girl.

YUE

Dreams

I STOOD AT THE EDGE OF THE SEA—blue, green, dappled with pink, a rainbow of coral blooms. A kayak made from the shell of an abalone calls to me, and I sit in the center with an oar made of pearl, light as air, in my hand.

I place it into the waters of the Pacific and paddle north.

I fly over the whitecaps, one with the waves, craving the mystery before me.

I sound like my mom.

A glacier towered to my right, a clear aquamarine crystal, jutting up to the sun, worshipping. As I glide past, I feel a shiver of heat on my cheek.

The ice castle is a power center on the grid—like the mountain called Shasta, where one night under the Harvest Moon, a raging storm broke a sacred talisman.

Around the bend, the ocean becomes a flat tundra of ice, a treeless arctic plain, barren. It looks like a skating rink. It takes me back to when I was a little girl doing figure eights.

The sea moves faster and the wind bites hard.

My kayak becomes a wooden sled pulled by twelve Alaskan malamutes.

A lone figure looms in the distance. An old woman, hunchbacked, but not frail. Bundled in fur, she sits on the thick white skin of a polar bear like a magic carpet. Wrinkles crisscross her face, etchings of sun and wind, that draw the lines of time.

She motions to me and I am not afraid. I have known her in all of my lives.

Words are not necessary between us.

She opens her hand, revealing a small round stone, gray, nothing special except for its smoothness and a sheen so brilliant, it could have been a mirror for the North Star.

The Wisdom Keeper looks at me with indigo eyes. I have seen them before.

I want to dive into them.

She pulls a small chamois from the top of her fur boot and slowly rubs the stone, polishing it gently, deliberately.

She is showing me the way of patience.

To polish something takes time.

The quiet is interrupted by a hawk's cry, and a glacier calving. Chunks of ice pull away, rumbling, tumbling in slow motion, crashing into the sea.

The old woman hands me the stone. There is no more time for polishing.

No. More. Time.

She disappeares, leaving a beaded necklace on the ice.

On it hangs a bear, carved from bone.

          ❨

Yue opened her eyes in the time when night blends into day. She had her own dawning.

Pieces of the dream swam in her until she realized it was a visit from her mother, a gift, like the small bear she had given her before she died. *To protect you, my love, keep it with you always.*

And now, here she was with her sisters, sleeping on the plains, where a white buffalo calf had appeared, marking the beginning of a new cycle in time.

GOING ALONE

THE GIRLS SAT ON THE FLOOR eating apricots. No one remembered the horses flying them back to ARIA. They were dazed, still in awe.

"My mother came to me last night while we were still on the plains," said Yue. "It was a good dream."

Maia couldn't speak. The encounter with the prophecy was all-consuming, and she could think of nothing else. Yue didn't expect a reply. She understood when Maia needed space, but the copper hand of the compass began to shake, the way a pendulum does before it circles. The arrow landed on the Southwest.

This shook Maia out of her trancelike state. She looked at her buckle.

"We are to go to Compass Point 9.28," she said quietly.

"There are ruins there," said Ava. "Wait, and a cave! I dreamed about giant rocks last night. We have to go now."

"Let's give Maia time," said Yue. "Let's let her be."

"I'll be okay. I need to sit for a bit, and then we'll go."

It wasn't like Maia to wait, not these days, but she wanted the moment with White Buffalo Calf Woman to last.

Falcon walked outside to saddle Aveer. She had birds on her mind, white birds. She didn't know why.

❮

The girls landed on the vast Sonoran Desert. Ava, determined to find the cave, went ahead. She was a wanderer, like her aunt. But this time Ava walked with purpose, like someone with a destination in mind. *I will find the stolen piece*, she said to herself. *The cave is here, somewhere. It was in my dream.*

They all had dreams now—important, vivid dreams, strong guidance leading them closer to the stolen crystal. Ava saw petroglyphs drawn on the wall. A bird, a winged horse, and a broken horseshoe. *Was this somehow linked to the cave in France*, she wondered, *where the origin story of Apollo and the horseshoe was written?* Ava tuned into her gift of hearing before there was a sound, sensed it coming . . . a strong wind blowing into the canyon with the ferocity of the Goddess Kali, who with her sword destroys darkness and transforms it into light.

This wild wind fueled the fire inside of Ava. *It is a warning*, she thought.

The shriek of the wind barreled through the canyons and made the horses nervous. They knew the winds heralded the shape-shifters in the sky. Ava screamed out to the girls, but she was too far ahead and the wind was too strong for them to hear. She radioed to her sisters, warning them of what was coming as she scanned the rocks for a place to hide. She spotted a hole in a giant boulder and took cover in the nick of time. Aze saw that Ava was safe and ran back to the others.

The mistral lashed the rock. Ava felt the earth beneath her shake and heard a loud crack as the two-ton boulder flipped, blocking her exit. The shaking and the roar of the wind ceased. All she could hear was the echo of her breathing and her pounding heart. She leaned against the rock wall—it was cold and icy, a glacier on her back. But it wasn't the chill that made her shiver. Rather, it was the fear that she would never get out. She thought about hot and cold and how temperatures were changing, affecting life on Earth. Ice was melting, oceans were rising. Storms raged. So did fires. She remembered the volcano in Hawaii, the earthquake last year in California, how Gaia cracked and shuddered. These images flashed in her mind along with those of floods in the Midwest, destroying the crops and washing away fields.

These thoughts knocked Ava back to reality. If she didn't get out of here, she would die, and if they didn't find the crystal, others would, too. She used the fire in her belly and all of her strength, placed her hands on the wall, and pushed with everything she had. She bent her knees slightly for leverage and pushed again, so hard that she felt a pain shooting up her arms. She tried one more time, but her wrists gave out. She knew she was hurt.

She was mad at herself. She was wrong to have gone ahead. *Why do I always have to prove myself?* Yes, this was her turf, her terrain. Maybe so, but now she realized she'd been foolish. *I can't beat myself up. My wrists already hurt enough*, she thought.

She prayed her sisters would come. She began to hum a song her Aunt Rosa used to play about a white raven.

STRONGER TOGETHER

*T*HE QUEEN WAS USUALLY TUCKED safely inside, but today, she poked her head through the opening of the hive and flew. *Odd behavior*, thought Sophia, who was in the meadow tending the honeycomb. *Why would she leave?* The single queen bee only leaves the hive to lay her eggs—and only when the bees swarm, which is usually once a year.

The queen flew back in and out again, this time landing on Sophia's hand. They looked into each other's eyes, and in the reflection of the queen's black iris Sophia saw a white raven looking back at her. The girls were in trouble.

The red crystal on her belt buckle lit up and buzzed. She heard Falcon's breathless voice. "She will die if she doesn't get out! Sophia, you have to help!"

"Who will die?" asked Sophia, calmly.

"Ava! She went into a hole in a giant rock and the wind came and flipped it over. It's too heavy to move. She'll suffocate!"

"Slow down, Falcon. Use your breath," said Sophia. "And your eyes. Look for the cracks in the rock. Blow into them to warm her. Tell Maia to hold onto you as she grounds her feet into the earth. Where's Yue?"

"She's here—standing next to me," said Falcon.

"Good. If a cloud comes, it will probably shift into a Fire Dragon. Yue can use her water. You've got this. Hang on until the White Raven comes. What's your compass point?" Sophia asked.

"9.28," answered Falcon.

Sophia nodded to the bee and ran to the house where her dreamcatcher hung. She looked directly into the center of the hoop. Light came through the crystal like a dagger, straight and fast, creating the shadow of a bird on the wall. The shadow transformed into a raven as white as snow. Sophia opened the door and sent it on its way. As the White Raven flew, it grew in size as it got closer.

As Raven got closer to 9.28, the wind churned like a storm at sea. The girls shivered in the heat, shuddering at the thought of a fire dragon coming in. Four loud *ca-caws* came rolling down the canyon.

White Raven swooped down and with her strong talons, lifted the boulder to free Ava who looked up to see the bird in flight, getting smaller and smaller, and then gone.

She picked up a fallen white feather beside her feet, a feather from the bird who had saved her life.

Yue's jaw dropped. "Where did that raven come from?"

"Sophia sent it," said Maia.

Ava had tears in her eyes. She felt weak. She hated having to be rescued, but what felt even worse was putting the sisterhood in danger. She turned to them, and before she could utter a word, they circled around her. No reprimands, no asking why she had gone off alone. She was safe now; that's all they cared about.

❨

Exhausted, they returned to ARIA. Maia walked directly to her shelf of herbs and made a poultice of chokecherry and birch. When she was done, she gently placed the medicine on Ava's bruised skin.

Ava looked into her friend's eyes. "I don't know if I can do this," she said.

Maia remembered when she had said those very words to Sophia.

"I could have been killed," said Ava, her voice trembling. "What if Raven hadn't come?"

"But Raven *did* come," said Maia. "There are powers protecting us."

"Being trapped inside that rock. Maia, I had no air. I couldn't breathe. If Falcon hadn't called Sophia, what would have happened to me?"

"Did Falcon call the White Raven, or did you?" asked Maia.

Ava stared at her sister. "Oh. Oh, Maia. The song. The song I sang when I was trapped and scared was about a white raven. . . Oh, Maia. So, Falcon called for help, and kept me warm while I was in the rock. And Yue stood guard while you kept everyone rooted and grounded. And I am the one who sang in the raven. We all did it. Together."

"Teamwork." said Maia. "The Crystal Warriors are stronger together."

"I don't feel strong, and I thought of quitting."

"Do you think I haven't crumbled?" asked Maia. "I've questioned myself many times. We all have. But there's no going back. Besides, even if you could go back, we wouldn't let you."

"I wouldn't go," said Ava. "Not now. I have songs to sing and fires to build."

Always stronger together, thought Maia. Now that Ava was taken care of, Maia needed to take care of herself. She needed solitude. She was still numb from their morning on the plains.

Stones can speak, trees have their own language,

they are part of our old knowledge

—Joy Harjo

GRASSHOPPER MEDICINE

MAIA'S GRANDMOTHER TOLD HER that when she needed to find peace, she went to the mountain. After Ava's close encounter with death in the desert, Maia's nerves were raw. She saddled Terra, flew to the top of Albiqui where she knew of people etched in stone. A woman's profile in the granite. The outline of an elder. A man, a boy. Faces. Souls trapped in stone, caught between the physical and spirit worlds.

Maia wanted to sit on the rock and hear their stories, and then release them. But she didn't know how and wondered if her grandmother did.

I want to take each stuck soul into my hands and let them know it's okay to leave, that their time on Earth is done, she thought. *Go now. Be free.*

Maia scanned the giant rock. The sun was bright and there were no clouds to leave shadows on the granite wall.

Are they the Stone People, she wondered, *the record keepers of Mother Earth?* Her grandmother had told her they were the Ancient Ones of the whole planet—that they had held the history of this world since time began.

On the medicine wheel, the Stone People lived in the direction of the North, the place where Maia was born. Maia's stone collection took up an entire table in her bedroom. It was by the window, so the sun lit up the veins in each rock, highlighting the grains and patterns, and stories.

Her favorite was red jasper, the sacred Nurturer Stone. Her mother told her that it was considered the blood of Mother Earth herself and was used to call down the rains.

Maia sat on a rock, holding the gift that White Buffalo Calf Woman had given her. She felt the smooth jasper in her hand. The simple act of holding it made her feel stronger and more grounded. She began to rub it between her fingers. *It will give me courage*, she thought. *We have so much more to face.*

She remembered the day she found the four stones for the Sisterhood. Each one had a code, a kind of memory. *I know when we find the missing crystal, it will make the horseshoe the most powerful crystal on Earth, maybe even the Universe.* She drank the last of her water and thought of Yue, and how the ocean was a part of her soul, and how what lived in them was like family.

Yue is like a mother to the ocean's creatures. She needs family, Maia thought. *If I were taken from an orphanage as a baby, and flown to another country, I would need that, too.*

Maia's mouth felt dry. She licked the salt off her arm. The dried sweat tasted good and would help her stay hydrated.

Nature knows what to do, she thought, *it always does. Even when she is angry, and the floods come and wash crops away, when the rivers move houses, when the levees break and the trees are ripped from the soil, disrupting the underground web and the conversations between them. She knows what she's doing, even when she's destructive.*

Looking up toward Father Sky, she said, "Please show me, lead us to the crystal."

A grasshopper landed on her lap, its large eyes looking into her own.

She grinned down at the long-legged creature. "So," she said, "We have to keep moving forward. We have to take leaps of faith! I hear you, little one."

Wasn't this entire mission a leap of faith? She broke down and cried, desperately missing her mother, the one who normally helped her through things. Now she was alone. Well, alone except for this silly grasshopper doing yoga on her knee. She giggled a bit as she wiped the tears with the back of her hand and sat up a bit straighter.

It was time to guide the others with a looser rein. They would split up the searches, and sometimes if it felt right, go on their own. It was time.

WOUNDS AND BRIDGES

AIA'S MOUNTAIN SOJOURN told her they all needed down time, together and apart. Today was that kind of day.

Yue was on the ledge brushing Mazu. Ava sat quietly in the shade, her back against the stone, tuning her guitar.

Falcon and Maia were deep in conversation in the cave.

"It's sad," said Maia. "We're fighting to keep our sacred lands, struggling to keep our customs alive. Some are struggling just to have enough to eat, and decent health care. The indigenous peoples of this country are speaking out, but so far, it hasn't made much change. I'm so angry."

Falcon listened. "I know you're mad, and I understand. And I'm sorry. So, so sorry for what was taken and what is still an injustice."

Maia and Falcon had touched upon this in their letters, but never spoken of it face to face.

"My mother's ancestors were born in Eastern Europe—in a tiny village in Poland," said Falcon. "They were poor and lived on potatoes and beets and love. They tried to escape the Holocaust," Falcon went on. "Some of them fled and survived. Others died in the camps. Six million people were killed at the hands of the Nazis."

"So much tragedy," said Maia. "Both cultures lost so much." She reached her hand out to Falcon, and a tear ran down her face.

"My grandfather's sister had a number tattooed on her arm," said Falcon.

"A number? Why?" asked Maia.

"That's how the prisoners were identified," explained Falcon. "Sometimes I hide my Star of David. There's so much hate. Then I get mad at myself for being a coward, for not being proud of who I am."

"The Star of David is a beautiful symbol," said Maia. "It's perfect geometry. Above and below. It's balanced."

"My mom says it's the masculine and the feminine," said Falcon. "I'm not quite sure what that means."

The two girls sat, holding hands, thinking about generational wounds, another bridge between them, another thread of connection.

Yue floated in and plopped down on the floor. Ava joined them with her guitar. She had overheard Maia and Falcon talking about their ancestors. She thought about her Aunt Rosa. She had only met her aunt twice before she died, but in those two encounters, the connection was strong, threads stitched tight like her mother's embroidery. The first time Ava heard her aunt pluck the strings, she went into a trance. The music stayed in her body, moving through it, long after the notes were gone.

"Ava, I love when you play," said Falcon.

Ava held the guitar. The wisdom of the ages lived in the strings and became Ava's inner soundscape, the canto that lit her fire. Aunt Rose knew the instrument known as One Thousand Voices belonged with her niece, that it would be in the right hands.

As Ava gently strummed, the walls hummed along with the notes and the crystals lit up. The sound bathed them all, refueling them for what was ahead.

Fire and Water

*A*VA AND YUE WENT BACK TO THE DESERT where Ava
had been trapped by the rock, the rock that stole her
breath.

Ava knew it wasn't the wind that had held her hostage. It
was the cloud playing tricks, the Fire Dragon that had followed them to the Great Plains. She was obsessed with finding
the cave from her dream. So, she turned fear into courage, and
returned with Yue by her side.

As they searched for the cave, they couldn't ignore the
ground they stood on. They became archaeologists, digging,
hoping to find an object or a story—any breadcrumb that
would lead to a small, hollow crystal, just two inches long.

They roamed for hours and found nothing but sherds of
old pottery.

"This could be a thousand years old," said Ava, as she turned
the hardened clay in her hand, one edge a small smooth lip
indicating that it came from a vessel of some kind. Maybe a
bowl, or a drinking cup. Black lines, drawn with ancient ink,
likely made with berries or soot, went diagonally across the
sherd.

Ava imagined Native women sitting along the banks of the
river, washing their pots and bathing their children.

"My feet need a rest," said Yue, as she hunted up a patch of shade. Sweaty and flushed from the heat of the high noon sun, she cooled herself down by daydreaming of oceans and coral reefs.

"Did you ever hear of the starfish called the Crown of Thorns?" she asked.

Ava was adjusting her buckle. The signals were weak.

"Sounds like a video game or an alien invader," said Ava, not really paying attention.

"Crown of Thorns has no brain."

"How can it survive if it can't think?" Ava asked, eyes rolling. She was focused on the buckle and getting frustrated.

"It has a nerve ring that coordinates everything, like command central, and has hundreds of tiny tube feet with eyes at the end of each leg." Yue drank some water, satisfied with her scientific explanation.

"You're so weird sometimes," said Ava. "This isn't working," she said, still fiddling with her buckle.

"You know what's weirder?" said Yue. "It pushes its stomach out through its mouth, and secretes digestive juices to liquefy its prey."

"That's completely disgusting," said Ava.

"No worse than scorpions," said Yue.

"True."

Ava didn't understand the oceans' ways. The desert was her world, parched except for winter storms or the summer monsoons.

"You like snakes, right?" Yue asked.

"What does a snake have to do with a sea star?" Ava asked, shifting her weight as she shook the buckle.

"A snake sheds its skin and new skin grows back. Is that so different from a starfish growing a new leg?" said Yue.

"A snake doesn't shed its skin because it's been hurt," said Ava. "It sheds its skin because new skin is underneath. The molting makes room for it to grow." She paused, then her eyes locked with Yue.

They burst into laughter for no reason. It felt good to be together, to be friends, to be out of doors, to have a goal. To talk about what they knew and loved.

If Falcon were there, she would have bellowed out a snort. Maia would have giggled, putting her hand over her mouth like someone with a secret.

Ava shook the buckle, again, then pressed a crystal. It didn't light up or reveal any kind of GPS code.

"Something is wrong," she said, getting worried. "I think we should go back."

"But we didn't find the cave," said Yue.

"It's too risky to be here. Something is messing with my buckle, and yours could be next."

"I wonder if that liquid metal we saw when we flew over Cathedral Rock is interfering with the signal," said Yue.

"Maybe."

Yue felt a humming coming from the center of her buckle. "Mine is working." She pressed the crystal. Maia's voice came through.

"You need to get to ARIA," she said. "Now."

Falcon and Yue took off, without even asking why.

STAR PEOPLE

*A*ZE DID A HARD LANDING on the edge of the ridge. Ava somersaulted down like a Roman rider, an acrobat on horseback. She hit the ground and ran into ARIA Headquarters, followed by Yue.

"What happened to you?" said Falcon. "We were worried."

"I was trying to recharge my buckle. Something's not right—it's not holding its power," said Ava.

"You flew over Cathedral Rock, didn't you? "said Maia. An hour earlier, the golden arrow had indicated that they should go search there, again.

"We flew over it this morning, "said Ava.

"We saw metal. It was moving and shimmering like mercury on top of one of the spires," said Yue.

"Which spire?" asked Maia

"The one that cracked when it got hit in the lightning storm."

It must be interfering with our GPS, thought Maia.

"And yesterday there was a flash flood in Antelope Canyon," said Yue.

"And it's not even monsoon season," said Ava.

It hadn't rained in months.

"It's a warning," said Falcon.

At her words, the wind began to blow. It whipped against the cave, howling like a crying wolf. Falcon's power needed tempering. When she was anxious, the strength of her own wind moved through her like thunder. But maybe it wasn't Falcon. What worried Maia was that the wind could also be from one of the clouds they'd seen, like those that shape-shifted into snakes with open jaws and fangs.

Maia held out her hand for Ava's belt and inspected the buckle, holding it up to the portal of light. She slowly turned it from side to side, looking for a crack. The crystals all seemed to be intact.

They sat in their designated spots on the compass etched into the floor. Ava picked up her guitar and plucked one of the strings. The wind stopped. The vibration echoed beyond the canyons, through the forests, and above the rivers. It went all the way to the edge of the continent and up into the Milky Way. This was the call of the Crystal Warriors. An SOS to the Star People Maia had known since childhood. They were asking for help from the heavens.

Hopefully, they would get it, on Cathedral Rock.

☾

They landed on Compass Point 5.34 in the late afternoon. It wouldn't be long before the sun began to drop to the other side of the earth.

They needed the sun. The stolen crystal might be the shimmer on the spire.

Ava was worried that if it was there, on Cathedral Rock, the lighting strike might have cracked it into hundreds of pieces.

Then what?

The horses hovered over the red rock, which was bathed in a purple haze. They would need to stay very steady, so that the girls could hold a miniature telescope and scan the rock. Falcon squinted through the lens at the shimmering metal. She saw lines and letters that she didn't understand. Maybe Greek or Sanskrit. She wasn't sure. She handed the telescope to Maia. The words and symbols were foreign to her, too, but what was familiar was the color green. The silver changed before her eyes, turning into an emerald light.

"The missing piece is here," said Maia. "And the lines and letters are part of the Codes." Elated, Maia's heart skipped a beat. *Could we have found it?* she thought.

"The crystal is not here," said a kind voice, floating down from the sky. "It's another trick. So are the Miners."

Ava looked up. She knew about the Miners, and was used to hearing voices from the stars, but this was a first for Yue. She kept turning to see where the voice was coming from.

Maia's heart sank.

"Go back to ARIA, before another serpent comes." Then the voice and the shimmer were gone.

Maia knew it was the Star People talking. The Crystal Warriors would listen and return to ARIA.

Secretly, Ava had other ideas.

Tricksters and Compassion

*A*VA BURNED TO GO BACK. Her desire to find the cave she had dreamed of was too strong. She had to return to the mystery of Cathedral Rock.

She and Maia stood toe to toe and fought. Maia begged her to listen to the council of the Star People, but Ava left anyway, left to find out if her dreams were as important as the dreams of the others.

Aze did a whirl over the giant stone mountain. His movement was so abrupt, Ava had to grab his feathers to steady herself. She looked down to see what had caused the quick shift from their planned landing on the ridge.

The sandstone beneath them flowed in layers like an ancient ocean. On the surface was a long thin crack that ran parallel to a ley line. Slowly, the static waves of stone began to move. The crack widened with the sound of shattering glass. Before horse or rider could react, they were sucked out of the sky, into a spiral dance, down into the dark velvet night of the earth.

Ava panicked, trapped inside rock again. But she heard Maia's words: *There are powers protecting us.*

Horse and rider were deep in the dankness of this underworld. It didn't smell like forest moss after a rain, though the air was cool and heavy.

Ava felt a breeze on her left cheek, followed by a gentle tug on her hand. In the pitch black, she couldn't see what was leading them deeper into the earth, further away from the crack opened to the sky and the light.

"Aze, get ready, I'm going to make us smaller, invisible, in case we need to be hidden." Ava willed their bodies to contract into the smallest version of themselves, beings so tiny that they almost weren't there.

But they *were* there. And so were others.

Ava looked up to see hundreds of glowing orbs moving on the rock, soft golden lights, green around the edges. *Green around the edges,* she thought. *More pieces of the Crystal Horseshoe?*

She moved closer and saw that the light came from tiny headlamps. *These must be the Miners,* she thought.

They were everywhere, chipping away at the rock with iron tools.

Ava knew about mining that took from the earth without care, the pillaging of gold or titanium or quartz from the depths. And in some places, coal—stripping it from the mountaintops, then burning it to light the world, leaving soot and carbon in the air, poison in both fresh and saltwater.

The Star People said the Miners weren't real. But Ava saw them with her own eyes—they were here, looking for something, too. *Maybe the crystal.*

I hope granite doesn't feel pain, she said to herself as she watched their tiny hammers. They didn't seem to notice her. Her mind wandered to the Stone People, the spirits of the ancient people trapped between worlds, etched in giant edifices, homage to the gods. They were not here, or there, but stuck between heaven and earth. Maia had seen them when she went to the mountain.

The chipping of stone got louder. Her sensitivity to sound heightened the noise to a level that was almost unbearable. She and Aze hurried past the Miners without notice, saved from being captured and interrogated. She was smart to make herself invisible.

She pressed the searchlight on her buckle to light her way now that she was around a bend...and stopped. The walls were covered with etchings. She wanted to read them like a book.

Maybe this is the cave of petroglyphs? Is this the cave from my dream? She saw on the wall before her a sundial, an antelope, a flower of life, an infinity wave. She went over to a medicine wheel and lightly touched the South, her home.

These circles and symbols have hidden meanings. Surely, they hold clues.

Something moved, emerging from the stone. The outline of the Goddess Artemis, protector of the earth, pointed her arrow to a tiny circle, much smaller than the rest. Ava moved closer. Next to the circle was a golden hook, and on it, a bronze key. Because she was so small, it took all her strength to fit the key into the hole and turn it. The door swung open.

She entered while Aze kept watch.

Inside, the chamber was cold. Icy minerals grew down from the ceiling, glowing blades of stalactites in shades of pink and gold. Ava was spellbound by their beauty, but knew they were dangerous if they fell. Ava vibrated with the music of constantly dripping water. Her lips were blue, and she shivered. She was deep inside the womb of the Mother and wondered why it wasn't warm. She tried to call up the fiery energy of the earth. She imagined the soles of her feet growing roots, like a Grandmother Tree boring into the ground, tapping into the heat that comprised the core of our world.

Usually it warmed her, but today her efforts failed.

Wind bounced off the walls, rumbling like soft thunder. Where could the cold be coming from?

Pulled like a moth to flame, she went around another bend and found herself standing in front of a crystal cut in the shape of a pyramid. It had a pink sheen and was surrounded by a clear globe, perfectly placed on a pedestal carved of citrine.

Wait, she thought. *The stolen piece is green, not pink. Is this another trick?*

Ava felt a vibration, a flickering moving up and down her spine. As it grew more intense, she looked at her fingertips which glowed with the same pink light as the crystal. The light expanded to fill her body and she began to grow until she had regained her normal size. The power of the stone was stronger than her own. She knew she had to get out.

She made herself small enough to escape the chamber and ran to where Aze was waiting. He shook his feathers, and they were sucked back up through the crevice. When daylight came in view, her panic subsided. *What was I thinking?*

The Star People were right. The beings called the Miners were tricksters, intent on throwing the Crystal Warriors off course, and maybe even causing them to give up and go home.

But she was home, about to land at ARIA, and all she could think about was her own selfishness. Why were her dreams more important? She slithered into ARIA, their ARIA, their place, knowing that she would be facing Maia, and the rest. Maia.

This isn't the first time, thought Ava. *I got trapped in a boulder because I insisted on going ahead.*

The girls were sitting on the floor, totally silent. Maia stood up, her usually kind face, harsh and unforgiving.

"I have no words, right now," said Maia.

"I know, I know, but..."

"I can't right now."

Maia turned away and caught Yue's eye. They had just talked about Kuan Yin, how compassion and forgiveness healed the world. Maia was trying to find that understanding within herself. How could they move forward as a tribe without it? But how could they move forward with everyone going their own way?

She had heard Sophia warn Ava about her fiery nature, and how her passions could take over. This wasn't about Maia. It was about Ava!

Maia softened.

Ava felt a vibration, a flickering moving up and down her spine. As it grew more intense, she looked at her fingertips which glowed with the same pink light as the crystal. The light expanded to fill her body and she began to grow until she had regained her normal size. The power of the stone was stronger than her own. She knew she had to get out.

She made herself small enough to escape the chamber and ran to where Aze was waiting. He shook his feathers, and they were sucked back up through the crevice. When daylight came in view, her panic subsided. *What was I thinking?*

The Star People were right. The beings called the Miners were tricksters, intent on throwing the Crystal Warriors off course, and maybe even causing them to give up and go home.

But she was home, about to land at ARIA, and all she could think about was her own selfishness. *Why were her dreams more important?* She slithered into ARIA, their ARIA, their place, knowing that she would be facing Maia, and the rest.

This isn't the first time, thought Ava. *I got trapped in a boulder because I insisted on going ahead.*

The girls were sitting on the floor, totally silent. Maia stood up, her usually kind face harsh and unforgiving.

"I have no words, righ.t now," said Maia.

"I know, I know, but . . ."

"I can't right now."

Maia turned away and caught Yue's eye. They had just talked about Kuan Yin, how compassion and forgiveness healed the world. Maia was trying to find that understanding within herself. How could they move forward as a tribe without it? But how could they move forward with everyone going their own way?

She had heard Sophia warn Ava about her fiery nature, and how her passions could take over. *This wasn't about Maia. It was about Ava!*

Maia softened.

She approached her sister and took her hand. Then she touched the wolf charm on Ava's necklace. "I understand you are a wayfinder, but we need to find our way together. Come sit in circle—the four of us together."

HARMONY

*A*LIGHT SHOW OF PURPLE RAYS brought Ava into a higher world where she dreamed of Saint Germain. He played the violin. It made sense that she would dream of him, the keeper of the flame.

In the dream she stood with him. He was much taller, with long gray hair framing a kind face. He wore white robes embroidered with golden thread.

They entered a cavern that was lined with crystals of pink and white. He told her that he was taking her to the Cave of Symbols.

"But I've already been there," said Ava. "I went deep into the crevice of Cathedral Rock."

"My child," he said. "Walk with me."

"Where are we?" she asked.

"We've entered Table Mountain."

"In Wyoming?"

"Yes, in the Grand Tetons."

They walked further into a vaulted chamber that was humid and smelled sweet, like violets. The room was enormous. Saint Germain raised his hand toward the center of an archway. The doors opened, ushering them into a long, narrow tunnel.

Ava hesitated.

"You are safe with me," he said.

They walked to the end and into the Cave of Symbols. It was pristine, a laboratory with light boards and numbers scrolled on glass walls, giant microscopes . . . a room of epic proportions where inventions were born.

Ava saw sine waves moving through a crystal box, a continuous motion that appeared to be measuring physical space and time. It looked as if it were sending signals.

"What is that?" she asked.

"It's a radio. It communicates with other planets in the solar system, with the center of the earth, or with any point on the earth's surface," said Saint Germain.

Ava caught her breath. *It's the same principle as our belt buckles*, she thought.

"What's in there?" she asked, looking at a closed door.

"More laboratories," he said. "Scientists are perfecting past inventions found in the cities at the bottom of the Atlantic Ocean."

"Those cities are real?"

"To those who think they are, yes. They have been protected since the sinking of Atlantis," he said.

Protected by whom? she wondered. She was afraid to ask too many questions.

Ava looked over to a woman sitting on a crystal stool. She was wearing a white lab coat and goggles. She was bent over in a pool of light, carefully inspecting something too small for Ava to see.

"The scientists here are updating discoveries to right the planet. But man must learn to harness greed, selfishness, and the desire to control others. Otherwise, our efforts are for nothing. The need for power has destroyed land, air, water, and food. It has made us less compassionate," said the saint.

So there is hope, Ava thought. "But how will mankind see the errors of their ways?" she asked.

"Do you not hear Gaia? She is already speaking," he said.

Ava nodded her head. Of course she heard the cry of Mother Earth.

"Come," he said kindly.

They came to a crystal elevator and descended into the heart of the mountain, into a room that looked like a symphony hall with a domed ceiling that was sky blue painted with clouds. On the stage were instruments of all kinds—an organ, a piano, violins, a mandolin.

"These are used by the masters to generate harmony. It is the great balancer for the planet. They play in 528 Hz," Germain said.

"What's that?" asked Ava.

"It's the vibration of love."

Saint Germain, of the Purple Ray, now stood in front of a piece of glass, his multiple reflections like the fractures within a kaleidoscope.

"The cosmic mirror. You are not ready for this, but you will be, one day soon."

Saint Germain disappeared into the mirror and Ava woke.

☾

Ava looked at her dreamcatcher and saw a purple flame in the center stone. She lay still for a long while, trying to make meaning out of her dream.

She remembered Saint Germain's words. "Harmony is the great balancer of the planet." She said it out loud more than once, to make it stick. She thought about music, and how harmonies are notes that enhance other notes. For the planet, harmony meant all things living together, in support of each other, in balance. But this was not the world she was living in.

The kind man said I wasn't ready for the cosmic mirror. I don't even know what it is, she thought. *Maybe it means you look into the silver and see a reflection of the Universe? Isn't that like looking into ourselves?*

She'd ask Yue about cities at the bottom of the ocean. *He'd said it was Atlantis, right?*

But the thing that made Ava most curious was 528 Hz. The love frequency. *I wonder if my guitar knows?* she thought. She needed to play, to feel her fingers on the rosewood. She would wait until tonight when they were all together and she was surrounded by the comfort of her tribe. Maia was leaving the next day on a solo journey, and they wanted to say goodbye.

"The land knows you, even when you are lost."

—ROBIN WALL KIMMERER, author of
*Braiding Sweetgrass: Indigenous Wisdom,
Scientific Knowledge, and the Teachings of Plants*

CHAI

MAIA SPOTTED THE MAZE from Terra's saddle as they flew overhead. The circle of stones was nestled between two large mounds of earth that looked as if two bowls had been placed upside down and covered in a blanket of velvet grass, greener than any Maia had ever seen. The mounds were so exact she thought they must have been made by human hands. She wondered how long ago, and by whom.

She directed Terra with a slight nod. They gently landed on the soft grass, Compass Point 12.48, careful not to disrupt the pattern of stones, stones of rose quartz, pale pink with white veins, no two the same.

Perhaps there was a lost crystal hidden in between. But she didn't think that's why she had come.

Maia stepped down from Terra's strong back and onto the spongy grass. When she bent down, she saw it was a carpet of tiny plants that smelled like thyme. Honeybees would bury themselves in their fragrance, noses deep into the center of the flower, but there were no bees here. Not one.

The land was empty, barren except for this circle of old stones, gateways to the path that led to the center. Maia knew from books that the labyrinth was an ancient symbol that combined the circle and the spiral into one meandering path.

Maia wanted to walk it slowly, empty her mind, and find her way to her own center, a place that could show her something she might not know she was searching for.

She took off her boots and looked at the bright-colored socks Falcon had given her. *What's your Superpower?* was woven into the cotton fabric. She still wasn't sure what her answer to that question was. She tossed the socks aside and stepped onto the soft earth with her bare feet.

A long time before, Maia's grandmother had told her about the earth's living energy and how it mingled with their own. She said it could even change a person's mood. A month earlier, Maia had read in *National Geographic* that this practice was a real thing called "grounding." Scientists said that the earth had countless negative electrons that traveled up through the soles of bare feet, stabilizing systems, making us just feel good.

Maia wondered why science needed a special study to come up with that. *Just go outside, and ask the ancestors.* They paid attention to what was around them. Maybe there was more time to notice.

Maia stood at the opening of the labyrinth. It was an entryway, an invitation. She looked over her shoulder at Terra. His feathered mane caught the wind as he gazed directly at the girl. *Go on, walk the path. You cannot get lost.*

Maia opened her heart to the four directions of the Medicine Wheel before she stepped into the circle. The ground felt moist.

This is odd, she thought. It wasn't morning, there was no summer dew, and everything in this landscape was dry.

Maybe there's a freshwater spring bubbling underneath, she thought. *Or a well?*

She pushed away her thoughts and walked on. Before she got to the next ring, she felt like she was in a trance. Everything fell away . . . the sound of wind and birds, the sun's heat, her worries. It all disappeared.

Maia was inside of herself. Her mind was quiet, empty, open to whatever appeared.

What will happen if I walk with my eyes closed, she thought. She tried it, and moments later, a single letter floated across her lids. She didn't recognize this alphabet. *Was it Greek? Or Hebrew?* The letter looked like a house without a roof. A three-sided box of soft, slightly curved lines. Then the strokes moved and re-organized themselves into the number eighteen. The moment Maia recognized it as a number, it fluttered and became the outline of a mother holding her newborn child.

This was not the first time Maia had seen the number eighteen. When the girls had sat along the banks of the Colorado River, mapping out their route to North Dakota, clouds over the grandest of canyons had left shadows on the rock. They'd appeared as a flock of birds in perfect formation. The V had nine birds in each line. As they moved across the almost evening sky, Falcon explained that eighteen was *chai.* Spelled like an Indian tea, it was the Hebrew word for life.

Mother. Birth. Life. Death. With bare feet on the ground, Maia tuned into Gaia, and all that she had given to every species on the planet. How generous she was, this Mother Earth.

The closer Maia got to the center of the labyrinth, the more she could hear the call of her heart, the closer she became to the center of herself. She stepped into the fire of her thoughts, allowing them to burn away, leaving room for truth.

On her way out of the labyrinth, Maia scanned the paths one more time. The lost piece was not here, but she had gotten something else. It was time to give birth to something new. But how?

The Crystal Horseshoe knew.

☾

"What was the labyrinth like?" asked Falcon. "Did you find anything?"

"Chai," said Maia.

"Tea?"

"No," laughed Maia. "*Chai* means life! Remember when we saw eighteen birds flying over the canyon? You told me about eighteen, and what it meant.

"It's pronounced, 'hi'," laughed Falcon.

"Well, the symbol came to me during my walk, and then it shifted into a mother with a baby. Everything is pointing to one thing: Rebirth. A new way of being here on this earth."

"Like the white calf," said Falcon.

"Yes. Like the white calf."

"On my way back, I heard the word *ayin* on the wind."

"*Ayin*, really?" said Falcon, surprised. "It means 'eye' in Hebrew. It has to do with seeing beyond, in relation to time. It's about vision. It tells us to look at more than what's in front of us—you know, to see ahead, what's five or ten or one hundred years down the road. My mom told me a story about a very old man who was planting fruit trees in his garden. He knew they would never mature in his lifetime. His grandson asked him why he bothered with their planting if he would never eat the fruit. His grandfather said he was planting trees for the next generation. What we do in the present impacts the future. That's vision," said Falcon. "That is *Ayin*. It opens our eyes to see what's hidden, not yet visible. But what could be. It's about possibility and planting seeds."

"You are perfect as the East," said Maia.

Falcon put her arm around Maia's shoulder. "And you are perfect as the North. Do you think we're getting closer to the crystal, Maia?"

"I do. Let's hold that vision. We don't see what's hidden. Until we do."

FALCON

writes

LAST NIGHT I DREAMED I was a bird nestled in my basket made of twigs. I sat in the top of an oak tree, rooted in an ancient forest.

A monarch landed on my back. She held a note in her wings written in butterfly calligraphy, delicate and fluid with little curls. There, on tiny parchment made of birch, was an invitation to join her kingdom as they migrated north from Mexico.

"We want to show you something," she whispered.

I was honored, of course, but why me?

I politely accepted the invitation, as if asked to a tea party with my favorite dolls. I couldn't contain my excitement. I would be with the millions of winged ones on their yearly expedition.

I don't know how I got there, but I found myself on the branch of an oyamel fir tree. The breeze was warm and wet, smelling of summer, sweet like ripe mangos. I sat cocooned in a blanket of orange, tucked into clusters of sleeping butterflies. Their wings were closed, and they completely covered the trees—not an inch of bark was visible.

The one who had borne the invitation landed on my beak. I don't know how I recognized her, but I did. I had named her Madame Butterfly in my mind.

"We head north soon," she said. "Those who are lazy will take advantage and ride on your back. There may be hundreds of them clinging to your feathers. But they know their sun-compass and will lead. They will guide you to what it is you must see."

"Is it the crystal?" I asked.

She didn't answer.

Then I asked if she would be coming.

"Why yes," she said as she left.

I slept in the orange jungle until I was nudged awake by the sound of rustling leaves. Thousands of wings unfolded, revealing nature's perfect symmetry, the black lines of a tiger, the markings of the monarch.

The air smelled of cinnamon. I was hungry, and tired of apricots. I longed for apple crumb cakes, the kind my mother made, the ones I served to my dolls at our tea parties. But there was no time for nostalgia, and birds don't eat cake.

In one swift motion, I was lifted into the air and on my way. There was no time to think about what was happening. We moved across the sky with Madame Butterfly perched between my eyes.

"The routes are genetically ingrained," she said. "Let go and allow the direction in our DNA be your autopilot."

I thought that was a fantastic thing, to know where we were going without having to think.

We flew over the Rio Grande, a sliver of green snaking through deep canyons. This water was the lifeblood for lowland farmers. Long stretches of the river, though, had dried to a dusty ribbon of sand. In the next breath, because time did not exist, we were on the other side of the Rockies, moving quickly over snow-capped peaks. Before long we came to the vast prairies of the Midwest. The butterflies that had been my passengers began to drop away until I was left alone, with Madame on my beak as navigator. Below us, wheat stretched out like a beige carpet, until a large circle of green came into view.

"Isn't it glorious?" she asked.

I thought it an odd word from a butterfly, but she was right. Nestled in the brown wheat was a piece of art, a mandala of greens in forest and lime, lights and darks, a kaleidoscope of shapes with paths running through them like a labyrinth.

Gardens within gardens.

We hovered over this circle of life, and my intuition told me that this perfectly designed bounty was here to show me something.

It wasn't about finding the crystal tucked inside a blossom. It was about finding a new way for the future. I imagined New York City rooftops, once strips of hot black tar, now bursting with circles of verdant life. Mandalas of green at schools, at playgrounds, in tiny backyards, gardens within gardens, here and across the world. Sustainable communities seeding change, growing food, reclaiming the ancient practices that honored the Earth as a goddess, as a perfect provider, the center of every living thing.

I saw that this would have to be the new way.

I asked Madame Butterfly how she knew that this was what I always dreamed about.

"It wasn't me," she said. "Nature knows everything."

I woke up, thinking that Diana was the butterfly, showing me what was possible, the way she did when we planted rows and rows of seeds and drank the juice of tomatoes once they became ripe.

Tikkun Olam

*T*HE NIGHT WAS SILENT until a lone wolf cried, stirring Ava from a deep sleep. Wolf, her pathfinder, the guide she had always longed for, was calling.

What direction are you giving me? Ava asked. *What do you want me to see?* Ava heard a voice from her dreamcatcher. It whispered, "Play the strings."

Maia, Falcon, and Yue were still asleep, so she took her guitar outside. She plucked the string that made the color yellow, the color of wolf's eyes. The note was met with another cry. This one longer and louder than the first. When the howl died away, Ava went inside to see if her dreamcatcher had something else to say. The green morning star shone bright.

"Maia, Falcon, Yue . . . wake up!" said Ava. "You have to see this."

The girls rubbed the sleep from their eyes and sat up.

The center of each dreamcatcher glowed green, illuminating the walls of the cave with moving symbols, numbers, and words. The morning was a light show, images projected onto the red-rock screen.

Maia grabbed her journal and began to draw. Falcon's quill pen moved across the page. Yue committed everything she saw to memory. Ava held out her guitar, inviting the information into the hollows and the heart and the strings.

The Codes revealed an assemblage of records in all the languages of the Universe. Ledgers and letters, in Hebrew, Arabic, Mandarin and Cantonese, Russian, Latin, Greek, and English. The Romance languages. Writings in Middle English, Anglo Norman, Celtic, and Hindu. Egyptian hieroglyphs, runic symbols, and *zhuanshu*, the seal script calligraphy from China.

It all came so fast.

Languages of Africa—Bantu and Nilo-Saharan, and languages of indigenous peoples from Peru and North America, moved across the walls.

Falcon scribbled drawings—Phoenix, Eagle. Raven and Dove. Spider and Snake. Coyote and Fox, Fish, Frogs. She couldn't keep up.

The sun, fire, and a volcano came to Ava. So did musical scales, a harp, a wooden flute, the Great Pyramid, and the symbols for all the religions in the world.

Yue's eye caught waterfalls and fish, rivers and rock, floods, tsunamis, trees floating underwater, and women in forests dancing on moonbeams.

All of it came in and out of view, except for one constant: the emerald green thread of light that lived inside the Horseshoe. It wove through every letter, every symbol, every creature, binding them as one.

But the thread was frayed at the edges, almost torn.

Then ARIA went dark. The girls sat in silence. They were stunned from the visual commotion, this download of information. Stunned at how abruptly it had all gone away.

❦

Maia closed her eyes. When she opened them, the green glow had reappeared and formed one illuminated symbol.

"Look," she said. "The Tree of Knowledge. The Tree of Life. The Tree of All There Is. Whatever the name in whatever culture, it is the breathgiver, and we give ours in return. The Codes are about connection. *Mitakuye Oyasin.* We are all related. We are all one."

"Humans don't act as if that's so," said Falcon, her voice trembling.

Yue looked up from the floor. She didn't know if she was sad or overwhelmed. "We've forgotten what's important."

"Not all of us," said Ava. "Those who built towers and kingdoms and borders, the ones who fight over land, *they* are the ones who forgot. The more they own, the more power they have."

"Calm down," said Yue. "You're getting fired up!" The other girls grinned. It was usually Falcon who joked.

"I will not calm down," said Ava. "And how can you, of all people, say that? You fight. You fight hard for the oceans and the reefs. You didn't get as far as you did by being quiet."

"You're right," said Yue. "I love your fire."

"We will not be on the sidelines," said Maia. "Youth will lead. It's our future. We cannot give up."

"No, we can't," said Falcon. "*Tikkun Olam.*"

"What's that?" asked Yue.

"It's Hebrew for *repairing the world.*"

"It feels so big. We're just girls," said Yue, as she touched the charms that hung on her neck.

"We are Crystal Warriors," said Ava.

Maia put down her journal and leaned into Yue.

"Have you lost faith?" she asked gently.

"No, but we don't have answers," said Yue.

"But we have courage," said Falcon. "And purpose. And heart. And vision."

"We all do," said Yue.

"And the dreamcatchers just gave us knowledge and a message," said Ava.

"Trees," said Maia. "Going back to our roots, to simple ways."

"People don't want to change," said Yue. "Not really."

"We were never supposed to take more than we need," said Maia.

"Earth Mother is forcing our hand. She's sacrificed for us for so long, and now we must sacrifice for her," said Falcon.

"I don't see it as a sacrifice. It's just a new way of being in the world," Maia said.

They sat in silence, contemplating the truth of Maia's words. Ava was getting tired of apricots, but she took a bite of one anyway.

"The leaders are not listening," she said. "We're in for a fight."

A hint of green still glowed in ARIA. Maia looked at the dreamcatchers and bowed her head in gratitude.

"Trees," said Maia. "We must go to the trees."

Outside the cave, a wolf called to the moon.

Turtle and Time

*T*HE ENCHANTED ROAD is not in a storybook. The road is real, and it takes you to Compass Point 8.08 and The Painted Forest, a rare stand of rainbow eucalyptus, in Maui. Trees with layers of jewel-toned bark were perfect camouflage for an ancient green-edged crystal.

The morning after the dreamcatcher light show, the Crystal Warriors flew to the island in the Pacific. While still in the sky, they spotted a narrow coast road weaving through the lush landscape with curving switchbacks carved across the mountain, zigzagging around waterfalls and groves of bamboo.

As they dipped over the sea cliffs, Yue gasped. *This looks like home.*

The ruffled edges, where land and water met, had sandy beaches the color of coal, remnants of volcanic eruptions that shaped this land. The girls and horses descended onto the mountain that rose from the ocean like a crown. It was as green as the tree frogs that joined the chorus of birdsong, chattering conversations that let the world know the day was new.

"The air is so wet here," said Ava. "It feels good on my skin."

"Like a long drink," said Yue. "I am so tired of dry and brown! I needed this."

"We're in the arms of the Earth," said Maia. "Smell the soil, so rich and thick and moist!"

"Look over there!" said Falcon, pointing to a portal into the forest. "That looks like a trail." Yue wished they could stay beside the sea.

The path called them into a sea of green, a dense, dark green beneath the thick canopy. They stepped slowly. To rush the magic of this place would be a waste, and besides, they felt as safe here as they did at ARIA. They were hidden from the enemy.

Yue stared upward. When her eyes adjusted, she saw that some of these trees were two hundred feet tall with trunks six feet around. And they were not green at all. They had fairy tale streaks of color from roots to crown. The layers of shed bark made a carpet of vibrant color beneath their feet.

"Rainbow trees," murmured Maia.

Ava touched the bark, rubbing her fingers over the surface, wondering what color fire it would make when it burned. "It's smooth in the middle and rough along the edges," she said.

The colors transformed from dark green to blue, to purple, then changed to orange and reddish tones before transitioning back to brown and shedding again. The color changes went in cycles, and each tree appeared to be in its own phase, changing at its own pace.

"Like a snake shedding its skin," said Ava.

"The same message keeps coming through," said Maia. "Renewal."

"What do you mean, Maia?" asked Falcon.

"We are being given another clue into the ways of the Codes. When nature isn't compromised, it can renew itself."

"Do you think the crystal is here? This is a big forest. How will we know where to begin looking?" asked Ava.

"Let's ask the dreamcatchers," said Maia, as she pulled hers out of her pouch. "Wouldn't it be cool if the souls of these trees could communicate with the Codes of Nature through the center stone?"

Everyone, including the horses, crowded behind Maia.

The dreamcatcher breathed in her hand. The crystal began to beat like a heart, and the green edges glowed stronger with each pulse.

"My hands are tingling," said Maia. As she spoke, the wide purple strip of bark on the tree became a shiny mirror.

Is this the cosmic mirror that Saint Germain said I wasn't ready for? thought Ava.

A turtle appeared on the surface of the mirror.

"A turtle?" said Yue.

Falcon turned to see something coming slowly down the path.

"It's a hawksbill," said Maia. She tried not to sound too excited, and show reverence for this sacred visitor. "She brings ancient wisdom. It's the second time I've seen a turtle in the forest."

The giant turtle was four feet long, and Falcon guessed she must have weighed 350 pounds. She moved slowly, but with determination.

Yue got flustered. "Wait. It will *die* if it can't get back to water," she said.

"Keya will not die," said Maia.

"Isn't that your mom's name?" asked Falcon.

"Yes, and in my language, it means turtle. She symbolizes long life and adaptability, and she is a guardian of the world. She is Earth," said Maia, as she touched the turtle charm she wore around her neck.

"Why is she here, in the rainbow forest?" asked Falcon.

"Turtle is about time. And the power and wisdom of the thirteen moons." Maia bent down and pointed to Turtle's back. "See those? She's got thirteen big scales and twenty-eight small ones around the shell. The Lakota have thirteen months in a year because of the new moon. Each moon has twenty-eight days in the cycle, from one to the next."

"Everything has a meaning," said Falcon, "and connects to something else."

"That's what the green light keeps showing us," said Ava. "The threads."

Maia looked at Turtle and felt a slow rush of sadness. "The crystal has broken. So has the soul of the world," she said.

"No, it hasn't," said Yue. "Turtle is telling us that in order to keep going, the world must adapt to change."

Air and Water

*P*ower rests in a grain of sand, Yue wrote, *especially when it sits in the dunes that rest in between two mountain ranges, far away from any shore.*

Yue put down her pen. "Are you awake?" she whispered.

Falcon rolled over. "I've been dreaming about blue herons."

"I've been dreaming about sand. Will you come with me to Colorado?" asked Yue.

"What's in Colorado?"

"The Great Sand Dunes, the highest dunes in all of North America. Maybe Raven buried the crystal there. Maybe there are blue herons, too."

"There are no beaches in Colorado."

"These dunes are in the mountains where there was once a giant lake. It dried up," explained Yue.

"Well, sand *is* made of quartz," said Falcon, "and minerals and mica. I've seen it under a microscope. It sparkles like crystal. That's a good idea."

"The winds shift the sand into patterns. You'll like it there."

"We'll leave tomorrow," said Falcon. "Now I have to sleep." She rolled over. Yue wondered, not for the first time, how she went to sleep so fast.

☾

When Yue opened her eyes at dawn, a blue heron feather rested on the blanket at the foot of her bed. She wasn't sure if the feather was meant for her or for Falcon.

They sat in a circle as they did each morning, reading the compass. Today, the copper arrow pointed due north, Compass Point 7.19, the heart of the Great Sand Dunes.

Yue started to laugh.

"What is so funny?" asked Ava.

"I dreamed this last night," said Yue. "Falcon has already agreed to go with me."

"Find your water source first," said Maia. She always worried about Yue not getting enough to drink.

Yue looked at the intel on her buckle. "It shows two mountain streams, the Medano and Sand Creeks, and over two hundred bird species. Look Falcon! Heron!"

❨

The temperature was a perfect seventy-two degrees. Azure skies and just enough tailwind carried the horses to the riparian wetlands and high alpine tundra where a kaleidoscope of jewel-toned colors waited, home to hundreds of plant species. A balanced ecosystem diverse with plant and animal life surrounded the Dunes, and these mountains were home to many apex predators like mountain lion and bear and eagles. The elk and deer were plentiful.

"The crystal would feel at home in a place this beautiful," said Falcon.

But as they flew toward the dunes themselves, the colors began to fade. When they reached Compass Point 7.19, the only color was gray. The terrain was a wasteland, a photograph in black and white, a landscape of gnarly tree trunks, twisted limbs with no life on their branches. The plants were naked, not one leaf, as if winter had come, stripping them of their clothing.

The sand of the dunes was not the soft sand it once had been, with ripples and patterns of lines that changed with the winds. It was harder, like rock, with deeper tones of gray, almost volcanic.

"It's dead." Falcon's eyes filled with tears, the only water in the whole place. "I hope this land can come alive again one day. Let's go, Yue. The crystal isn't here."

"How do you know that?"

"I don't see it being in a place that's so . . . dead."

As they turned toward the horses, two blue herons flew by.

"Is it a sign?" said Yue.

"Maybe we should stay," said Falcon. "When you woke up, there was a feather by your foot. And I had a dream about herons. I don't want to go back yet. I need a little time."

"Taos is on the way to ARIA," said Yue. "We can stop there. That might give us a boost!"

Within minutes, the horses landed in the mountains near the Taos Pueblo, a community built of red clay almost ten centuries ago. They left the horses outside of town and walked around the square with the few tourists. Some of the Pueblo residents sat inside their homes with the doors open, selling paintings, sculpture, and jewelry.

"We've seen ruins all over the Southwest, but this tribe still lives here," said Falcon, amazed at this discovery.

"I'm sure Ava knows this place. She lives not far from here."

"How was this built?"

"Earth mixed with water and straw, and then poured into a mold where it hardens like concrete. My dad loves ancient architecture. We saw a film about old structures from around the world. The bricks and forms are dried in the sun, but the rest is hard to explain," said Yue. "The thick walls keep out the cold and retain heat."

"You should see the walls in our apartment," said Falcon, laughing. "They are so thin, I can hear the neighbors talking next door. I have to listen to music with earbuds." She looked around at the burnt-orange structures. "Intelligent architecture."

"Nothing wasted." said Yue.

Yue and Falcon were lifted out of their bad moods after seeing the wasteland of the Dunes.

"There's a lake up here called Blue Lake," said Yue.

"Maybe there are Herons?" asked Falcon.

"They wouldn't be here," said Yue, "but we can't go anyway."

"Why not?"

"It's sacred land. Only those in the First Nations are allowed onto it for ritual and ceremony."

"I saw a little church on the way here," said Falcon.

"Do you want to go?" asked Yue.

"Yes. The only church I've been to is Saint John the Divine. It's in New York. Every year they have a New Year's Eve Concert for Peace," said Falcon. "I've been going with my parents since before I could walk."

"Your parents sound nice."

"They are. I'm sorry your mom died."

"Yeah, me too. But she's here. Especially in nature. Especially in water."

"I know you told me once before, but how old were you when you were adopted?" Falcon asked.

"I was a baby," said Yue. "I've only lived in California."

"I've only lived in New York."

"It must be easy to fit in there. So many different kinds of people," said Yue.

"It is easier there, but when I'm in other places, I don't feel like I fit in at all."

"Still?" said Yue, surprised.

"Still."

"I know what you mean," said Yue. "Sometimes I don't know where I belong. I feel White. I'm part of a White family. But then I look in the mirror and see myself and know that I'm not white at all. I mean, I am. But I'm not."

"I get it," said Falcon. "I struggle, too. So, imagine being biracial, *and* Jewish. And I have a crush on Diana. There's no club for me at school."

The girls laughed, and after all of the drama, the messages, the mission, it felt good. Better than anxiety or tears or battles.

"Maybe there isn't a club," said Yue. "But there are whole movements. Black Lives Matter. Pride. You can marry whoever you want."

"I marched in New York City with my parents—everyone stood together—Black, White, Asian, Hispanic, gay, Muslim. It felt good," said Falcon.

They walked, arm in arm, into the Santuario of Chimayo. It was built like a small barn and smelled of dirt. Clean dirt, not city dirt. Guests of the sanctuary could take home a little scoop of that dirt that was said to have healing powers. Yue and Falcon gathered the floury silt in their hands and put it into their medicine bags.

Sunbeams streamed through the eight windows, making shadows dance on the thick clay walls. Aged wooden benches lined the nave. The two girls sat down and began to pray, not to a particular saint or to Buddha or to a god. They prayed *to* humanity *for* humanity. They prayed that those in power would wake up and move toward a more sustainable path. They prayed for change.

They prayed for Mother Earth.

They walked out of the sacred structure into a cloudless sky, a ceiling of blue over hues of red clay and a one-thousand-year-old community built on cherished land.

As they walked back to their horses, two blue herons flew across their path.

"That's odd," said Falcon. "You said this isn't their habitat. Do you think they're the herons from the Dunes?"

"They must be. They definitely want to tell us something. In China, they're called 'cranes.' They symbolize longevity and peace."

"This morning, Maia told me that when you see a blue heron, the medicine is air and water."

"So they came for both of us with a message of possibility," Yue said. "They usually stand on one foot and are solitary."

"I saw young cranes at an exhibit at my favorite museum," said Falcon.

"The Museum of Natural History?"

"Yes—you remembered! Cranes have long spindly legs. They look awkward. I feel that way sometimes," said Falcon.

"Spindly and awkward?" said Yue.

"Tall and skinny . . . the same thing," said Falcon.

"Maybe they remind us to be strong enough to stand alone. Alone is not a bad thing," said Yue.

Falcon paused. "That is true. The message of the Heron . . . it is okay to be alone. But I enjoyed today, being with you, I mean. And we know . . . we are stronger together."

"Yes," said Yue. "We are."

FALCON

writes

I FEEL AWKWARD about a lot of things, but I'm not the only one having a hard time pooping out of doors in the wild. Yue pretends she's fine with it, but I know she's not. She was shy when she had to go at the Dunes.

Here I am, riding horses that fly, meeting clouds and storms and snakes. I can handle all of that. But I am not a bear. The joke that bears poop in the woods never made me laugh. Squatting like it's nothing, burying my poop with dirt, isn't the easiest thing to do for someone who grew up always having a bathroom nearby. Does this mean that I am spoiled?

Cowgirls do it all the time. So do women whose work is out of doors where there are no places to flush. Ava laughed at me and told me straight out that I need to *cowgirl up.*

So every morning I walk down to the creek and follow the rhythm of my nature. I think about the Bear and the Coyote, the Cow and the Rabbit, the Deer, the Bird, the Fish, and every other living thing, even the plants. They follow their rhythms without self-consciousness, hesitation, or self-doubt.

I am learning to let go of what I no longer need. I'm also finding a connection to a lost part of myself. I feel a kinship to the Indigenous women who came before. We are all the same. We all have to squat on the creek bank in the morning. We are Earth. We belong. The remembering is in my bones.

Awakening

A LEOPARD LIZARD scurried across the hot ground, running on its hind legs. The horses didn't move nearly as fast. Feet heavy with heat, they dragged along as the girls journeyed through the flat Monument Valley landscape, red buttes and spires against a backdrop of blue sky.

The Navajo, who live here, talk about this land as though it were alive. Totem Pole Rock is a god held up by lightning. El Capitan is a supporter of the sky.

Months ago, before the circle came together, Maia dreamed of standing on the edge of this desert, high on a ledge against a pink-stained sky. As the sun sank in the west and the wind spoke, Maia felt a peace she had never known. When Maia had told Ava about that dream, Ava showed her a photo on her phone and asked her if it was what she had imagined.

"I've been there before. Even though I've never been."

The night before, Maia and Ava agreed that going to the Navajo Reservation was important. Now that they were here, Maia wanted time alone. She asked the others to stay close but give her space. She stood facing west, and felt the separation between herself and the land fall away. She renewed her vow of loyalty and reawakened something else.

We don't have to heal Mother Earth. She knows how to do that. Our mission is to heal ourselves.

The message of the valley was clear. She had known it all along.

(

The ARIA sanctuary, usually cool, was brutally hot. They seemed to have brought the heat back from Monument Valley.

"Yue?" Falcon asked.

"Meters," she said. "At twelve meters, you'll find manatees and the staghorn coral, which got its name because it looks like the horns of a deer."

"We have lost her to the ocean," said Falcon.

"Maybe that's a good thing," said Ava. "I would not mind diving into the water right now."

Maia was chewing on blackroot, which helped with thirst. "Want some?"

Yue was too deep in thought to hear the offer, but Ava held out her hand.

"At that depth, the water is still blue," Yue went on. "The sun's rays cut through the surface like flashlights." She spoke like she was swimming in the water, seeing every detail, as if she were a fish taking notes.

"Polar bears go down twice the distance . . . don't you love that bears can swim?" Yue asked, looking up. "They have no gills, but they can hold their breath for a long time, like free divers."

"What's a free diver?" asked Ava.

"A human fish. Someone who skindives without an oxygen tank. Like in the movie, *My Octopus Teacher*. They take one breath, hold it, dive as deep as they can then rise back to the surface."

"How deep?" asked Maia.

"The record is 122 meters."

"That's not a human fish! That's a super-human!" said Falcon.

"The pressure is crushing," said Yue.

"If you thought the crystal was under the sea, you'd go down that deep. I know you would," said Ava.

"You think so?" Yue was glad Ava believed in her. "Diving might be in my blood. Fishermen in China still dive for pearls. You know that a meter is 39 inches and a bit, right?"

Yue's ocean dive was a good distraction and cooled them all off.

"At what depth does the ocean get totally dark?" asked Falcon.

"The Midnight Zone. No sunlight at all."

"How do fish see?" asked Maia.

"Some make their own light. They glow," said Yue.

"Oh, like in the bio bays?" said Falcon. "I canoed one at night once."

"What's a bio bay?" asked Maia.

"Water where microscopic organisms glow in the dark. Only five exist in the world. The algae light up like neon, in blue and green. It's like being in the stars," said Falcon.

"Is Atlantis a real place?" asked Ava.

"Some say it's a lost city. It hasn't been found, but that doesn't mean it's not there," said Yue.

"Hidden things," said Maia.

Yue stopped talking.

"You have that look," said Maia. "Are you thinking about plastic?"

"I'm always thinking about plastic." Yue detested everything plastic, including fake people who pretended to be something they weren't, or who were nice to your face, but mean behind your back.

"Tell us more about the sea," said Ava, hoping to lighten Yue's sudden shift in mood. But it was too late.

"Corporations don't need to use plastic or Styrofoam food trays. Schools and cafeterias should ban them, and so should salad bars and packaging companies. Know how long it takes for Styrofoam to decompose? Five hundred years. You could circle the entire earth with one day's production of those cups."

She was right to be angry.

"Microparticles get into landfills, and soil, and eventually the water, and all the things that live in them. Scientists have found these tiny particles of plastic even in the Midnight Zone."

"How deep is the ocean?" asked Maia.

"It depends. The Hadal Zone is six thousand feet. More people have gone to the moon than have gone to that depth."

"If the crystal is in the deep, we'll never find it. Pass me an apricot?" said Ava.

"I want to see the ocean," said Maia.

That evening, as the sun went down across Shiprock, cooling their mountain above the sea, Maia looked out across the valley. She had gathered purple sage for their nightly fire. The scent would mingle with the wood smoke, the kind that clings like wrapped arms.

Snails and Fireflies

*I*F COLORS HAD FLAVORS, this one would be spearmint ice. Cool patches of greens and blues brushed against the coast. From two thousand feet up, the scene resembled an abstract painting. The shore was dotted with salt marshes, reeds and grasses crowding the edges, providing soft nesting places for flamingos, sandhill cranes, and darting dragonflies.

The morning after Yue's musings about the ocean, the compass pointed them to water. Maia would stand on the sand for the first time.

The horses landed at Compass Point 9.04, on the white bluffs of Bonewood Beach. As Maia and Yue dismounted, a cloud rolled in, muting the bright tropical hues, turning the landscape into an eerie gray and putting Maia on alert.

Giant sculptures dotted the beach . . . salt-washed skeletons of live oak and cedar, a graveyard of trees that once grew in an underwater forest, dead limbs and torsos now bent by the wind. Roots sunk deep into the sand.

"This is . . . another world," said Yue.

Maia stood quiet. She had never been to a beach, let alone one like this. She watched the waves touch the sand, listened to their language, soothing and constant, hypnotic. She smelled salt air mixed with seaweed. She wondered where the turtles laid their eggs.

Maia wanted to linger, to get to know this new place, but she knew they had a job to do. They moved through twisted forms, bending to examine the different bark. Some of the trees were smooth and white, stripped of their roughness, as if whittled with a knife and then rubbed with oil. Others were covered with raised lines. Maia traced them with her fingers, stopping when she came to a protruding mound of bark, a large hollow knot. She peeked in and saw what looked like blue pebbles packed together like a robin's nest with tiny eggs. But they weren't eggs. They had openings at both ends.

"What *are* these?"

"They're some kind of snail," said Yue. "They're hiding inside their hard shells. They're smart. They found a safe place. See?"

Even dead trees harbor life, thought Maia.

She remembered all of the bugs and grubs and things that lived in the crevasses of bark, how mosses grow on fallen logs, minuscule trees if you looked close enough. This was a hopeful message. Life exists even when we can't see it. *Somewhere on this beach of bones there must be a clue*, she thought. *Otherwise, why were we called here? It can't be just because I wanted an adventure away from the dry, hot desert.*

Maia and Yue walked the beach barefoot, stepping around the seaweed where gnats feasted and foam left its watermark. They smelled the dead and alive things that mingled here at the seam of ocean and land.

Yue pointed down the beach where a thick trunk curled itself into an archway.

"Like a window or a doorway of some kind," said Maia.

"Should we go through it?" As much as Yue loved the ocean, she wasn't comfortable here. She was chilled and clammy, and felt a bit seasick even though they were on dry land.

"We don't have to," said Maia, as she picked up a piece of sea glass at her feet, enjoying how it caught the light. But the light dimmed, covered by a cloud that took away the warmth. She dropped the glass. Maia's expression turned from curiosity and delight to fear.

Yue touched her on the arm. "It's okay. That is a lenticular, a rare cloud that forms over oceans. It looks like a flying saucer, doesn't it?"

But Maia saw more. She saw an eye in the cloud and knew they were being watched. Terror washed over her as they heard a crushing sound. Before they could respond, they were caught in a wind tunnel, instantly becoming as light as air, like astronauts beyond the pull of gravity. In an instant, they were sucked, as if by a giant straw, through the arch.

It was no longer day. And they were no longer at the beach. They were on a field of grasses and in a sea of fireflies. Maia remembered catching them as a child. She would cup them in her hands and study which parts of them lit up. Sometimes they would sit in her palms for a long time as she watched them have conversations, blinking to each other in patterns and rhythms.

"It feels like being inside a Christmas tree!" said Yue.

"To me it's more like being in the stars."

"Where are we?" asked Yue, as she reached down to her ankle. It felt wet. *It must be blood*, she thought. She bit her lip and tasted salt.

"I don't know, but look, over there—do you see it, the green light?"

"Maia, it's coming closer! It's the Crystal! Catch it!"

Maia jumped up and grabbed. The whole world was in her hands. But when she opened her palms, nothing. They were empty. It was a trick.

"The cloud brought us here. Why?" asked Yue.

"To weaken us, to make us lose hope."

"Never," said Yue, wincing in pain.

The wind kicked up again, and the power that had pulled them through the portal sent them flying back. This time they were pushed rather than pulled and dumped back onto the sand of Bonewood Beach.

They lay still, their mouths parched and their energy sucked dry.

When they finally stood, Maia and Yue saw their horses lying down near the bluffs. Maia was worried. Usually, the horses stood while waiting. The girls crawled to their mounts and rested their heads on their warm bellies. The feathered manes were tangled, their breathing quick. Maia soothed Terra, stroking his neck. She whispered, "We will be okay." The saucer-cloud gone, everyone wanted away from this place. But their bodies ached, the cloud had taken all their strength.

Maia saw the blood on Yue's ankle and reached for her medicine bag. She moved the bottles around until she found the broadleaf plantain. She placed a poultice on Yue's wound and the bleeding stopped quickly.

Blood, thought Maia. As she worked, she confided in her friend. "Yue, can I tell you something? I still haven't been in my moon time. It's embarrassing."

Yue cocked her head. She remembered Maia mentioning this in the chat room, a lifetime ago.

"I still haven't bled. I haven't gotten my period," Maia explained.

"You're not missing anything. It's a pain," said Yue.

"You don't understand. In my culture, menstruation is a sacred thing. Part of the moon cycle that holds the power of birth, life, and death."

"Death?" echoed Yue.

"The end of one cycle and the beginning of another."

Yue had never thought of it that way. "It will come when your body is ready."

"I *am* ready," insisted Maia.

"The timing is not in our control," Yue wanted to comfort her friend. "Trust in the natural flow of things. Like the river."

Yue's wisdom did comfort Maia. It was good to hear these things from someone other than her mother who always said, "Patience, my child. Root yourself in the Earth and feel her warmth in your womb. It will come."

The river. She liked having both images now. Maia looked over to the dead limbs of the trees that held life. The snails had moved ever so slowly in their tiny wooden nest. They reminded her of Turtle and the hard, protective shell she wore on her back.

Maia touched the charm on her necklace and remembered how Turtle Island had come to be, and how Earth was aging daily. Sometimes it felt as if her heartbeat had dulled. Today's cloud could not distract them from the truth. Firefly had come to tell them that the light was still there, the world would be rebirthed, and renewal would come when humanity learned to flash its light in rhythm with the Mother's heartbeat.

It might be at a snail's pace, but change was on its way.

They had to find the Crystal, and the snail's pace wouldn't do.

AVA

writes

" SHE WAS A GENTLE GIANT, with nicks on her skin and barnacles on her belly. I dreamed I was riding on her back. She was thick and rubbery and moved slowly in the warm sea, swimming on the surface, moving gracefully in the clear water.

I wish I could swim like that. But there's no place to swim at home. The creeks are shallow and, usually, dry.

The sound of the sea soothed me. *Swoosh, swoosh.* Is that what a baby hears when it's growing inside its mother? I wish I could remember.

I felt the soul of this whale, older and deeper than the waters. She told me that she was *a swimming library.* "I'm the Record Keeper. I carry the history of Mother Earth," she explained in her language. "I was sent to Earth by the ancient people who live on Sirius, the star."

A Star Person sent a Whale?

She went on to tell me that she holds the knowledge of everything that's happened on this earth. Everything. The dates when the lands and rivers and oceans were formed. When the mountain ranges thrust up toward the sky. When the animals began to walk about.

She recorded when man came and populated the world, taking over, making buildings and bridges, factories and farms. She knew when the world became so lit up, it could be seen from space. *From space.*

Whale recorded the timeline and history of this planet.

"Nothing stays the same," she said. "The Earth is always changing. Humanity must change with it. It's time for a new and higher frequency."

That word again. Frequency. It spoke to me, the way my guitar strings do. But that was not the whale's main message. Her message was about change. Perhaps even a kind of evolution.

Then she sounded the number 528, over and over. She was insistent. The same numbers that I heard with Saint Germaine.

"528 . . . 528 . . . ," said Whale. "You must play."

THE COLOR OF SOUND

*A*VA LANDED AT ARIA after a solo journey, exhausted. Her fire had gone out. She stood at the opening of the cave and hesitated. Memories of being caught in the boulder flashed in her mind—the darkness, the icy cold, no oxygen—thoughts of dying and never being found. And the crevice. Deep inside the earth with the Miners. What if ARIA closed her in?

She reminded herself that this was *their* cave, the place the Crystal Warriors went for renewal, *their* haven, *their* home. Still, her breathing quickened, her heart beating fast. *Why is this happening? This is ARIA. What is wrong with me?*

Ava didn't feel much like a warrior, but she took the first step. *That's what I have to do when I am afraid. Just take that first step.*

It was warm inside, and so was the sweet welcome of her tribe. Yue brought over apricots for her tired friend.

"Thank you. I'm going to sit," said Ava. "I need to rest." The other girls moved about their tasks, leaving Ava to recharge.

White rays came through the portal above. Her mama called them the fingers of God. Her fingers had their own magic. As tired as she was, she needed to play and perhaps the music would relight the fire inside.

Her wrists were almost healed. Maia had continued to bind them in herbs, adding crushed comfrey leaves. Ava bathed in the rainbow that came from the stones embedded in the walls. Sophia had told them that each color was linked to the energy centers of the body. The energy centers were called chakras.

"Violet, at the top, is linked to the Crown, our highest level of knowing. Indigo comes next and rests between the eyebrows. It is called the third eye. It opens one to wisdom and insight. Aquamarine is linked to the throat chakra. When we focus on that color, we find the words we need. Green, like the emerald, opens the heart. Opens us to love. Yellow topaz is the energy of the solar plexus, the power center for personal strength. Yellow helps us refuel."

Now, Ava was drawn to the yellow light. But her favorite was the orange carnelian, known as the singer's stone, a beautiful combination of fire and song. Sophia had told Ava that the stone would energize and center her after battle.

Ava let the seven stones do their work.

When she felt renewed, she lifted her guitar.

She plucked the seventh string. The vibrations became purple rays, a reminder of Saint Germain.

Could a frequency really be love?

She called up some intel about 528 Hz on her buckle.

"In the ancient musical scales, the Solfeggio frequency 528 Hz, resonates at the heart of everything that exists in the Universe, including the sun, pyramids, circles, squares, rainbows, and snowflakes. The number 528 is fundamental to the ancient pi and phi, the Golden Ratio. Evident throughout natural design, it is the musical mathematical matrix of creation."

Math.

"It reverberates with nature, from the trees to the bees, vibrating at the same frequency. It has color."

Colors! Ava was fascinated.

"This mysterious frequency of love, 528 Hz, has the power to transform our world, whether by eliminating pollution from our oceans, healing our DNA, or overcoming our hate and conflict. Sound brings harmony and healing."

"Falcon, where is Compass Point 5.28?"

Falcon pressed the stone. "It's a rose quartz mountain on the East Coast. In Massachusetts."

"The witch trials," said Yue, in a scary voice.

"That was in Salem," said Falcon.

"But were they witches?" asked Yue, who had been enthralled by the witches of Celtic myth, before her focus on climate took over her life.

"They were women who honored nature and the earth," said Falcon. Diana had told her about the goddess religions, the earth-based matrilineal cultures, on one of their forest walks. "They performed rituals around the seasons and the rites of passage."

"Most indigenous peoples looked at the cycles, the position of sun, moon, and stars," said Maia. "It's not that different."

"No, it isn't," said Yue.

"The number 528 keeps coming up for me," said Ava. "Especially as a frequency of sound. I think we need to go to that quartz mountain, the one at 5.28. Maybe I can explain along the way."

MONUMENT MOUNTAIN

THE GIRLS FLEW OVER the Berkshire Hills and the quaint New England town of Great Barrington, Compass Point 5.28. The horses circled Monument Mountain, a small but potent quartzite peak. As they came down and around the north face, a large bald spot of rock with veins of pink, black, and gray glittered in the noon sun.

Falcon spotted a spire rising from the ledge. There were stories about this place; this land that was once the home of the Stockbridge Munsee Band of Mohicans, the People of the Waters That Are Never Still.

A local legend tells of a Mohican woman falling to her death from one of the knife-edged summits. A pillar of stone marks where she had stood. Now called Peeskawso Peak, it means virtuous woman.

What would this mountain hold for the virtuous Crystal Warriors? When the girls landed, they made the horses small, tucked them into a patch of myrtle, and began their search.

Ava wanted to be still and listen for the sounds of 528. She longed to know what the frequency of love sounded like.

Today the trails on the mountain, hard packed by foot traffic, were vacant. The girls walked alone as if some invisible power had cleared the path. Falcon didn't feel like this was a mission, but more like a hike up a pink mountain. She wished

Diana was here. This place reminded Falcon of their forest walks at camp.

Falcon tripped, landing on the other side of a fallen log. Yue reached down to help her up.

"You okay?"

"Fine," said Falcon, annoyed at her own clumsiness. She had lost her focus thinking about Diana.

"Look at those mushrooms," said Yue, pointing to the base of a giant oak.

"The hen of the woods," said Falcon. "My mother sautés them in butter."

"Maybe one day we'll eat more than apricots." said Yue. "I would do anything for a cheeseburger."

Ava groaned. "And I'd do anything for a bowl of my mother's *chile verde*, with her homemade tortillas. And then a shaved raspberry ice from the cart on the corner."

Maia chimed in. "A baked sweet potato, mashed, with lots of butter. And Twizzlers, of course . . ."

"Of course!" laughed Falcon. "Mangos. I want a mango from the side of the road in Costa Rica. I never eat the hot dogs from the food stands in the city, but right now, I could eat two!"

The girls chattered about food as they went along the Mohican Monument Trail.

"It smells good here," said Ava. The evergreens, maples, and birch didn't grow in the Southwest she knew. They all paused and looked up with her. She waited for the song of the wind, the whispers that floated between branches.

Please let 528 show its voice, she thought.

A sudden sweeping breeze rustled the leaves, prompting a crow to cry out and fly. Thunder warned of a coming storm, and within minutes, a crashing rain and wind forced them to seek cover in a cave near the path.

"I don't want to stay in here. It makes me think about when I was trapped. I can't breathe," said Ava, with panic in her voice. "Let me out!"

"We are with you," said Maia, as they surrounded her. "We're okay."

Maia wanted to think they'd be fine, but she wasn't so sure. She didn't know what kind of storm this was. *Is it a deterrent from searching, or just a summer storm?* she wondered.

"I know the story of this boulder cave," said Falcon, thinking a tale might be a good distraction from Ava's fear and the worry on Maia's face. "In 1850, two writers, Nathaniel Hawthorne and Herman Melville, were on this mountain when a storm hit. They took cover in this very cave."

"Right here?" asked Yue. "How do you know?"

"When we were reading *Moby-Dick*, my English teacher told us. She said they were stuck for a long time and talked for hours. Some of the ideas for Melville's novel were hatched right there that afternoon," said Falcon.

"I love that," said Yue, who was fascinated by the story of the giant whale.

"A whale," repeated Ava, no longer worried about caves and tight spots. "I dreamed about a whale! She was insistent about 528 Hz. We must be in the right place!" As the storm continued, she told them all she knew about the love frequency, and about the number 528.

Sheets of water pelted down, cascading like falls over the entrance to the cave. It had a red tint, the color of blood. As the storm raged on, they all fell silent, sure there was danger on the other side.

Yue shivered. They huddled closer. Ava put her hands over her ears. A thunderous sound rolled through the mountain, not thunder, though. A cloud had followed them to 5.28. Was it a warning? Greed's way of saying, "You have no power"? Or were they trapped and in real peril?

Maia turned away from the others and pressed her buckle, an SOS to Sophia.

"What is it?" said Sophia instantly.

"I'm not sure about this one," said Maia.

"What does the air smell like . . . did the temperature warm?

As Maia ran outside, the girls grasped at her arms to keep her back, but she was too fast. She was drenched, so it was hard to tell if it had gotten warmer or if the chill came from her rain-soaked skin.

Sophia looked at the dreamcatcher. Onto her wall, it projected the shape of an obelisk—a tall four-sided monument ending in a pyramid. She didn't understand the message but saw the numbers *212*.

Maia spoke into the buckle. "Sophia, it smells like rain, that's all, a little ozone but not much chlorine. And no iron. And it's warm, even though I'm cold," she said.

"It's a trickster," said Sophia.

"Then why is the water tinged with red?" Maia asked.

"It's trying to break you down. Don't let it. Look it in the eye. Then look for an obelisk on the mountain. And the number 212. It will give you information."

Maia stood, hands on hips, and spoke. "You. Have. No. Power. Here!"

The cloud bellowed, disappeared into itself, and left a sun halo behind.

Ava hurried out of the cave. Her boots stuck and sucked in the mud. "Maia. Look. This is the only place that it stormed."

Maia gazed around them. The rest of the mountain was bone-dry. It was dark where the girls stood, but everywhere else was filled with light. Light that moved in waves.

What about 528, Ava thought, as she stared at the light. *Are you in there? Are you in the light?*

All was still.

"I think coming here was a waste of time," she said.

"No, it's exactly where we need to be," said Maia as the other girls crawled out to join them.

"Sophia said to look for an obelisk and the number 212."

Falcon perked up. "An obelisk, and 212?"

"Do you know it?" asked Maia.

"I might."

Falcon led them along the trails until they came to a wall of pink stone. Falcon put her hands on the rock. Warmth spread through her fingers and into her arms. Then she turned and stood with her back against the solid quartz.

"You have to feel this," she said. They each stood and felt the power and heat of this rock, this mountain, and the earth. Falcon turned to put her forehead against the veins and saw something shimmer inside the stone. It took all of her vision to make out the shape of a tiny obelisk.

Engraved inside was the number *2.1.2.* Her hunch was right.

"We need to go to New York City," she said.

CRYSTAL TOWER

*I*T RISES LIKE A PRAYER to the sky, and when the sun hits it at dawn, it glistens like a million mirrors.

Falcon was standing near the Oculus, a building on the southern tip of Manhattan. The white structure looked like a dove with wings of steel. It sat in the shadow of what could be the tallest man-made crystal on earth, an obelisk monument named Freedom Tower, Compass Point 2.12.

Today, a small black cloud hovered over the tower, and it worried Falcon. It also made her wonder if the missing piece was close by, maybe in the tower itself. This was not a remote place and many people could get hurt if the cloud chose to expand and show its rage.

Like Falcon, Yue was comfortable in a city. She loved being on an island surrounded by water, and she could taste the salt in the air. If she walked a few blocks south, she could see past the harbor to the great Atlantic.

Ava felt a different kind of energy. She couldn't stand still. The sounds of the city pulsed in her blood. Even at daybreak, whirling sirens sounded from the streets. This was unfamiliar music, and while it energized her, she missed the gentler songs of the desert. She had read that once this land was the home of the Lenape tribe. They had cultivated this land, this island flanked by rivers that flowed into the ocean. Now, it was a grid of concrete with very little green.

Maia was shell-shocked. Never had she seen so many cars and people. They were all in a hurry. They carried briefcases, walked dogs, wore headsets as they jogged. Occasionally, a bicycle would whiz by. When the girls had flown over Times Square, her heart sank. She wondered how many kilowatts it took to light up all of those billboards. So much energy. Sophia would be devastated.

On their way south to the edge of the city, Falcon had taken a detour. She wanted to show them a statue called "The Fearless Girl." Four feet tall, hands on her hips, this tiny little girl in a dress appeared as a powerhouse of strength as she stood head-to-head with the bronze sculpture of a charging bull. Falcon pointed out that she held her ground outside the New York Stock Exchange, the temple of American capitalism. Yue thought she could have been part of their cowgirl sisterhood—a fierce-looking warrior, with her own superpower.

The girls arrived at Battery Park, an open space to do their work, a few steps from the obelisk. Falcon saw Yue eyeing the entrance to the Seaglass Carousel. *Fish.* Falcon leaned on her shoulder, "We'll go later."

They would all need a salve of childhood magic. In fifteen minutes, the cloud had grown five times its original size. It was still small, but likely wouldn't stay that way for long.

"We need a plan," said Ava.

"I want to move it out to sea and drown it," said Falcon. "I'll need all of you to stand and hold me from behind."

They moved into position without questioning. This was Falcon's call. She closed her eyes and breathed deep, filling her chest, her belly, her whole body. Today, she would be a tornado, funneling every ounce of energy and power. She would focus intently on her target, making sure her wind was on point, like an arrow. Her strong gust shot up toward the cloud. A gray infinity sign wrapped around the metallic black shape like a lasso. As it was yanked away from Freedom Tower, the cloud morphed into a black raven, dark wings passing over the white Oculus. Falcon's lasso gave it one last hard pull, tossing the bird-cloud over the park and into the ocean where the saltwater waves swallowed it whole..

A tall, crowned woman stood in the harbor, her green patina catching the light. The Statue of Liberty raised her torch as if to say, "Well done."

Falcon's wind power was strong. Combined with the sun, it could light the world. *Solar and wind could solve a lot of problems*, she thought. *Why is it so hard for people to make the change?* She looked at the clusters of giant buildings and saw the answer. Money and the love of power moved decision-makers around like chess pieces on the board of New York City's financial district. It was hard to change greed or teach it anything about the soft growing things so easily buried.

Falcon's body was spent. She wished she could see her parents and tell them about her day, as she always had. Maia's soft voice interrupted her inner thoughts.

"Sophia would be so proud of you."

"She'd be proud of you, too, Maia."

"Do you think the crystal is here, Falcon? I see some signs," said Maia. "Freedom Tower. Statue of Liberty? The Codes are about justice, fairness, balance."

"The scales *have* been tipped," said Ava.

"Maybe the missing piece is hidden in the planetarium, in the dome of stars," said Yue.

"It's possible," said Falcon. "We'll have to come back."

"Did you like growing up here?" asked Yue.

"Yes and no," Falcon answered. "But mostly yes. But I'm changed now. I need green spaces, and there's not much of it in the city, except for Central Park. We should go and get the horses."

Terra, Aze, Mazu, and Aveer had turned themselves into painted bronzes and were hiding themselves on the park's famous carousel.

"They must be tired of circling," said Ava.

"I'm going pop into the Seaglass. It is right here," said Yue. I'll be quick."

What was once the New York Aquarium was now a huge, chambered nautilus. Thirty massive fiberglass fish, all different species, were illuminated from the inside. As they swam, their colors changed. Yue went to the angelfish and sat inside. She thought it would make her happy, but it had the opposite effect. She left before the ride began.

《

The Crystal Warriors braved the C Train, the underground silver bullet that went up the center of Manhattan Island. The subway was crowded and loud as the steel wheels churned up the tracks. Nobody made eye contact. Heads were down and people were in their phones.

The disconnection between human and human did not go unnoticed by Maia. She felt closed in. And sad. She missed home, where there was solitude and time to just be still.

The train came to a stop at 59th Street. The girls walked up the stairs single file and out into fresher air. Horse-pulled carriages were lined up, waiting for tourists, in front of a big hotel called The Plaza.

"That's cruel," said Ava. "Horses don't belong on city streets."

"I know," said Maia. "They need to graze. Let's go rescue ours."

Terra, Mazu, Aze, and Aveer blended in with fifty-seven fanciful horses, poles moving up and down as they went around and around. The girls watched as the horses went by until they claimed their own. As they climbed into the saddles, everyone shape-shifted into the tiniest versions of themselves. Sophia had taught them well.

In a very short time, the horses and girls where home on Crystal Ridge. After New York, they all needed quiet and rest. Maia needed peace. She fell asleep thinking about ley lines.

GREAT WHITE GULL

"Now, explain again? What are ley lines?" Falcon asked.

"They align sacred sites," said Ava. "A lot of people don't believe in them, but I do."

"What do you mean? What do they look like?" asked Yue.

"Have you ever been on an airplane and looked at the back of the magazine, where it shows the flight routes? Now, imagine that there are lines that connect certain places, and they form shapes like triangles, or even circles if you trace them," said Ava.

"Kind of like a grid," said Maia.

The four girls were seated in the circle in ARIA, eating apricots and waiting. They had tried to saddle up earlier and look for ley lines, but a huge wind had stirred up the dirt and obscured the ground. Maia was grateful for the crosswinds, even if they were sent to discourage the mission. She needed to replenish her energy after being in New York. The strain was beginning to show. Dark circles under her eyes stained her skin, the blue tinge deepening as the days went on. Her sleep was restless. Instead of dreaming, she wrestled with worry and her biggest questions. *When will we find the crystal? What if we don't find it at all?*

As the rainbow from the walls seeped into her body, strengthening her energy, the arrow moved on the compass.

Yue glanced at Falcon.

"Compass Point 2.07. Water."

Falcon heard the air whisper a message. *Ride the wind. Go east. Toward Vega, the main star of the Summer Triangle.*

Ava's clairaudience heard it, too. "Ley lines in the sky," she said.

Falcon bounded up from the floor. "It's the Eastern Seaboard. "We haven't searched the surface of the ocean."

"Do you think the crystal is in the sea?" asked Yue, practically jumping up and down.

"Who knows. We've looked everywhere else," said Ava.

"The glistening of light on the water would be perfect camouflage," said Yue.

Falcon turned to Yue. "We'll go. You and me."

Ava's face reddened. She didn't have to say a word. Maia understood. Ava was sensitive about being left out. Maia rested her hand on her friend's shoulder. "Stand in a waterfall with your feet on the rock, grounded into Mother Earth."

Ava took a deep breath. She imagined water streaming down and through her body, cooling her fire, but not putting it out. Yue and Falcon came and stood next to her.

"We didn't mean to—"

"I understand," Ava interrupted. "You are air and water, East and West. Maia and I are here, ready to head out if we need to. We divide and conquer," said Ava.

Maia was grateful for the time to rest.

Falcon and Yue mounted their horses and took off toward the coast and the blue-white light of the star Vega, the brightest in the Lyra constellation. They flew over Nebraska and Iowa, taking in the shapes, the geometrical patterns of the Midwest farms—patches of greens, browns, and tans—an earth quilt of lines coming together, squares and rectangles and circles. The colors were not as vibrant and healthy as they had been a week ago. Today, a thin gray overlay, like wax paper, blanketed the land. Yue could taste how the essence was lost to a new breed of farmer—corporations that messed with the DNA of plants, modifying seeds along with the order of the natural world, the very principles of life.

Dread came over Falcon. They had to find the crystal soon. She lifted her eyes and shifted her focus to Compass Point 2.07. Sensing her determination, Aveer sliced through the clouds. They needed to get there before sundown. Otherwise looking for a crystal on the sea would have to wait.

The highest point on the Eastern Seaboard, the Monhegan Cliffs jutted up from the ocean, ancient dark granite with veins of copper and white that sparkled when the sun hit them. This would be a good place to stand with the super-powerful, pocket-sized telescopes that Sophia had given them. They made a smooth landing, despite Yue losing her cowgirl hat to the wind. She wanted to reach for it, but instead held her breath as it floated down like a feather to land on a twisted branch of windblown pine beside the nest of Great White Gull. The bird took Yue's hat in her orange beak and flew toward them.

When Great White Gull got closer, Yue blinked in disbelief.

"What is it?" asked Falcon. "What is that with your hat?"

"A white gull. No, a *giant* white gull. I think she is as big as a whale!"

Yue knew the white gull was a guide, a keeper of visions, a protector of the oceans. Yue had learned that a meeting with a seagull, like a dolphin, opened communication with the sprites who lived in the waters. Maybe this would be helpful on their search.

Great White Gull floated down on the wind. She hovered, sun streaming through her white, black-tipped quills, spread out like a fan. She landed on the wide slab of rock where Falcon, Yue, and the horses stood in awe. Yue gently took her hat and bowed her head in gratitude. Gull blinked. Her eyes were midnight black—glossy like wet ink—dark and deep like an ocean. But in the middle of her pupil, a tiny point of light expanded like a morning star.

Gull had a gift for Yue. Tucked beneath her wing was a gold coin, ancient and worn. She dropped it at Yue's feet. Yue cautiously picked it up. It was icy cold in her hand. She examined it, recognizing the engraving as the Morrigan.

The myth of the Morrigan, also known as the Phantom Queen, told the story of a dark goddess from old Ireland, associated with war, destiny, fate, and death. She was a shape-shifter and often appeared as a black raven, an ominous sign for those who saw her prior to battle.

The Morrigan, Yue thought. A chill went through her.

"Was the Morrigan the raven we fought—the black cloud that turned into a bird over the Freedom Tower?" asked Yue.

Gull shook her head.

Then why the coin? thought Yue. *Oh, there must be another side.*

From their perch upon the cliff, Yue spotted a whirlpool in the distance, swirling waters that went into a rabbit hole under the sea. *Could the voices of the wells live here?* she thought. She knew they existed in Celtic myth, but could they be here in the Atlantic? Or was it a trick, a distraction from skimming the ocean with their eyes—a diamond-faceted surface, and a brilliant hiding spot for a stolen crystal.

It was not a time for thinking about the wells or coins or myths. Not while they had the sun. They began to hunt between the whitecaps, eyes focused on the glittering sea. When night fell, the full moon rose, the Strawberry Moon that came but once a year, the kind that seemed to cast pink rays of syrupy light on everything it touched. The Star of Vega was another beacon. They traversed the waters on horseback, following the lanterns of stardust and moon. Yue had a feeling the crystal they were seeking was here, somewhere, and didn't want to leave. She was drawn to the whirlpool she had seen earlier, for the voices.

Too tired to go back to ARIA, they signaled to Maia, letting her know they were safe and staying overnight. Great White Gull led them to Cathedral Forest, a magical place in the middle of the island not too far from her nest. She would watch over them as they slept.

WATER SONG

*A*S THE MORNING LIGHT DANCED through the trees, Falcon and Yue reveled in the feast of blueberries plucked from this magical forest. After weeks and weeks of apricots, the change *was* delightful . . . and this forest *was* magical. Though these trees weren't covered in layers of colored bark, they held their own mysteries . . . tiny doors to tiny houses built by the faeries who lived and slept and partied in the roots.

In the night, Yue had dreamed of the Morrigan, and the churning whirlpool they saw on yesterday's search. What if the crystal was spinning inside, deep in one of the wells, the place in the dark Celtic story where the maidens were held and silenced for using the powers of the earth to heal?

"Have you ever seen shapes in the water?" asked Yue. "They have hidden messages."

She popped a blueberry in her mouth.

"What do you mean?" Falcon asked.

"A scientist from Japan studied water and proved that a person can change its structure with their thoughts," explained Yue. "Positive thoughts create crystals. Another experiment used a certain frequency of sound. The water went from cloudy to clear."

"Ava would like that," said Falcon.

"It's based on scientific research," said Yue.

"And you know this how?"

"My mother showed me photographs in a book. You can't see the crystals without a special camera. They look like snowflakes. Have you ever heard of people talking to plants to help them grow? It's like that."

Falcon's mother had a garden on the windowsills in their apartment. One ivy grew especially long. She never cut it. She was worried the leaves would feel the snip. "My mom doesn't talk to plants," said Falcon, "but there's always music in the house. She once told me her plants were happy because of Mozart."

"See?" said Yue.

"So, you think if a million people got together and sang on all the beaches in the world, the oceans could be healed?" asked Falcon. Now she was really missing Ava.

"It won't get rid of the plastic," sighed Yue. "Do you remember when that great Blue washed up in Monterey?"

"I think I saw it on the news?" said Falcon.

"That whale changed my life. It died from pounds of plastic in its belly. If my mom were still alive, she would have been called in."

"Wasn't she a researcher for the Aquarium?"

"Marine biologist," said Yue. "When I was little, I sat in the dark exhibit room for hours imagining I was climbing the giant kelp forest, just like Jack in his beanstalk."

"Like me in the Planetarium."

"You should have been a star," said Yue.

"You should have been a Mermaid," laughed Falcon.

"I could not take my eyes off the jellyfish. They make their own light. If only humans could do that, it would raise the happiness in the world."

"In China people think jellyfish are a delicacy," said Falcon.

Yue wondered if someone from her birth family had eaten them. She would never have that answer. She didn't even know their names.

᚜

A cool breeze rustled the leaves in the forest by the sea. Yue closed her eyes and thought about coral. She had discovered that one species looked like a zinnia, a flower-burst of perfect geometry. But nothing astonished her more than the mandalas at the bottom of the sea. The male pufferfish, the size of a small kitten, spent days wiggling his body, creating tiny currents that pushed the sand into patterns, raised mandalas that became a safe nest for the female to lay her eggs. Yue wondered who'd gotten the idea for mandalas first . . . the pufferfish or the Tibetan monks.

"Falcon, do you think the crystal might be hidden in a snowflake, maybe on top of a mountain!?"

Falcon thought for a moment. "Black Raven could have hidden it in a place like that."

Yue popped the last of the blueberries into her mouth before taking out the gold coin and rubbing it between her fingers.

"I'm ready," she said. "Come, let's go to the wells."

The girls walked Mazu and Aveer to the edge of the forest where a shimmering and vast Atlantic Ocean came into view.

The crystal might be floating at the surface right within our grasp, or maybe it's way down at the bottom of the well, thought Yue.

Ava had warned Yue that the well could be a lure, a trick, a magical spell to pull her down into the depths. Yue was cautious, but had to go. She thought about the maidens and what they sacrificed to heal the earth. Was she willing to sacrifice herself?

Yue leaned down on her horse, whispering in her ear. "You are Mazu, named after the Chinese goddess of the sea, the protector of seafarers. Lead us."

Mazu responded by getting into position.

Yue reached into her bag and took out the coin, holding it to the sun.

"The Goddess Morrigan also helps warriors to be brave during battle, to help bring victory," said Yue.

"Ready?"

They lifted swiftly into the salty air, making thunder over the ocean. The wind was warm and loud, rushing around their ears. As they got closer to the whirlpool, the wind quieted, and Yue could hear voices, female voices . . . murmuring and wailing in an achingly sad song.

She wanted to reach down with her hand and pull the women out. Mazu made a sideways dive, moving away just as the underwater currents collided. The whirlpool turned, getting louder as the churning vortex gained velocity. When the maelstrom began the slow collapse into itself, Falcon saw a piece of cloud turn itself into a dark curl.

The Wave Cloud, she thought, bracing herself. It rose above them and Yue knew it could crash down and sweep them into the swirling pool, where they would be forever lost. She and Mazu danced sideways around it with Falcon and her horse following. She used her powers of love and breath to create a miniature tornado. The cloud spun down, down into the funnel, and got sucked into the vortex the very moment the whirlpool fell into itself.

Yue moved toward Falcon and saw that her skin was turning blue. She had no breath left. As she struggled to get air, Yue came from behind to give her some of her own. When Falcon was breathing normally again, a large shadow crossed over them. It was White Gull offering her back. Gull had been watching from her perch, knowing they might need help. Now they needed rest. They would sleep in her nest overnight. She would feed them fish, and maybe more blueberries.

Tomorrow it was home to ARIA.

SHADOWS AND LIGHT

Yue lay awake in ARIA, staring at the ceiling.
"I saw a number in my dreams," she said.
"So did I," said Falcon.

All four of them sat up on their blankets and compared notes.

Compass Point 9.07 on the next full moon.

They all had identical, vivid dreams during the night.

Falcon looked up 9.07 on her buckle. "It's a place called Denali. It says it's a sacred mountain in the middle of a grid."

"Black Raven stole the crystal from a mountain," said Maia, "so it makes sense for him to hide it on another."

Yue held up her buckle, looking at the moving words that trailed over the map on the tiny screen. "Denali is a powerful vortex in a zone where there are others. The ley lines form a triangle. See how they align?" she said, pointing to the message.

"Let's go!" said Ava.

Patience, Yue thought and smiled, remembering her dream about the spirit of her mother, patiently sitting in the icy tundra, polishing a stone, not rushing.

"The full moon is in four days," said Yue. "We must wait."

Ava rolled her eyes, picked up her guitar, and quietly plucked the strings. The tension in the cave was building. The pressure to complete this mission was high, and they were getting prickly with each other.

Maia wanted licorice. Instead, she chewed her nails. Falcon went into her own cave of words, where writing gave her peace and clarity.

Yue turned to Ava, "It's cold in the far North," she said as a bridge and peace offering.

Ava sighed, "I know."

"We have the warm furs that Sophia left for us, and the boots," said Maia.

Each day of the wait, the girls went off alone to hone their powers and gather their strength. Each night, they watched the moon get rounder, glowing pink until it was full. On the fourth dawn, Falcon went to the horses who had been resting for three days. Four girls, four horses, heading to a remote and vast wilderness, in search of a crystal in the oceans of snow.

As they flew over the Rockies and into the far North, the wind chill cut like a hundred knives. The girls shivered, despite the fur, and their muscles tensed to hold in their body heat. Their teeth chattered. Fog swirled from the horses' breath and icicles dangled from feather manes.

The raw, rugged peaks of Denali spiked up through the icy mist. The tallest mountains in North America, they were also the most treacherous of the Alaskan Range. Here, the snow didn't melt and it was hard to imagine that any life existed here at all.

The girls called up their courage, strength, and resilience. They tapped into the spirit that lived inside, the bravery that would power them through. Tenacious to the core, they were blazing new trails. Nothing would break them. Not even this ice that froze their bones.

They slowly descended into the gripping cold. The snow-caps were deep, dense, and sharp. *Can we even land here?* wondered Yue. It might be impossible to see the crystal snowflakes, the shapes in water she'd mused about.

Denali is the perfect place for the stolen piece to hide, buried in the crystals of snow, thought Maia.

Falcon squinted, focusing on a circular ledge. *A good landing spot just below the summit of the mountain.*

They moved downward in a slow spiral, wind howling against their backs. Their horses, in peak form, landed gently on the ledge. Coated with a star-dusting of ice, the ledge was surrounded by raised, rounded edges like a giant crystal nest.

Inside the nest were etched patterns: intersecting circles, infinity signs, triangles, formulas, and the geometry of flowers. The nest held recordings of every place they'd searched—all of the compass points of sand and seas, rivers and rock, fields and forests—all of the places they had seen from above and below.

They were on top of the world. And stunned into silence.

Moonbeams lit the earth, casting pink shadows that curled along the curves of the landscape. The heavens opened up and luminous curtains of green wafted down like silk ribbons against the night sky. The northern lights, nature's most spectacular light show, cradled them in a blanket of mystery.

Maia was certain the crystal was here. She quickly messaged Sophia to join them. The time was right.

"Look," said Yue, pointing to Maia's pouch. It glowed green, like the lights.

"It's my dreamcatcher!" said Maia as she quickly pulled it out.

A green, pulsing light shone through their leather pouches. The center stones were energized in a way they hadn't been since being broken apart.

Sophia and Apollo appeared in moments, as if time did not exist, as if they had been waiting for this call. Sophia dismounted and stood, regal as always, wearing a cape of feathers, white like pearls. She and Maia hugged long and hard. Maia didn't want to let go. She remembered something she had written in her journal during training. *Sophia smells of the earth in all of Her seasons. Pine and cedar in winter, lilacs in spring. And in summer, her fragrance is warm rain. In the fall she smells of apples and apricots and oak leaves ready to let go. She never wears perfume.*

Everyone gathered around. Seeing Sophia again made it all feel right.

"I've been all over the world," whispered Sophia, gazing in a full circle. "I've never seen a place like this." She walked around the icy nest, crouching down at times to look at the delicate work. Maia wondered if the symbols had been drawn by a talon, or a beak.

"These are Codes," whispered Sophia. She looked up, searching the sky. As the northern lights faded, the full moon took her rightful place in the sky. Her pink glow turned blue, illuminating all of Denali, until a dark shadow moved across the moonscape.

"What *is that*?" asked Yue, slight panic in her voice.

They looked to Sophia for an answer, but her eyes were on the shadow. *What if it's a shape-shifter,* she thought, *like the cloud on Shasta. All of the crystals could be stolen.*

The shadow took form with wings, giant wings. As it came closer, two shiny green eyes caught the light.

"Black Raven," said Sophia with a note of fury in her voice. "Hold onto your pouches. Don't let go," she yelled, as she stood in front of the girls.

"It can't be," said Maia, her voice shaky. *This can't happen now, not here. There's too much beauty.*

As Raven circled over them, Maia noticed that this bird didn't have carbon feathers, black like coal. She saw plumes of white with a tail of green. This was not the black raven that had stolen the stone on Mount Shasta. This was the raven who had shone in the eyes of Queen Bee, the bird who had come through Sophia's dreamcatcher, landing as a shadow on her wall. This was the White Raven that Ava had called in with her song.

Ava had tears in her eyes. "I know her," she said, almost to herself.

"This must be her nest," said Falcon.

As she circled over them, three piercing *ca-caws* sounded in warning. They watched as White Raven banked swiftly toward the north. Black Raven appeared out of nowhere, moving fast. Maia held her breath as the dark, giant bird slammed against White Raven's side.

"Leave her alone!" cried Yue. "Everyone, use your power!"

White Raven didn't waver until she was slammed again, slammed so hard she dropped toward the valley.

Maia grounded herself into the mountain. She spread out Mycelium threads to anchor the other girls and Sophia in the earth's power. These strong threads of connection held the Crystal Warriors steady as the attack of the Black Raven roiled above.

The moment Ava felt Maia's steadying strength, the flame inside her ignited to a roar. The flame began to sing. Ava lifted her voice into a long note, the note she had heard in the seventh string. She sang it pure, again and again. The love frequency rang out sweet and true, lifting White Raven just as Black Raven circled around to steal the pouches that held the crystals inside.

Yue held very still, like a calm pool. She reflected the powerful clarity that Sophia earned through years of guarding the Earth. That clarity helped to direct the flow of her thoughts and guide Falcon's wind. With the power of the wind giving her strength, White Raven attacked, her talons digging deep into and across Black Raven's chest, tearing through the heart of his evil.

Blood stained the snow.

White Raven grabbed her wounded enemy and flung him across the skies. Each girl focused her vision on coming to White Raven's aid, adding distance to her throw. Black Raven twisted in the winds before falling to his death, leaving bloody feathers in his wake.

"She's been fighting for us," whispered Sophia.

White Raven circled back, exhausted. She had more to do. She moved a brick made of ice and lifted something in her beak. The stone glowed like the finest emerald. The girls stood behind Sophia as White Raven bent down and dropped the found crystal into Sophia's hands. The bird looked at them with wise eyes before taking flight. She sounded four *ca-caws*, which echoed across the lands.

Sophia and the Crystal Warriors stood staring at the sacred object they had been searching for, hoping to find for so long.

"She must have hunted down Black Raven and taken back the stone," said Maia.

"She's been protecting it," said Sophia.

"Why didn't she tell us that she had it? And that it was safe?" asked Yue.

Sophia gazed at her with knowing eyes, understanding the frustration. "I think she wanted time to pass," said Sophia, "so that you could become strong warriors."

"This is her nest, right?" asked Falcon.

"Yes, and these are some of the Codes, but not all of them," said Sophia.

Sophia opened her hand, looked at the crystal, then closed her fingers again. She placed her hand on her heart, dropped to her knees, and began to sob. The girls held her as she cried. Relief flooded her body as did the love of these girls.

They would return to Montana, put the pieces together, and make the Crystal Horseshoe whole again. And then, a new kind of work would begin.

Healing

*M*AIA OPENED THE ROUND CLOTH flat beneath the big sky on Montana soil. The white cloth represented a medicine wheel, hand stitched with Buffalo, Eagle, Coyote, and Bear.

The night before, when the girls had slumped exhausted into the Silo, Maia had removed the pieces of the Crystal Horseshoe from the centers of the dreamcatchers, undoing her mother's work, unlacing the sinews. She had placed the fragments inside the Golden Box. Sophia slept with the box in her hands.

Now Sophia led them toward the creek, horses by their sides.

"That clearing looks like a good place," pointed Falcon.

"Yes, and we can hear the water," said Yue.

The sisters scattered four eagle feathers from their dreamcatchers around the blanket and took their places in the circle.

Sophia placed the Golden Box in the center as Maia called in the four directions. When she opened the box, green light spilled over the sides.

Sophia had been wise to keep them together overnight. They glowed stronger, the power of sharing their energy was already aligning the Codes.

Maia began to move them around, like puzzle pieces, until they took the shape of a horseshoe. Nothing was missing, and the breaks were clean. Strands of gold and white light made soft, sizzling sounds, like butter bubbling in a skillet. Four of the pieces began fusing themselves together, but the weaker crystals, the end pieces that had been separated from the others all of this time, needed help.

Earth, air, fire, and water could bring healing.

Ava crouched down, kissed the tip of her finger, and began to softly hum her song. Her finger first glowed pink, then orange, like the sunset against rock. "Here we go," she said softly, as she used her fire to liquefy the crystal. "Like blowing glass." The broken pieces began to meld together.

"I think that's good," said Ava, as she moved to the side so that Falcon could take her spot.

Falcon closed her eyes and called up air, the light filled kind that came from the east. She blew into the horseshoe, cooling the molten crystal. She handed the horseshoe to Yue. Earlier, Yue had collected water from the falls. She blessed it with intent, creating crystalline snowflakes, and poured them through the horseshoe, washing away any debris. When Yue's part was completed, she turned to Maia who put the sage into the abalone shell that Yue had given her. Ava lit the sage with her fingertip. Falcon fanned it with an eagle feather and her breath.

Maia held the Crystal Horseshoe above the burning sage. As the smoke rose through and around it, so did prayers to Mother Earth, Father Sky, to the sun and the moon, to the plants, the animals, the waters, and humans around the world. Maia prayed for clarity and vision, strength and wisdom, and the medicine that sage brought to the feminine. She prayed for the *anima mundi*, the Soul of the World, which lived in the Codes of Nature, the essence of all life.

No More Apricots

W E DID THIS," said Maia. "All four of us. Together."
She stood in the middle of the Silo and held up the
Crystal Horseshoe. Then she placed it on the table
on a cloth of silk and spun around in a circle, arms toward the
sky in jubilation. "We did it!"

"And now we have to go back to school!?" said Ava.

The girls groaned.

"We are the Earth Teachers now," said Maia.

Yue picked up the Crystal Horseshoe and watched as the
scrolls moved and hummed inside. "Ava, will you play?" asked
Yue. The vibrations of the seventh string filled the room,
swimming in waves around them. Ava began to sing the love
song, her song without words, her song to Mother Earth. As
the love frequency faded, streams of sunlight filled the silo.

"It's like a party in here!"

"A light show."

The Crystal Horseshoe pulsed green, the color of the heart
chakra, a clear, strong message that love was a powerful Code.

"Do you think that love is the most powerful healer?" asked
Maia. At her words, the green light began to weave around
and through them, the same green thread that the dreamcatchers had shown them that night in ARIA. But this time,
the threads were strong and whole, instead of weak and frayed.

"Unity," said Ava.

"Connection," said Yue.

"Everything is interwoven—humans, animals, earth, air, water, planets, stars. The only thing that can heal it all is love," said Maia.

"Is that too simple?" asked Falcon.

"It's not all sweetness," said Maia.

"No, it's not," said Yue. "Think of it this way. If a scientist invents something to clean the oceans, the intention behind that would be love. I mean, why work so hard on something to clean the oceans if not out of love?"

"Diana told me about a couple who bought a farm where the soil had been abused, used up. A farm where nothing could grow. And they brought the dead soil back to life. Eventually, the biodiverse ecosystems grew a paradise. Love was *totally* behind that," said Falcon.

"A food paradise." said Ava. "I'm hungry."

"Mother Earth can heal herself," said Maia. "If we get out of the way just a little bit. But people need to heal. I hope we can heal ourselves."

"Maybe we have to get a little mad. I think outrage is love rising," said Ava. "We are fired up, angry about the state of the planet. We have to fight for her, sometimes hard and loud, in solidarity. Doesn't that fight also come from love?"

"It does," said Yue. "Outrage helped me get rid of plastic bottles in my town."

They stopped talking, for a moment.

"If I eat one more apricot . . ." said Ava.

"What is that smell?" said Falcon, eyes wide.

"Oh, my god. Real food. I smell real food," said Yue.

They all turned as Keya appeared at the top of the spiral staircase.

"Mom!" Maia jumped up from sitting cross legged on her bed. But she couldn't hug her mother, the platter of food barring the way.

Behind Keya, Isabella surprised them with her own tray. Ava shrieked. Sophia laughed, coming up the stairs last, her own arms full. After Maia moved the Crystal Horseshoe to an out-of-the-way place, the women set the feast on the table and accepted the arms of these strong, unstoppable girls.

"Cheeseburgers!" said Yue, melting.

"The bigger the better," said Isabella, smiling as she handed Yue the most perfect burger she would ever taste. Food kept coming. The table was laden with bags of nori, more bowls and platters, and a box of mangos sent by Falcon's parents with a note tucked amongst them. *We love you to the moon and can't wait to see you! Mom and Dad*

Falcon took out her pocketknife and sliced the sweet fruit for her sisters. Maia bit into the slippery mango for the first time. It was juicy and sweet and tasted like heaven. She looked at her mom. "This might be better than sweet potatoes."

Keya laughed, and reached behind her back. Maia heard the familiar crinkle. Her mother handed her Twizzlers and said, "For later."

Ava took out her phone and their playlist filled the room. Isabella uncovered a beautiful clay platter piled high with soft steaming tortillas surrounding a pot of *chili verde*. She began to ladle out bowls.

"Are you missing your mom?" asked Sophia, as she put her arm around Yue's shoulder.

"I am, but I feel her here."

"I feel my ancestors, too," said Sophia.

"And all of you are my family now," said Yue. "I have many mothers."

"You do."

Sophia watched as the party swirled around her.

Maia was passing out Twizzlers and Ava was eating bowl after bowl of *chili*. She gave Yue a spoonful.

"Wow, that's hot, my mouth is on fire, Ava! Falcon, more mango please, I need something to cool me off!"

Sophia saw the strength in these girls. She saw hope, hope for the earth, hope for humanity.

The celebration continued well into the night. When Ava built the fire, they moved outside under the stars to dance, to sing, to drum, to tell stories about the quest. Ava sang the love song to Mother Earth, and to the mothers, to the daughters, to the women of now and of all time. To all Guardians of the Earth.

Queen Bee buzzed over and landed on Maia's shoulder, making herself right at home.

Epilogue

Four horses sliced through blue skies, eagle feathers swaying on the winds.

These equine chariots moved with purpose, as did the courageous riders on their backs.

Four girls, on a mission to restore the natural world. They flew over glaciers and streams, rivers and rock, oceans and deserts, forests and farmland—Crystal Horseshoe in hand.

As they raised the ancient talisman, light cascaded like an emerald waterfall, verdant and alive. It was the wisdom of the ages, love songs for the earth.

The Codes of Nature transformed darkness into light, and greed into generosity.

Sophia had handed the torch to Maia, who would fulfill her destiny, braided like sweetgrass to her circle of four.

Together, they walked
as sisters of the earth

Dedicated to my parents, Lee and Sy Novack, who by example, led me to becoming a seeker, and showed me that the questions are often more important than the answers. And to my loving family, who were bright beacons of encouragement as I found my footing, and who picked me up when I stumbled along the way.

ACKNOWLEDGMENTS

*I*F IT WERE NOT FOR THE NATURAL WORLD, this book would not have been written. You grew me and taught me about the interconnectedness of all living things. Thank you for inspiring me with your heartache and beauty— it is you who called me to write this story.

Thank you to the many teachers whose wisdom appeared at the just the right time—you have as come as dear friends, as chosen sisters, as spiritual seekers, and as circles . . . circles of women who showed me what sisterhood looks like—an important theme in this book. You know who you are. Many were early readers. You listened and laughed, over wine, under peach trees, on porches and in jeweled box sanctuaries. You said, "Keep going," so I did.

With huge appreciation for the When Words Count Retreat in Vermont, and Steve Eisner. You have created a place where writers can become authors. That is quite something. To Marilyn Atlas, and Steve Rohr, how lucky to have had your energy and brilliance. I'm glad I listened. To Ben Tanzer, you've been my rock. As my book coach you kicked my ass in the best way. As my publicist, you and Wiley Saichek are knocking it out of the park. Thank you, my friend.

Also from that circle: Sharyn Skeeter for her thoughtful guidance, and Asha Hossain—book cover design goddess. Peggy Moran, thank you for your eagle eyes; and Amber

Griffith, your sustenance, smile and fresh brewed coffee will not be forgotten. Nancie Laird Young—meeting you early on in Vermont was a gift; we instantly connected, as friends, as mothers, as writers-in-crime, thank you for keeping me sane. I can't wait to read your book. And Carole, thank you saying, "Let's go."

Deepest gratitude goes to Dede Cummings, my publisher at Green Writers Press, who loves words and the natural world, who believed in me and in this book. You are a kindred spirit. GWP could not be a more perfect midwife for this book. To my editor, Rose Alexander-Leach, for pushing me, and pushing me again, for championing my endurance, for seeing things that I didn't, for being so gentle and wise. To Ferne Johansson—your thoughtful questions, suggestions, and eye for detail were invaluable. Cassandra Taylor, thank you. Emma Irving, just wow. Your continued support throughout the process has been beyond appreciated.

To Amy M. Hale, author, cowboy, master of words, dear friend and FW. You came in at the eleventh hour, shiny pen in hand, and made this book better—because words matter, because the story is the thing. I will never forget. You also showed me the desert you love, where I slept under the stars, and learned more about the nature of wild things and myself.

To Cathy A. Smith, my friend, artist, and Lakota guide, you made sure I got it right. I am forever grateful for your sensibility, sensitivity, artistry and kinship. To artist Alexis Estes, Woksape Oke Winyan, Seeks Knowledge Woman, member of the Lower Brule Sioux, you give with your full heart. Together, we will build cultural bridges of healing. I can't wait. To Great Grandmother Mary Lyons, Ojibwe Elder, and author, who blessed this book when it needed blessing. And to friend, author, and climate justice rock-star, Jennifer Browdy, Ph.D., for your guidance and generosity.

Thank you to all those who gave your time and words and loved this book, even before it was ready for prime time: Nina

Simons, Clare Dubois, Lance Rubin, Jana Laiz, Courtney Maum, Jennifer Dennison, Holly George Warren, Adrian Brannan, Kat Livengood, Ellen Feig Gray, Hope Fitzgerald, and Carrie Waible. Bouquets of love to Deb Chamberlin and Diane Pearlman. To Carrie Grossman for her voice, and Diana Baur for her eye.

I'm appreciative for the writing places in nature: Sedona Summer Colony Artist Residency, Ghost Ranch Inn and Rancho Nambe in New Mexico, Port Clyde Maine, The Mount in The Berkshires. Places where I hiked red rocks, journeyed into forests, walked on beaches or just sat, listening for the messages. To the hawk and the ant, thank you.

Lastly, to Carmen Baraka, Spirit Warrior Raven Woman, an elder of the greatest integrity, for her wisdom, encouragement, and recognition of the importance of my work as a bridge to healing. Carmen fought for Indigenous people's land and water, for the empowerment of women and girls, and for bringing the Rainbow Tribe together. Your star is shining bright. Aho, Sister.

Mitakuye Oyasin. We are all related.

"We showed that we are united and that we, young people, are unstoppable."

—Greta Thunberg,
UN Youth Climate Summit,
New York City, 21 September 2019

RESOURCES

❪

Call Up Your Cowgirl Spirit
and Learn How You can Be
a Voice for Mother Earth

Zero Hour

www.thisiszerohour.org
Founder: Jamie Margolin, Author. *Youth to Power: Your Voice*
and How to Use It. With a foreword by Greta Thunberg.

The mission of Zero Hour is to center the voices of diverse youth in the conversation around climate and environmental justice. We are a movement of unstoppable youth organizing to protect our rights and access to the natural resources and a clean, safe, and healthy environment that will ensure a livable future where we not just survive, but flourish.

Bioneers:
Youth Leadership and Education Program
www.bioneers.org

An incubator for thousands of youth and educators to deepen their passion and power through self-expression, skills development, mentorship, and deep relationship-building within the broader community of Bioneers. The program has produced some of the most dynamic, engaging, and cutting-edge programming within the Bioneers kaleidoscope and it continues to shape the work of youth movements, activism, and education.

Tree Sisters
Founder: Clare DuBois
www.TreeSisters.org

TreeSisters has funded the planting of over 15 million trees across twelve locations in Brazil, Borneo, Cameroon, India, Kenya, Mozambique, Madagascar, Nepal and West Papua.

Jane Goodall
www.rootsandshoots.org
USA Youth Program

You want to do something about the problems facing your community and our world—social justice, pollution, climate change, and more—we provide the support, resources, tools, and leadership training to empower you take action and lead change.

Earth Guardians
www.EarthGuardians.org

Earth Guardians has become a global movement providing a platform for hundreds of youth crews in over sixty countries to engage with some of the greatest issues we face as a global community.

jewishyouthclimatemovement.org

Dedicated to mitigating climate change by empowering teens, mobilizing communities, and taking action. JYCM believes in using Jewish values as a motivation to create a more equitable and sustainable world for all.

www.period.co

A period product that won't end up in landfills or oceans. It's kinder to you, and the planet.

Books

Braiding Sweetgrass for Young Adults, by Robin Wall Kimmerer.

Generation Green: The Ultimate Teen Guide to Living an Eco-Friendly Life, by Linda Sivertsen and Tosh Sivertsen.

Youth to Power: Your Voice and How to Use It, by Jamie Margolin.

Girl Warriors: How 25 Young Activists Are Saving the Earth by Rachel Sarah.

Parenting 4 Social Justice: Tips, Tools, and Inspiration for Conversations & Action with Kids by Angela Berkfield, et al.

Notes

528hz: https://www.mindvibrations.com/528-hz/.

Joy Harjo quote from *Beautiful Writer's Podcast*, with Linda Sivertsen.

To download a discussion guide for teachers, book clubs and organizations, go to www.barbaranewmanauthor.com.

PART OF THE PROCEEDS OF THE

DREAMCATCHER CODES GOES TO

ORGANIZATIONS FOR CLIMATE JUSTICE

AND ENVIRONMENTAL ACTIVISM.

ABOUT THE AUTHOR

Barbara always wanted to be a cowgirl. Growing up in New York didn't stop her. She took that can-do spirit and became an award-winning global creative director, leaving an indelible mark on brand culture. After hearing an NPR story about the American cowgirl, she was so inspired, she followed the spark, left the ad world, and found herself in Montana, Wyoming, and Texas filming a documentary about their lives. It was out west where Barbara fell in love with the natural world, the power of the landscape, and what it means to be an environmental steward. It was also where she connected with indigenous elders and their wisdom teachings.

Barbara is an advocate for building cultural bridges and emboldening women and girls. She has facilitated leadership programs for schools, Girl Scouts of America, and other organizations, and was part of the think tank that inspired the Fred Rogers Center for Children's Media and Education. She lives with her family in the Berkshire Mountains of Western, Massachusetts, on Mohican tribal land. This book is her love letter to Mother Earth and all her daughters.

Visit: www.barbaranewmanauthor.com